Death of a Blue Blood

A *Murder, She Wrote* Mystery

OTHER BOOKS IN THE *Murder, She Wrote* SERIES

Manhattans & Murder
Rum & Razors
Brandy & Bullets
Martinis & Mayhem
A Deadly Judgment
A Palette for Murder
The Highland Fling Murders
Murder on the QE2
Murder in Moscow
A Little Yuletide Murder
Murder at the Powderhorn Ranch
Knock 'Em Dead
Gin & Daggers
Trick or Treachery
Blood on the Vine
Murder in a Minor Key
Provence—To Die For
You Bet Your Life
Majoring in Murder
Destination Murder
Dying to Retire
A Vote for Murder
The Maine Mutiny
Margaritas & Murder
A Question of Murder
Coffee, Tea, or Murder?
Three Strikes and You're Dead
Panning for Murder
Murder on Parade
A Slaying in Savannah
Madison Avenue Shoot
A Fatal Feast
Nashville Noir
The Queen's Jewels
Skating on Thin Ice
The Fine Art of Murder
Trouble at High Tide
Domestic Malice
Prescription for Murder
Close-up on Murder
Aloha Betrayed

Death of a Blue Blood

A *Murder, She Wrote* Mystery

A NOVEL BY

JESSICA FLETCHER & DONALD BAIN

Based on the Universal Television series created by
Peter S. Fischer, Richard Levinson & William Link

AN OBSIDIAN MYSTERY

OBSIDIAN
Published by the Penguin Group
Penguin Group (USA) LLC, 375 Hudson Street,
New York, New York 10014

USA | Canada | UK | Ireland | Australia | New Zealand | India | South Africa | China
penguin.com
A Penguin Random House Company

First published by Obsidian, an imprint of New American Library,
a division of Penguin Group (USA) LLC

First Printing, October 2014

LIBRARY OF CONGRESS CATALOGING-IN-PUBLICATION DATA:

Bain, Donald, 1935–
Death of a blue blood: a novel / by Jessica Fletcher & Donald Bain.
pages cm—(Murder, she wrote) (An Obsidian mystery)
"Based on the Universal Television series created by Peter S. Fischer, Richard Levinson & William Link."
ISBN 978-0-451-46825-3 (hardback)
1. Fletcher, Jessica—Fiction. 2. Women novelists—Fiction. 3. Aristocracy (Social class)—Fiction. 4. New Year—Fiction. 5. Murder—Investigation—Fiction. I. Fischer, Peter S. II. Levinson, Richard. III. Link, William. IV. Murder, she wrote (Television program). V. Title. VI. Series: Bain, Donald, 1935–
Murder, she wrote.
PS3552.A376D43 2014
813'.54—dc23 2014015562

Printed in the United States of America
10 9 8 7 6 5 4 3 2 1

Set in Minion

PUBLISHER'S NOTE

This is a work of fiction. Names, characters, places, and incidents either are the product of the author's imagination or are used fictitiously, and any resemblance to actual persons, living or dead, business establishments, events, or locales is entirely coincidental.

To my wife and collaborator, Renée Paley-Bain,
whose touch is evident on every page

From the deepest desires often come the deadliest hate.

—Socrates

Like all the best families, we have our share of eccentricities, of impetuous and wayward youngsters and of family disagreements.

—Queen Elizabeth II, 1989

Death of a Blue Blood

A *Murder, She Wrote* Mystery

Chapter One

James William Edward Grant, seventh Earl of Norrance,
and
Marielle Grant, Countess of Norrance,
request the honour of your presence
at their
New Year's Eve Ball
Castorbrook Castle
Chipping Minster
Gloucestershire

"Great old pile, what, lass?" George murmured to me as we both leaned forward in our seats to capture the view through the windshield of the twin towers of Castorbrook Castle.

I patted my shoulder bag, which held the precious invitation, and shivered in excitement. I've been to many wonderful places, but this would be my first New Year's Eve ball in a castle.

"Built in the eighteenth century, in the style known as

Gothic," our driver called over his shoulder. "It bears a resemblance to the Palace of Westminster, doncha' think?" He was referring to the building where the Houses of Parliament meet in London.

"A smaller, less ornate version," I agreed, "minus Big Ben."

"If you put a giant clockface in one o' them towers, it'd come pretty close." The driver crested the hill, leaving behind the avenue of plane trees. He turned left, taking a route around a large pond, the surface of which mirrored the banks of rhododendrons along the shore and reflected the tips of the towers shimmering in the water.

"Looks like we won't be getting in any ice-skating," George said to me.

"Good thing, since I didn't bring my skates."

"Too early in the winter for that," the driver called out, eavesdropping on our conversation as he had been the entire two hours from London. "Don't get snow out here before January, most years anyway. You'll find a bit o' frost about in the mornin'. Might see a flake or two before the New Year, if yer lucky. Been raining on and off—why I suggested we start out when we did. Don't fancy driving these hills in a storm."

"Thanks, Ralph," George said as the car pulled to a stop in front of the impressive entrance, where a series of arches, flanked by evergreens festooned in red ribbons, led to an interior courtyard.

"Happy to oblige, George. I'll be at the cousin's in Stow on the Wold a few days if you change your mind and decide you don't want to miss the fireworks on the Thames." Ralph handed him a card on which he'd written a phone number.

George tucked it in his vest pocket. "I'll keep it in mind."

While the men retrieved our luggage from the space next to the driver's seat, I tugged on the hem of my tweed jacket, smoothed away the travel wrinkles of my skirt, and inhaled the sharp country air. No one was out front to greet us, but perhaps they hadn't seen the car coming or heard the crunch of the tires on the gray gravel. We'd arrived a little earlier than expected. Ralph had taken the afternoon off from his usual duties as a London cabbie to drive us to the Cotswolds, where we would welcome in the New Year as guests of Lord and Lady Norrance, friends of my British publisher, which was how I'd landed on the invitation list.

Ralph cocked his head at the building as he wrestled my rolling suitcase to the ground. "Yer host, Lord Norrance—you call 'im by his title, Jessica—is seventh generation," he said. "Opens the place up to the public every summer—many of the great houses do now, you know—and does the occasional wedding or some such. Not a bad setting to launch a new life together, what? Wish I coulda done that for my daughter, Allie, and 'er beau, but 'er mum says, 'Save yer pennies. A pretty picture won't keep 'em warm in winter.' Too practical by half, that one."

"She was very wise," I said, taking the handle of my bag from him.

"Ralph's a dreamer," George said. "That's part of his charm. But you'd have empty pockets, old chap, if it weren't for your wife, Kay." George clapped Ralph on the shoulder as the driver closed the hackney's door.

"True, and don't I know it."

A former bobby, Ralph had retired due to injuries sustained during a crackdown on gangs by the Metropolitan Police—the drug pusher was caught, but Ralph's knee was a casualty of the operation. Opting out of a desk job, he'd exchanged a life pursuing criminals for one escorting tourists, although many of his customers turned out to be his previous law enforcement colleagues. My companion, Chief Inspector George Sutherland, was one of them.

George Sutherland and I had met years earlier during a trip I'd taken to England to be the weekend guest of Marjorie Ainsworth, the reigning grand dame of British mystery writers. Marjorie had become old and feeble and was confined to a wheelchair, and I felt this might be the last time I would see her alive. Despite her advanced age and failing health, she'd recently completed what was being touted as her finest literary effort, *Gin & Daggers*, although there was growing controversy over whether she'd had the help of a ghostwriter.

Yet none of that mattered to me. Simply being able to spend a weekend with this wonderful and wise woman, whose books set a high bar for any of us other writers of crime fiction, was a joy to contemplate. However, I wasn't the only guest that weekend at her imposing manor house outside London. A number of others had gathered, which made for spirited conversation, some of it occasionally contentious. Because she fatigued easily, Marjorie had retired to her bedroom the first night of my stay after having played the generous and welcoming hostess.

At three o'clock that morning, I was awakened by a sound coming from the direction of her bedroom. Was it a weak female voice crying for help? I got out of bed and went to find out. Marjorie's bedroom door was ajar. I stepped inside and approached her bed. What I saw horrified me. Marjorie Ainsworth was sprawled on her back, a dagger protruding from her chest like a graveyard marker.

Because of her fame, the investigation wasn't left in the hands of the local constable. Scotland Yard was called in, and Chief Inspector George Sutherland arrived to spearhead the inquiry. Not only was he charming; he was undeniably handsome, six feet four, impeccably dressed, and with eyes that were at once probing and kind. We ended up working together to bring Marjorie's murderer to justice, and in the process we developed what might be called a mutual infatuation. Over the years, it became obvious that we were attracted to each other beyond solving murders, and we wondered whether one day we would give life to our romantic inclinations. It hadn't happened, at least not yet, and time spent together was limited. That was why I'd leaped at the chance to spend New Year's Eve with George at Castorbrook Castle.

"I'm Scotland Yard's favorite cabbie," Ralph had informed me when George introduced us. "Unofficially, of course. Had to bone up on Yard history when I was in training. Couldn't let those nobs in their fancy offices know more'n me."

London cabbies are required to go through an intensely challenging program, learning the history of three hundred twenty places of interest as well as how to find all the streets in the city, a process that can take years. Those in training—"Knowledge boys," and more recently "Knowledge girls"—often make multiple attempts at passing the test, as many newly minted lawyers do in taking American state bar exams. Ralph had passed on his second try, a source of great pride.

"Don't lose that number, now." Ralph started up the engine. "Ta, George. Ta, Jessica. See you next year!"

We waved Ralph off.

"Mrs. Fletcher, Mr. Sutherland, my sincerest apologies."

George and I turned to see a gentleman in a tuxedo hastening toward us, followed by a rough-looking man lumbering behind him. The second man was brushing his hands against the sides of his heavy trousers, raising small clouds of dirt with each pass.

"I'm Nigel Gordon, butler to Lord and Lady Norrance. We were only just alerted to your arrival. You weren't due for another two hours." He looked at his watch. "Angus will take your luggage up for you." He indicated the man behind him. "Please follow me. The family will soon sit down for tea. Would you care to join them straightaway? Or would you prefer to freshen up before the introductions?"

"I'd prefer to freshen up," I said.

Nigel hurried us across the interior courtyard and into the entry hall, a vast marble space with fifteen-foot-high columns joined by pointed archways and flanking a half dozen closed doors and one open one. I barely had time to notice the intricate carving between the arches, the huge holiday-themed floral arrangement standing on an oak table, the medieval statues, the velvet-covered benches, and the elaborate Oriental rug underfoot before the butler ushered us through the open door to the base of a broad staircase, where a redheaded woman wearing a large watch on a chain around her neck awaited us.

"This is our housekeeper, Mrs. Powter, who'll show you to your rooms," Nigel said.

"We do have a lift if you find the stairs wearing," Mrs. Powter said, eyeing us up and down.

"Actually, I'd welcome the stairs right now." I smiled, but she remained impassive.

"Could do with a bit of up-and-down after the long sit," George added.

"When you're ready, Mrs. Powter will show you to the drawing room where the family are gathered," Nigel said, giving us a quick nod. "Please excuse me. I shall see you shortly."

He was gone before we could thank him properly, and he was not the only member of the household in a rush. Mrs. Powter set a brisk pace trotting up the steps. The staircase curved around to the second-floor landing before continuing on up. George and I were afraid to stop and catch our breath for fear of losing sight of our escort. Mrs. Powter was halfway down the hall when we reached the third floor.

"I hope these will be satisfactory." She stepped back from the open doors to adjoining rooms.

I walked into the first room. "Oh, this is lovely."

It was a sun-filled square with a four-poster bed, the gold and filigree canopy of which almost touched the ceiling fifteen feet above our heads. The walls above a paneled wainscoting were covered in blue silk. A pair of what might be ancestral portraits stared down at the bed and across to the window, which overlooked a garden two floors below.

"Very nice," George said. "I see Angus has already been here." He tapped the top of my suitcase, which had been laid on a bench at the foot of the bed.

"He must have taken the elevator," I said.

"No doubt. Or else he's in training for the hundred-meter sprint."

"I wonder if your room is as nice."

"Let's go see."

Mrs. Powter was still on guard in the hall. "Will you need assistance unpacking?"

"I think we can manage by ourselves," I said.

She looked at her watch. "I'll be back to collect you at half past three. Will that be sufficient time?"

"We'll be ready and waiting." I resisted the urge to salute.

She walked briskly to the end of the hall, opened a door to what was probably the back stairs—or perhaps the elevator—and disappeared through it.

"Seems we've put them out by arriving early," George said.

"We're not *that* early, are we?"

He made a show of looking at his watch. "We're not due here for one hour, thirty-five minutes and—ten seconds, give or take a second."

"Oh, dear. Is it just as rude to be early as it is to be late?"

"Nothing of the kind. Besides, you'd think people who are capable of putting on a New Year's Eve ball would have all the details worked out by now."

"I suspect that if I had a hundred people coming to my home for a party, I'd feel pressured, too."

"You, my lass, would take it all in stride. Now let's take a peek at my living quarters in Castorbrook Castle. How do they compare to yours?"

"Pretty much the same," I said, entering his room, "although your ancestral portraits appear to be sixteenth century, while mine are of a later vintage."

"How do you figure that?"

"These gentlemen are wearing ruffs." I gestured at the stiff ruffled collars under the double chins of the aristocrats depicted in the paintings. "Mine are wearing cravats."

"I bow to your superior knowledge of historical neckwear, and to your powers of observation."

"I happen to be reading a book on the Renaissance now. The author spends a lot of ink on clothing, jewelry, and hairstyles."

"See how handy it came in?"

I laughed. "I think I'd better go unpack before Mrs. Powter returns with our marching orders."

"And I'll do the same. Shall I knock on your door at twenty-five past, just to be safe?"

"I'd appreciate that."

I unpacked my bag as quickly as possible, shaking out a blue dress I planned to wear down to tea and hanging up the rest of my clothes in a tall armoire. Buildings of Castorbrook Castle's vintage don't have closets unless the owners have added them in a modernization.

A door fitted into the paneling opened into an old-fashioned bathroom with a claw-foot tub. I washed my hands and face at the pedestal sink and used a linen towel folded atop a small round table next to it, then changed into my dress. I wrapped a plaid shawl around my shoulders—the Sutherland tartan, a gift from George—in anticipation of the chilly rooms for which English manor houses are infamous, and tucked a pair of reading glasses into my dress pocket.

Ready in no time, I turned in a circle, examining the contents of my room. In addition to the canopy bed and armoire, there were a single nightstand with a candlestick lamp, a small desk and chair, a marble fireplace with a coal basket inside, and, under the tall window, a built-in seat with an upholstered cushion. I crossed to the window, leaned on the cushion, and looked out at the view of the countryside's rolling hills and the gathering clouds in the distance. Cows were grazing on what was left of the grass in one pasture. The spire of an ancient stone church poked into the wintry blue sky from a valley beyond. Below me was a garden; the high stone walls enclosing it matched the limestone blocks of the house. I tried to picture where the walled garden was located in relation to the house, but we hadn't had time to get our bearings before Nigel had whisked us inside.

The garden had several gravel paths that ran along the back and sides, with concrete benches on which to rest and enjoy the views. The paths crisscrossed in the middle, leaving triangularly shaped beds in the center. Flowers withered from the cold waved on their brown stems, the only spots of green being a few holly bushes. Specimen trees and what I believed were bare rosebushes filled the beds at the far corners, but I couldn't identify any of the other plants from this distance.

A fragment of color closer to the building caught my eye, and I pressed my forehead to the glass to see what it was. It was not a plant, but a patch of purple fabric. Perhaps the gardener had dropped a cloth on the ground when he was working. Would that have been Angus? I knelt on the window seat and unlatched the window. A cold breeze reminded me that it was winter, but holding on to the casement, I bent forward. The wind ruffled my hair, and the purple fabric below billowed, floating off to the side—and revealing a leg and a dark shoe. They weren't moving.

"Oh, dear."

I raced to George's door and knocked urgently.

"Is Mrs. Powter here already?" George said, buttoning his vest and reaching for the jacket he'd left on the bed.

"No. Come look. Someone is hurt in the garden!" I opened George's window and directed him to look down.

"That swath of purple cloth?"

"Yes, and it's covering a leg and foot. I saw them when the wind blew the cloth aside. If she tried to call for help, no one would be able to hear her with all the windows closed. She must have injured herself in a fall and is unable to get up."

"We'd better go downstairs and investigate."

"Should we leave a note for Mrs. Powter?"

"No time. She'll have to find us later on."

We dashed down the hall to the door we'd seen Mrs. Powter open to find both the back staircase and the closed brass gate of the elevator.

"I'll take the stairs," George said. "Do you want to wait for the lift?"

"No, I'll follow you. You go ahead."

If I'd known I'd be running down the stairs, I would have chosen better shoes, but I managed to keep George in my sight as we descended several flights spiraling around the elevator shaft. We stopped on what we assumed was the ground floor.

"Which way?" he asked.

"I'm not sure."

"You take that hall. I'll try this one," he said. "If I don't find the garden, I'll look for someone to help. Call out if you find her."

George took off, looking into rooms on either side of the corridor. I went in the opposite direction, following the stone floor, glad of the shawl in the frigid air. At the end of the hall was a heavy curtain. I pulled it to one side to discover an opening that led into a large greenhouse, its tall potted plants blotting out the dimming afternoon light. The leaves of a tropical plant just inside quaked when I stepped into the room, allowing some of the cool air to follow me. On the wall to my right was a heavy glass-paneled door that led to the enclosed garden.

I held back the curtain. "George! Down here," I called. I opened the door, but it was very heavy. I looked around and noticed some wet dirt tracks on the floor. The plant was on a rolling stand. Clearly it had been moved before to hold the door open. I did the same thing and stepped into the walled garden. A woman was lying in a puddle just beyond the door. She wore only her purple dress and brown shoes; without a sweater or jacket, her attire was no match for the wintry day. I knelt next to her, pushing her blond hair aside to feel for a pulse on her neck. I couldn't find one. I lifted her wrist to try again and was surprised to find red stains on her fingers. I wondered briefly if she was a fan of pistachio nuts. When I was a child, they were often dyed that color, leaving my fingers and lips cherry red.

But there was no dye on this lady's lips, and from the gray color of her complexion, I guessed that she'd been dead for a while. How awful to die alone without the comfort of friends and family around you. I shivered and pulled my shawl closer as the icy air and brutal wind reminded me not to linger. I'd better go find George before there were two bodies in the garden.

I heard a bang and turned. The door had slammed shut behind me. I went to it, pulling and then pushing on the brass handle. It was locked. I peered through the glass to see if someone was inside. No one. "What do I do now?" I muttered, annoyed that I hadn't checked to make certain that the wheels of the plant stand were positioned correctly to keep it from sliding away.

I rapped on the glass with my knuckles, but they made barely any sound. I took off my right shoe and used the heel to knock on the door again. "Hello!" I shouted. "I'm locked out here. Help! Someone help!" There was no answer, only the muffled sound of a dog barking somewhere.

I stepped back and looked up at the side of the building. All the windows were shut, which meant Mrs. Powter must have discovered us missing and closed the ones in our rooms, probably grumbling about inconsiderate guests.

A gust of wind caught my dress, just as it had the one of the poor woman dead on the ground. My skirt flew up, flattening against my chest. I shuddered as I pushed down the billowing material. I wondered if I should cover the victim with my shawl, but it would do her lifeless body little good and leave me without a shield against the elements.

I walked to the outer path by the stone wall, climbed on a concrete bench, and waved, hoping someone might notice me from one of the myriad windows that overlooked the garden. There were lights on in a few of the rooms. I could see people walking back and forth, but no one stopped to peer outside. In fact, someone drew a heavy drape across a window, undoubtedly making the interior warmer by blocking the drafts. It was bitterly cold on the periphery of the garden, and water from an earlier rain had seeped into my shoes. Even my arm-waving exertions did little to warm me up.

I climbed down and looked across to the glass door. Several yards to its left, wedged between a bush and an ornamental stone column, was another door, a wooden one, which I hadn't noticed earlier. I hurried over. Stepping into a flower bed to get to what I hoped was an exit, I yanked on the handle. The door flew back to reveal a shallow closet, its shelves packed with flowerpots, garden tools, seed packets, boxes of Mole-Rid, bottles of insecticide, and bags of aluminum sulfate and lime. Even in the unlikely event I could have squeezed inside the closet, it wouldn't have offered much protection.

Well, George will find me soon, I thought as I retreated to the glass door. *He must be nearby.* I continued knocking on the panels with my shoe, and at regular intervals shouting into the wind. Minutes went by with no George. The sky darkened and the temperature dropped. The trees and bushes took on eerie shapes in the gloom. Had he gotten lost? It was not outside the realm of possibility, given the size of Castorbrook Castle. Could he have become disoriented and taken off in a direction away from where I waited? And if the staff was in the kitchen or readying the ballroom, they might not hear him call, just as they didn't hear me as I pounded my shoe on the door. I pictured George wandering the hallways, unable to find anyone to help.

Stop it, Jessica. He knows to look for you.

My teeth chattering, I switched shoes, taking off my left one and pushing my frozen right foot into the damp leather pump, and resumed banging on the door. My arm was tired, my feet hurt, and the shawl wasn't much protection against the currents of air swirling fiercely around the enclosed garden.

A bolt of lightning illuminated the charcoal sky, followed by a clap of thunder. I huddled against the door, but it provided scant shelter. I sank down, shoe in hand, and leaned against the glass, too tired to keep hitting the panes. I felt a drop of water on my head and pulled the shawl over my hair. I drew up my knees, making myself as small as possible.

Then the door opened behind me. I fell backward across the sill just as the rain began pelting down.

"Jessica, are you all right?" George said, lifting me up. "I'm so sorry. I never came upon anyone to ask for help. This place is huge. I got terribly turned around and had trouble finding my way back, until just now."

"Th-thank g-goodness you're here," I said, my teeth chattering.

George closed the door to the garden and groped along the wall until he found a light switch, bringing the indoor jungle to life. Graceful plants and exotic flowers bloomed in the warm, moist air, making quite a contrast to the climate I'd just escaped.

He wrapped his arms around me. "You're safe now. How do you feel?"

"I'm cold and miserable, George, but I'm a lot better off than that lady out there."

Chapter Two

"Who was she?" I asked George in a low voice.

"Apparently she served as lady's maid to our hostess."

"Lady Norrance?"

He nodded. "Her name was Flavia Beckwith. She'd been with the family many years. Drink your tea."

"Didn't anyone miss her?" I whispered.

"With all the hustle and bustle of the staff getting ready for the ball, no one thought to look for her."

I took a sip from the delicate china cup and replaced it in the saucer. I was wrapped in a heavy blanket in a wing chair in a corner of the drawing room near the tall Christmas tree, the branches of which held swags of gold ribbon, gold glass balls, and electric candles. George sat on an ottoman by my side. There were ten of us gathered for afternoon tea. George and I were the only ones who weren't members of the family, but a few other guests were expected to arrive at any moment.

Our hosts, Lord and Lady Norrance, had fussed over me in

my disheveled state, but they were understandably far more upset to learn of Mrs. Beckwith's demise.

"What in blazes was she doing in the garden?" Lord Norrance asked, glaring at his wife.

Marielle, the Countess of Norrance, raised a hand to tuck a loose strand of hair into her chignon. "I asked her to find a sprig of holly that I could use for my hair for the ball." She checked her image in the mirror over the fireplace. "I didn't ask her to go into the garden."

"Any sensible person knows it's far too cold to walk outside at this time of year," said a gravelly voice belonging to the Dowager Countess of Norrance, the earl's widowed mother. Honora Grant was a slight woman in her seventies, but her delicate appearance belied her tough nature. Earlier, when she had leaned on Nigel's arm as he escorted her into the room, she had pointed to a seat with her cane. "Put me over there where I can see everyone. Marielle, you know that's my chair by the fire. Find another place, if you please."

Lady Norrance obligingly vacated her seat so her mother-in-law could take it. Nigel placed a pillow he'd carried in on the chair, and Honora settled herself down. She cast a critical eye on the room's other occupants. "I hope you're not planning to cancel the ball because of this unfortunate incident."

"Oh! We hadn't thought . . ." The earl's wife trailed off.

"You really should, you know," said a young woman dressed in jodhpurs and boots. "We've had a death in the family." She released the scarf around her neck and shook out her dark blond hair.

"Nonsense!" the earl said. "This event has been on the social calendar for many months."

"Jemma, must you irritate your father?"

"Sorry, Mum."

"We could hardly cancel now," the earl said. "People are already arriving." He waved an arm toward George and me.

"And very welcome you are," said Rupert Grant, the earl's younger son, nodding at us, causing a curl from his carefully gelled hair to flop onto his forehead. He was a boyish-looking fellow in his mid-twenties. "Besides, Flavia would not have wanted to discomfort the family in any way." He leaned forward to pluck a pastry from a silver tray. "Isn't that right, Mother?"

"You're correct, of course, dear. Please take a plate and napkin. Mrs. Beckwith was dedicated to Castorbrook Castle and our family."

"Wasn't she the children's governess once?" the dowager asked.

"Yes, Grandmother," Rupert said, "but she needed another job when the three of us rudely decided to grow up." He cocked his head at his sister, Jemma, the horsewoman, and their older brother, Kip, who sat across the room and idly paged through a magazine. "And Mother gave the old girl another position."

"Ridiculous! She wasn't even trained." Honora thumped her cane on the floor. "Can't imagine she could have been a proper lady's maid without training. But then your mother probably doesn't know the difference."

Marielle flushed and looked to her husband for defense, but he was lost in thought as he stared into the fire.

Rupert popped up out of his seat, taking the tray of pastries with him. "Would you like to try one of these, Grandmother? They were made by our new French chef."

"What was wrong with the English one?"

"Clover is still in the kitchen," Marielle said. "We simply felt Chef Bergère would add an elegant touch to the cuisine, in particular for special occasions. He has been a wonderful change." She turned to her husband. "James, would you like a cream tart?"

"Don't encourage him to eat those sugary things. He's too heavy as it is. You'll give him a heart attack," Honora said.

The earl patted his stomach. "I don't think I've put on much, have I?"

"Nothing wrong with plain English cooking," the old woman said, but she allowed her grandson to put a piece of pastry on her plate.

"I like Clover's scones better than those," Jemma said, flinging a booted leg over the arm of her chair. Even from my seat some distance away, I could detect the aroma of horse that clung to her clothing.

"Nigel, would you please see if anyone wants more tea?" Marielle took a seat on an upholstered settee. The low table in front of her held a silver tray with a silver teapot, sugar bowl, and creamer. "Jemma, sit up, dear. Kip, where is your wife?"

"Sitting in the window seat with Adela," Rupert answered for his brother.

Two young ladies who'd been whispering together on the other side of the room looked up and waved. "Poppy's showing me her new ball gown," Adela called out. "You should see it, Rupe. I'm going to look like a poor relation. My gown is three years old."

"Cost me a bloody fortune," Kip said. "You'd think she was already a countess."

"Put that mobile away this instant," the earl said. "You know how I detest the use of electronics during teatime."

"And at the table, and in the library, and in the garden," Rupert said. "I daresay there are few places you tolerate them, Father. Perhaps we should send those two out to the cloakroom."

The young women giggled. Poppy tucked the cell phone away in her pocket, but not before a final check of the screen.

"Rupert, I don't need any smart talk from you," said the earl. "If you ever have an estate to run, you won't be so flippant about the responsibilities."

"Unfortunately, I'm your younger son, as you well know. I have no prospects for inheriting an estate."

"More reason for you to pursue gainful employment."

"You could change your mind and give me a piece of this one."

"I'll not break up Castorbrook for you."

"You've already . . ."

"Not another word. I've accommodated you enough. I trust you'll use this opportunity wisely. I won't be supporting you forever."

"Kip will take care of me. Won't you, Brother?"

"Leave me out of this."

"If you need a job, Rupert, you could always take Mrs. Beckwith's place," Kip's wife, Poppy, said, smirking.

Her companion in the window seat gave her a shove in the shoulder.

"I was just joshing, Adela. No need to get violent."

"You're always picking on Rupert, Poppy. Kip's being the heir doesn't make you Queen of the May."

"No?" Poppy said archly. "I thought it did."

While no one was paying him any attention, Kip slipped a small flask from his pocket and poured its contents into his teacup.

Honora, who had appeared to be dozing, lifted her head.

"Those young people are completely without conversation." She peered over her spectacles. "In my day—"

"Yes, yes, Mother." The earl cut her off. "We know everything was superior in your day."

"Well, I don't know what I said that prompted you to speak so rudely to me, James."

"I never intended disrespect, Mama. My mind is awash with a million problems. I'm upset over the loss of our staff member, the anticipated consequences, and how we will replace her on such short notice."

"Your wife should be able to dress herself in an emergency, I would think."

"Can we not discuss this now?" Marielle said.

While the family bickered, Nigel had picked up the tray and made the rounds of the room, stopping at each person.

"I'll have another cup," George told him when he'd worked his way to us.

"How are you feeling, Mrs. Fletcher?"

"Much better, Nigel. Thank you for asking."

"Our sincerest apologies for your regrettable introduction to Castorbrook Castle."

"No apologies necessary. I'm just sorry for the family's loss."

"Have the authorities been notified?" George asked.

"Yes, sir. Someone from the constabulary is expected shortly. I'm afraid there will have to be an inquest."

"Isn't that standard procedure when someone dies of unknown causes?" I asked.

"It is, but it's awkward timing with the ball tomorrow evening. Time is precious. With so much to prepare, the staff hope the business will be concluded before the start of the festivities."

"And the family must wish that, too, I imagine."

"I'll see if I can help him along," George said, lowering his voice. "Please let me know when the officer arrives."

"Of course, sir. And thank you for any service you can provide."

"Can you really speed up the inquest, George?" I asked softly when Nigel had moved away. "Won't the police have to interview everyone in the house? I understand the pressures of the social occasion, but after all, a woman has died, and she deserves the appropriate investigation."

"I would never interfere with the local authorities or their proper procedure. I hope you know that. But given the state of affairs, perhaps I can convince this gentleman to delay some of his inquiries until the day after the ball. Or, if he allows it, assist him in organizing his analysis so that it doesn't interfere with the efficient workings of the house. After all, that lady most likely died from exposure, which you very well might have done if I hadn't found you."

"And this lady, who is very grateful for your rescue, begs to differ with you. Without an autopsy, how can you say that was the cause of her death?"

"I'm not saying it emphatically. Heart attack, stroke are also possibilities. In fact, that's probably what felled her in the first place. But once she was incapacitated, hypothermia is not an unreasonable conclusion, given the circumstances. It only needs to be ten degrees centigrade—that's fifty in Fahrenheit—for a body to cool to dangerous levels. She was careless. The weather was wet. She was inappropriately attired to venture out of doors, yet she made that decision."

"And she got locked out, as did I. Are you saying that I was careless, too, George? I was inappropriately dressed for the outdoors."

"Of course not. Completely different scenario. Clearly she must have had some infirmity and was unable to return inside. Unfortunately, no one on the staff thought to look for her."

"Neither did anyone in the family. Why didn't Lady Norrance ask after her? She sent her on the errand in the first place."

"Agreed. However inattentive everyone was, I don't see it as an instance of willful negligence. Whether from the elements or from lack of medical attention to a fatal malady, the lady collapsed and died. Can you really come to any other conclusion?"

I felt as if our exposure to the family's squabbles had become contagious, and George and I were now communicating—or rather miscommunicating—in the same manner. I took a deep breath and sipped my tea. "It's entirely possible that she died of hypothermia, of course."

"I'm glad you see it that way, lass."

But I didn't.

Chapter Three

"So, Mrs. Fletcher, you were the one to discover the body of the deceased?"

"Yes, Detective Sergeant Mardling. I noticed the purple fabric of her dress when I looked out my window. Then George—I mean Chief Inspector Sutherland—and I ran downstairs to try to find the garden. I reached it first, but it appeared that she'd been dead for some time."

"Yes, well, when she died—the time of death—is yet to be determined."

"Of course."

There were five of us gathered in a ground-floor room down the hall from the greenhouse. The space was not much bigger than a walk-in refrigerator and equally as cold. Standing wooden shelves that ringed the room held cans and jars of preserved fruits and vegetables as well as crates of root vegetables. Mrs. Beckwith's body had been laid on a long wooden table and covered with a white tablecloth.

Detective Sergeant Mardling pulled it aside. "What's her age? How old was this lady, Mrs. Beckwith, as I believe you said?"

"Yes, sir, Flavia Beckwith," Nigel replied. "I believe she was in her fifties, but I cannot say with certainty. She was guarded about her personal information. I can ask the earl if he knows."

"Well, I can ask the earl myself, if it comes to that. Will have to speak to the earl at some point, won't I?"

Dudley Mardling was not the kind of police officer I expected, although I couldn't say exactly what an English detective was supposed to look like. He was short and plump with pink cheeks and curly sandy hair. Dressed in a green canvas jacket, he wore a gold watch and had buffed fingernails. His assistant, Constable Willoughby, was his physical opposite in every way. She was six feet tall, as narrow as he was round, with stick-straight hair brushed back from her face. Her uniform was wrinkled, and the grease marks on her hands suggested that she might be an avid weekend car mechanic.

"And who removed Mrs. Beckwith—or rather the body—from the garden and brought it to this room?" Mardling looked down at the table that held the deceased.

"I did, with the help of another member of the staff," Nigel replied.

"And you are Mr. Gordon, if I remember correctly?"

"Yes, sir. Nigel Gordon, butler to Lord and Lady Norrance."

"And the other staff member who assisted with the removal of the body? Is he here?"

"Not at the moment. That would be Angus Hartwhistle, our gardener. We couldn't leave her where she'd fallen. It was raining."

Mardling grunted.

Nigel rushed on. "Angus suggested this space because it is stone lined and the temperature is consistent. We use it as an auxiliary larder for vegetables. We trusted that this would serve you better."

"It was a well-thought-out decision," George said, nodding at Nigel. He turned to Detective Sergeant Mardling. "The garden is next to the conservatory, but that area is maintained as a warm, moist environment, which would have been conducive to more rapid decomposition."

"Appreciate your input, Chief Inspector. Do you have any official capacity in this matter?"

George coughed. "Not at all, Detective Sergeant. I am a guest of the earl and his countess, as is Mrs. Fletcher. It was simply our misfortune to find this poor soul."

"I certainly am aware of your rank with Scotland Yard, but since this is my investigation, I'm sure you won't mind if I continue the questioning."

"By all means."

"What do you suppose caused this?" Mardling gestured at the red coloring on the deceased's fingers. "Anybody know?"

"Perhaps a stain from berries in the garden," Nigel ventured.

"Did she like to cook Indian food?" Willoughby asked. "Some of the spices can leave you with marks on your hands." She looked at her own discolored fingers and quickly tucked her hands behind her back.

"I understand there is to be a big do here tomorrow night," Mardling said.

"A New Year's Eve ball," I put in.

"How many are expected?"

George and I looked to Nigel.

"One hundred forty-five, precisely, plus six musicians."

"All staying here?"

"Twenty-two guests have been invited to stay at the castle. The rest either reside in the neighborhood or are putting up at nearby establishments."

"Would have thought the castle had more than twenty-two bedrooms. Do you have more than twenty-two bedrooms, Mr. Gordon?"

"We have nearly fifty, sir, but many of them are not suitable to occupy as yet. The earl intends to redecorate as funds and time allow. The building is more than three hundred years old. A bit hard to keep up." He sneaked a peek at his watch.

I noticed that Nigel's cuffs were frayed and wondered why the earl skimped on uniforms when he was willing to host an elaborate ball. Of course, if Nigel had to pay for his own formal clothes, the butler might be trying to save money, but he seemed such a proper man, that didn't ring true.

"Were all twenty-two overnight guests in-house when Mrs. Beckwith went missing, Mr. Gordon?" Mardling asked.

"No, sir. Only these guests had arrived—Mrs. Fletcher and the chief inspector. Others have come since then, and more are expected momentarily."

A half hour earlier, my British publisher, Griffin Semple, had joined our group with a lovely young friend, Ruby Miller-Carlisle, who appeared to be an acquaintance of the earl's daughter, Jemma. On their heels, an artist, Elmore Jackcliff, whose name I wasn't familiar with, turned up. Lady Norrance seemed especially delighted at his arrival, although the earl did not, but he brightened when his business affairs manager, Lionel Fitzwalter, walked in with his wife. With the entrance of these guests, the family had put aside the contentious behavior they hadn't held back in front of George and me, and welcomed the newcomers with good cheer. The earl was regaling them with funny stories when Nigel alerted us that the police were here. We slipped out of the drawing room and followed him downstairs to the unheated storage chamber on the ground floor.

"How many work here? How many in staff?"

"Seven permanent, full-time staff." Nigel cocked his head at the body. "Now six. About a dozen part-time. But we hired on more from the village for tomorrow night, as we usually do for events. I wonder if you would be so kind as to excuse me. We're short-staffed tonight, and my service is needed upstairs."

"We'll detain you only a little longer, Mr. Gordon. Willoughby, use your mobile to call for the coroner's lorry."

Willoughby pulled out her cell phone but was unable to receive a signal. "Maybe it'll work outside." She flung open the door, surprising a woman in a long white apron who had her hand on the doorknob.

"Oh, my goodness, you gave me a start." The woman looked to each of us nervously. "Beg pardon, Mr. Gordon. Didn't know you had a meeting going on in here. I just need to collect the basket of onions. We're halfway through the coquille, and we've run out."

"Certainly, Mrs. Estwich. May she come in, Detective Sergeant?"

"Who is this, please? Your name?"

"Clover Estwich, sir. I'm the cook."

"Come away then," Mardling said, standing back. "Get what you need."

Clover scuttled in and grabbed a crate of onions, but the basket almost fell from her hands when she saw the body on the table. "Good heavens, Mr. Gordon. A body in my larder?"

Nigel grimaced.

"Did you know the deceased?" Mardling asked.

"Yes, sir. She was Mrs. Beckwith. We heard that she was found—dead."

"And how well did you know the deceased?"

Clover backed toward the door with her basket. "Not well, sir. She was kind of private, like, didn't mix much with the rest of the staff, not even for meals. May I go now?"

"Willoughby, take her name. We'll question you again, another time—Mrs. Estwich, was it?"

Mardling seemed to be bumbling along, repeating himself and asking questions twice. Yet I noticed that he remembered every name he heard without taking notes, and clearly wanted to be seen as in charge.

Clover spelled her name for Constable Willoughby, and she gave Nigel a baleful look. "Are you taking her out soon? I'll have to scrub down this room before we use it again. Of all times to put a body in my larder." She peered down at the onions with a dubious expression. "I don't know if I can use these now."

Nigel looked pained. "My apologies, Mrs. Estwich. We thought it for the best."

Clover sidestepped out the door. "Best to put a body in my larder? And use one of my finest table linens," she muttered as she hurried down the corridor.

"Mrs. Fletcher, I'd like to see where you came upon the body."

"Certainly, Detective Sergeant Mardling. If you'll follow me, I'll show you."

The five of us trooped down the hall, past the elevator and back stairwell to the conservatory. The hiss of the steam heating system was audible as we pulled aside the drape that covered the entrance to the greenhouse. Nigel went ahead of us to turn on the lights.

I hadn't really paid attention to the space my first time there. I'd been so intent upon finding the victim, and afterward upon getting inside to warm up, that I couldn't have given Detective Sergeant Mardling a very good description. Now my eyes roamed the room, noting the high glass walls and arched glass ceiling with a center ornamental cupola. The whole was supported by a framework of decoratively forged steel, the patterns cut into the beams making the structure appear light and airy despite the weight and strength of its construction.

A variety of exotic plants, some in flower, were arrayed on narrow tables that hugged the glass walls. Tall palm trees, as well as large pots of Norfolk pines, red and silver balls dangling from their branches, were arranged around a small furniture grouping, which included a metal table with a pineapple base, four matching chairs, and a garden bench. It was very appealing, despite the threadbare cushions, and I could imagine Lady Norrance entertaining her friends there. Yet, even though I hadn't familiarized myself with the greenhouse earlier that day, I had the distinct feeling that there was something I was missing.

But what?

It was pitch-black outside now and still raining, although the wind had died down. The only light in the garden came from inside the greenhouse. Nigel held the door while I pointed out to Detective Sergeant Mardling and Constable Willoughby where Mrs. Beckwith had lain.

"Willoughby, do you have a torch?" Mardling asked.

The constable pulled a flashlight from her belt and shone its beam on the puddles on the ground, but I couldn't see anything that would have been helpful to them. Shivering, I pulled my shawl closer, and George wrapped an arm around my shoulder, drawing me into the warmth of his side.

Mardling came back into the conservatory and shook raindrops off his jacket, while Willoughby stayed in the garden, turning in circles as she tried to get a connection on her cell phone.

"What do you think she was doing out there?" the detective sergeant asked.

"It seems Mrs. Beckwith was looking for something for Lady Norrance," Nigel told him.

"Ah, and how do you know this?"

"Lady Norrance mentioned wanting a sprig of holly for her hair to wear to the ball," I put in. "Apparently Mrs. Beckwith was sent on this errand."

"We speculated that she may have gotten locked out, collapsed in the garden, and been unable to rise to call for help," George said. "After Mrs. Fletcher discovered the body, this door locked behind her as well. There was a brisk wind at the time, and it was quite arctic, and she nearly became a victim of the elements. Happily, we found her before anything dire occurred. Mrs. Beckwith was not so fortunate."

Mardling grunted. "So it would appear. We'll have to confirm all this, of course. Cannot simply accept your analysis, even from someone as esteemed as a Scotland Yard inspector. Have to follow our own procedures."

"Of course."

George was convinced that there was no mystery in how Mrs. Beckwith had died, and I didn't want to embarrass him by disagreeing in front of the police. If they did their jobs well, as I hoped they would, they might come to the same conclusion. It wasn't that I believed Mrs. Beckwith had been murdered. She may have died exactly as George had assumed—of natural causes or from the cold. Since she was lying in a puddle when I found her, it must have rained. Between the cold and the damp, hypothermia was a good possibility. Even so, the victim of an unexplained death is entitled to a thorough investigation, not a quick assessment.

I've always been uncomfortable when people jump to conclusions. I can't count how many times I've argued with the sheriff of my hometown in Maine about this very thing. As Cabot Cove's chief law enforcement officer—and as a former New York City policeman—Mort Metzger had worked on many criminal cases, quite a few of them homicides, and I'd had occasion to help him. We'd butted heads whenever I felt he'd come to his conclusions before all the facts were in.

And all the facts were not in about Flavia Beckwith. Who were her friends? Did she have any enemies? Why had she gone into the garden without a coat or jacket? Was it possible that someone closed the door behind her, knowing that it would block her escape from the cold? Was it possible someone closed the door on me as well?

I looked at George, who smiled and squeezed my shoulder.

I dropped my eyes, ashamed. *You've been involved in too*

many murders and too many novels, I scolded myself. *Your imagination is running wild. Of course George isn't jumping to conclusions. As he said, he's merely speculating on what might have happened, and he could very well be right. Every death is not suspicious. Why are you fussing over this one?*

"What are you dreaming about, lass? You've been very quiet."

"Just feeling sorry for Mrs. Beckwith. What a miserable way to die, alone and cold."

"That it was. And you, are you warmed up now?"

"I am, but I'm also feeling tired and cranky. I'm sorry if I'm not good company."

"You're always good company, but you're probably hungry. We never got to sample those French pastries made by the new chef. You'll feel better once you've tucked into a good meal."

Willoughby grinned as she came back into the greenhouse. "Finally got through. They're on their way."

"We'll have the body removed, Mr. Gordon," Mardling said. "That'll give Mrs. Estwich a chance to clean up. I may want to spend some more time here after I hear from the coroner. We'll probably come back tomorrow to see this place again in daylight."

"Very good, sir."

"And if I can help in any way, I'm at your disposal," George said.

"Thank you, Chief Inspector. We don't get too many Scotland Yard higher-ups out here. We're just simple country police. Good to have your expert analysis on this case."

I thought I detected a tinge of sarcasm in Detective Sergeant Mardling's comment, but George smiled and held out his hand. "It was my pleasure. And if I may offer my congratulations on a capable service, I've read of the commendations given your constabulary. Well done!"

Mardling all but twisted his foot like a young girl receiving a compliment. "Thank you, sir! That's fine praise from a Metropolitan chief inspector."

George and the officers walked out of the greenhouse. Nigel pulled the plant on the rolling stand back to its usual position and put his hand on the light switch.

I lingered, my eyes roaming the room.

"Is there anything else I can do for you, Mrs. Fletcher?"

"No, thank you, Nigel. I'm ready to go." I sighed. There was something I was missing. I was sure of it. If only I could remember what it was.

Chapter Four

Dinner at Castorbrook Castle was a festive, if haphazard, affair, with the kitchen furiously preparing for the ball the following day and with houseguests and piles of luggage arriving with regularity. A buffet had been set up in the castle's state dining room, a cavernous—and chilly—hall with a gilt coffered ceiling and red velvet walls as backdrop for eighteenth- and nineteenth-century oil paintings. A long mahogany table, easily able to accommodate forty or more, was set with round leather mats beneath the Christmas tree–patterned bone china plates. Sideboards on opposite walls were decorated with evergreen bunting, fat gold candles, and spray-painted pinecones in between the platters of cheeses, cold meats, boards of whole and sliced bread, and a choice of three hot entrées to which guests were to help themselves. Nigel and another tuxedoed helper poured wine and refilled water glasses as a rotating round of diners entered, ate, and departed.

Lord and Lady Norrance had greeted most of their guests before retiring to another part of the house, probably to have a quiet meal together.

George and I sat next to my publisher, Griffin Semple, and the lady I assumed was his date, Ruby Miller-Carlisle. Griffin was the son of Archibald Semple, who'd brought many of my mysteries to the British public and had widened sales of my books to the European market. Archie had been a shrewd promoter, but he lived a self-indulgent lifestyle, eating and drinking to excess, which eventually led to ill health and if not exactly an early grave, at least a premature one. He died at sixty-three following a banquet hosted by the British-American Publishers Alliance.

Archie's son had taken over the business. While I doubted Griffin was gifted with his father's commercial talents, he had the good fortune to have inherited a thriving business and a knowledgeable staff.

As we ate, Ruby chattered excitedly about arrangements for the ball, the jazz band ("very modern"), and the food ("the chef used to work in a restaurant with a Michelin star"), and what she was planning to wear ("silk organza from Amanda Wakeley—she designs for the Duchess of Cambridge").

"I understand you're a friend of the earl's family," I said.

"His daughter, Jemma, and I share a bedsitter in town. We met at boarding school, but we were never close then. She's part of the horsey set, while I'm more of a 'Sloane ranger.' "

"I think I've heard that term before," I said, "but remind me what it means."

"A Sloane ranger is someone who likes to shop at Sloane Square in London, and everywhere else, for that matter. We're great fans of country sports and the clothes that go with them. I adore riding costumes, but I'd never get on a horse." She wrinkled her nose. "They smell."

Griffin set down a plate piled high with a generous portion of everything offered on the sideboards. "Has Rupert talked to you about his project yet?" he asked me.

"I didn't know that the earl's son was working on a project."

"Well, I don't know how far he's gotten. I think a lot will depend on you."

"On me?"

Griffin laughed. "You didn't think we were invited to the New Year's Eve ball out of the goodness of their hearts, did you?"

"I understood that I received an invitation because you and the earl have a relationship, and you thoughtfully asked that George and I be included on the guest list."

"We do have a relationship, sort of. Dad used to sell off selected works from the earl's rare-book collection whenever Norrance was short in the pocket. My father knew many antiquarian booksellers who paid top dollar for sixteenth- and seventeenth-century first editions. Those sales probably put a roof on this château."

"But what does this have to do with me?"

"Rupert fancies himself a film producer and has been casting around for properties he can bring to his former mates at Oxford to finance. They have a production company, but no scripts to film."

"I'm beginning to see the connection."

"Thought you might. Rupert asked me to suggest books that would make good movies. I thought of you. After all, several of your mysteries have been translated to the screen."

"And not all of them happy experiences. Didn't it occur to you that I might like to know about this in advance, Griffin?"

He shrugged. "Americans are always excited about meeting

members of the aristocracy. I figured it would be a good trade-off. You get to attend a ball, and Rupert gets—"

"Yes? What *does* Rupert get? Did you promise him anything?"

"Only an introduction, Jessica. I wouldn't commit you to something without your knowledge."

"That's comforting."

"Now don't get your knickers in a twist. It's going to be a great occasion. Norrance is planning a splendid fancy-dress ball, complete with French dinner service and fireworks at midnight. You'll love it. And, thanks to me, you and the inspector get to stay in a genuine English stately home, one that's not been taken over by a hotel chain yet. Might provide inspiration for your next book."

"Not everyone is invited to spend the night in Lord and Lady Norrance's home," Ruby put in. "Griffin and I are down the road at the Muddy Badger. Nice inn, mind you—isn't it, Griff?—but hardly Castorbrook Castle."

Griffin looked up sharply when Clover Estwich entered, carrying another platter. He stood. "They've just brought in more trout. I'll be right back."

"Oh, I'll come, too," Ruby said, popping up. "I love trout."

I sighed.

"A bit of a disappointment, is it, Jessica?" George said.

"Why didn't I remember that there's a price to pay for everything? I have to admit I have no one to blame but myself. I should have questioned Griffin more closely when he first broached the topic. I'm embarrassed to say I was swept up in the idea of having the opportunity to take *you* somewhere special, after having once stayed at your family's castle in Scotland. Pretty self-important of me, wasn't it?"

"Now, don't be down on yourself. Much as I love the Sutherland family seat in Wick, it can't begin to compare with the elegance and sophistication of this hall."

I'd been introduced to the castle in Wick during a trip to London with friends from Cabot Cove. George had invited us—all twelve of us—to spend time at his family home on Scotland's North Sea coast. Accommodating our group wasn't a problem; the castle now functioned as a hotel and had fourteen guest rooms, only two of which would be occupied by paying guests. It promised to be an idyllic holiday for me and my friends, and an opportunity for me to become reacquainted with George. It would have been all those things had I not encountered a woman in white in the hallway on my first night there. Her eyes were the color of copper, and a red stain grew on the bodice of her gown. I said something to her, but she was gone as suddenly as she'd appeared. That was my introduction to Isabell Gowdie, Scotland's most celebrated witch, who, it was alleged, haunted the Sutherland castle.

"Meeting" Isabell was upsetting enough. But when a local lass was found dead, killed with the same kind of weapon that had felled Isabell Gowdie, a pitchfork rammed into her heart, our holiday took a dramatically different turn. Despite that jarring intrusion into our vacation, a vision of the Sutherland family's dramatic castle, sitting starkly on a high, rugged cliff, an angry sky its scrim, and the dissonant strains of a bagpiper welcoming us, has remained with me forever.

* * *

"I must say, it is a treat to see firsthand, rather than on the television, how the members of the British aristocracy live," George said, "although with all their trappings of wealth, they don't seem to be any happier than the average Scottish burgher."

I smiled. "No, they don't, do they? I was surprised they spoke so candidly in front of us, given the English reputation for being reserved."

"I think they forgot we were there, tucked into a corner as we were. But such disharmony is not surprising. Families everywhere have their troubles. Don't know a one without. We simply were privy to the woes of the privileged."

Ruby returned to the table, her arm linked through Jemma's. "Have you met Lord and Lady Norrance's daughter? Mrs. Fletcher is the author I was telling you about, Jem. Jemma's going to write for *Nag and Dog* magazine."

Jemma rolled her eyes. "It's really called *Horse and Hound*, and I don't have the job yet."

"But she will. So, writer, meet writer." Ruby's smile was smug.

"We met Jemma this afternoon at tea," I said, "when we met you, Ruby."

"Oh, silly me."

"That's right," Jemma said. "You two found Mrs. Beckwith. Poor old thing."

"What happened?" Ruby asked.

"She dropped dead in the garden."

"Oh, my goodness. Was she a relation?"

"She was my governess."

"But you haven't needed a governess for years."

"She was my governess when I was little. After we were shipped off to school, my mother kept her on as lady's maid, but

I think my father would have been just as happy if she'd retired to the country somewhere. She should have."

"Why do you think that?" I asked.

Jemma shrugged. "He didn't like her, or she didn't like him. I can't remember why, if I ever knew. She mostly kept out of his way. But if she'd retired, she'd probably still be alive. I don't remember hearing that she was sick or anything."

"I remember now. Is she the one you used to call 'the tortoise'?" Ruby asked.

Jemma laughed. "She lived in an apartment in our old nursery on the fourth floor. My brother Kip said the only time she'd come out of her shell was when the House of Lords was in session and our father was away."

"Kip's such a clown. Will you miss her?"

"She's been around my whole life, but I didn't really know her well. My mother knew her better. They would play cards or watch the telly together."

"Does your father still attend the House of Lords?" I asked.

"He comes up to London on occasion, but I think he's more interested in meeting with his marketing people and finding craftsmen who can fix things. I shouldn't say it, but this castle just gobbles pounds and shillings. Too bad we don't have a movie or television show using *us* as a setting. They pay well."

"Maybe your brother could write a script and set the story here," George put in.

"Rupert? He barely knows how to write his name." Both girls laughed at Jemma's comment.

"Do you happen to know if Mrs. Beckwith liked to cook for herself?" I asked.

"What a strange question. I've no idea. I hadn't seen much of her lately, in any case. I live in town when my parents aren't entertaining."

"So Ruby was telling us."

"She was?" Jemma turned to her roommate. "What else did you say?"

"Only what's clearly obvious—that you like to ride and that you hurry home each weekend to exercise your horses." Ruby winked at us. "There may be another attraction in the stable, too. A tall, blond-haired one."

Jemma blushed. "Ruby, you're making things up again."

"Why not? I like the idea of the princess and the groom. It's such a romantic story, like a fairy tale."

"I'm not a princess, and he's not a groom. He's a licensed trainer. Anyway, we're just old friends, and please don't let my father hear you talking about us."

"The earl is very proud of his stable," Ruby told us as Jemma nudged her to keep quiet. "Do you ride, Mrs. Fletcher?"

"I don't," I said. "What about you, George?"

"The closest I've been to a horse was at Epsom Downs ten years ago for a charity fund-raiser."

Ruby sighed. "I love to get dressed up and go to the races." She turned to Jemma. "I got the sweetest wrap dress last week. I forgot to show it to you."

"Did you bring it with you?"

"No. It's a bit small, but I should fit in it by next June in time for Royal Ascot. But for now, I'm a free woman. Do you think there's any sticky toffee pudding left? I'm famished."

The young women excused themselves and drifted toward the buffet. Griffin had neglected to return to his meal, but I spotted him at the other end of the table having a serious conversation with Rupert.

I folded my napkin and placed it next to my plate.

"Feeling better, Jessica?"

"Much. You were right, George. I was hungry. Too bad it's so dark out. I could use some exercise now to work off this meal."

"There are miles of corridors in this house," George said. "Let's investigate some of them."

"I wonder if we could find Mrs. Beckwith's apartment."

He cocked his head and squinted. "Curious to discover if she cooked for herself? I wondered why you asked about that."

"She didn't take her meals with the staff."

"Beg pardon?"

"Clover Estwich, the cook we met this afternoon, said Mrs. Beckwith didn't eat with the staff. And just now, Jemma said she didn't get along with the earl, so it's unlikely she ate with the family. I'm just wondering where and with whom, if anyone, Flavia Beckwith ate her breakfast, lunch, and dinner."

"Maybe there's a take-away shop in the village."

"That could explain an occasional dinner, but would she eat out or order in for every meal?"

"Well, it's not unheard of."

"True," I said, "but with Castorbrook Castle having hired a French chef and still keeping its longtime cook, it would've been a shame if the family's former governess never benefited from the culinary expertise of the Grant family kitchen."

"Maybe Clover was exaggerating."

"Or maybe Flavia helped herself to whatever was in the refrigerator before or after others had eaten."

"That doesn't sound probable, but now you've piqued my curiosity about the lady."

I grinned at George. "I have to admit I'm curious about her in general."

"I think I see a trip to the fourth floor in the offing. Let's take that walk you're yearning for."

Chapter Five

The fourth floor of Castorbrook Castle had been the servants' quarters when the house was fully staffed. These days, however, while a few of the doors along the narrow corridor were locked, most of them opened into unoccupied rooms. Some were still furnished with low iron beds; narrow mattresses were rolled up on top of the springs, looking like the shells of giant snails.

The hallway lacked the patterned carpet that softened our footsteps one floor below. Instead, George and I walked carefully, conscious of the creaking boards and thin layer of dust that coated the level surfaces of the paneled wainscoting. In daytime, dim light would likely reach the long passage from the windows of the empty rooms, but at night, the only illumination came from brass sconces set high in the wall every fifteen feet. We'd found the switch for the lamps outside the door from the back stairwell when we'd taken the elevator as high as it would go, and then walked up the stairs from the third floor in search of Flavia Beckwith's apartment.

"So many empty rooms," I said softly. "Where do you suppose their employees live?"

"They probably commute from town," George replied in an undertone. "Supporting a staff round the clock—meals, laundry, utilities, and all else it entails—is a chore."

Whether it was the eerie nature of the deserted floor or guilt that we were trespassing in private territory, George and I hesitated to speak in normal tones.

"It must be an overwhelming responsibility—not to mention expensive—to manage a building this size," I said. "Still, the earl certainly spends a lot to maintain places the public—or at least his family and guests—will see, if the drawing room and state dining room are any example. I'm sure the ballroom tomorrow night will be spectacular, too."

"And don't forget the earl's stable, another costly luxury."

"With all that wealth, you'd think his wife's personal maid would live in a nicer part of the castle. This paneling could use a good dusting."

"Not a pleasant space, I agree. Are you certain we're in the right wing?"

"I'm not, but Jemma said the old nursery was on the fourth floor, and this is the only fourth floor we've found, so we may as well explore a bit."

George twisted a knob on a closed door, but it didn't open. "Even if we can determine which room was hers, don't be disappointed if it's locked."

"I won't be, but see that French door down there on the left? It's ajar. Maybe that's the former nursery."

We approached the open door, one of two glass-paned panels covered on the inside with sheer white curtains. I pushed the door all the way open and poked my head in the room, calling out. "Hello! Anyone in here?" Silence.

George felt around for a wall switch and flipped it up, turning on a bare bulb in a socket set in the ceiling and surrounded by a carved rosette.

"This must be it," I said. "Look at the wallpaper." A faded pattern of children riding ponies, sailing on ponds, and building sand castles filled the walls' empty spaces. In addition, an arched marble fireplace, centered on one wall, appeared to have been used recently. Half-burned coals, now cold, cradled new ones in the metal grate. Facing the hearth was a sofa covered in faded chintz with a soft woolen throw folded over one arm. A book was opened facedown on one of the cushions, probably taken from the bookcase to the left of the fireplace, where some of the volumes seemed to have been shoved in haphazardly, their spines to the wall instead of face out. Along with shelves of books—many of them children's books—a toy truck and stuffed rabbit sat next to framed family photos. I pulled one down and peered at it in the weak light. It was an old picture and had probably fallen off the shelf at one time; the frame was taped together. I showed it to George. "This looks like her, doesn't it?"

"At least twenty years ago," he replied. "She was quite pretty. Are those the earl's children, do you suppose? There are four of them."

The three boys and a girl were all dressed in blue jeans, barn jackets, and rubber boots; only the girl's long hair plaited into braids identified her gender. "Hard to tell at that age," I said, "but this one definitely looks like Rupert. Look at that curl on his forehead. His hair hasn't changed. Perhaps one of the other boys is a relative or friend."

I replaced the photograph and let my eyes scan the rest of the room. To the right of the fireplace was an efficiency kitchen with a half-size refrigerator under a wooden plank that served as a counter. There was barely room for the metal single-burner hot plate and a dish drainer next to the sink. Folded in the drainer was a linen dish towel with a picturesque view of an antiques shop and beneath it the words *Chipping Minster*. The label, still attached, said it cost one pound, which was less than two dollars and a reasonable price for a souvenir dish towel, although I wondered why she would buy a souvenir of the town in which she lived.

I knelt down to open the refrigerator and mentally catalogued its spare contents: a pint bottle of milk, several jars of condiments, a bag of almonds, two wedges of cheese, and a package of sliced ham.

"If she was preparing meals for herself, they were modest ones," George said.

"You're thinking of what Constable Willoughby said about the stain on Mrs. Beckwith's fingers."

George nodded. "I doubt she was experimenting with Asian cookery up here."

I agreed, but just to be sure looked through the salt and pepper shakers and jars of spices lined up neatly on a shelf above the hot plate and sink that also held four plates, cups and saucers, a frying pan, and two electric appliances, a teapot and a rice steamer.

George sank down on the sofa, picked up the book, and began paging through it.

Behind the sofa, just beyond a table holding a small Christmas tree and a stack of greeting cards, was a door. "Do you think that's the bedroom?" I asked.

"Go on in and see for yourself. I haven't read Robert Louis Stevenson since I was a lad."

I opened the door and stepped to the side, allowing the light from the main room's ceiling fixture to overcome the darkness. "Oh," I whispered. I groped along the right side of the wall, hoping to find another switch, but there was none.

"George, do you have a flashlight?"

"No."

"A lighter or match perhaps?"

George put down the novel and patted the pockets of his tweed jacket. "I have a lighter for my pipe. Will that serve?"

"I think so."

He reached over the back of the sofa and held it out to me.

I took it from him. "I think you may want to see this, too."

"Something wrong? What have you found?" He rose and came around behind me.

I held the lighter aloft, my eyes searching for a lamp. If my hometown sheriff, Mort Metzger, had been standing beside me, he would have said the room had been "tossed," police jargon for a ransacking. The place was a shambles. Drawers had been pulled from the dresser and spilled. Linens had been dragged from the bed and piled on the floor. The bedside table and lamp had been knocked over.

"Appears someone was looking for something," George said wryly. He stepped over the debris, righted the nightstand, and placed the lamp on it, straightening the shade before turning it on.

"They may have found it," I said, closing his lighter and handing it back to him. "The other room hasn't been ransacked."

"Perhaps the person was interrupted midsearch and abandoned the scene. I think we'd better not handle anything else. I'll alert Mardling that he should examine the deceased's living quarters, if this is indeed her space."

We walked back into the living room, closing the door on the mess behind us.

"Does this shine a different light on the case for you?" I asked.

"I'll reserve judgment on that," George replied, smiling. "Of course, someone could have simply taken advantage of the situation to hunt for money or jewelry. Thieves have no respect for the dead."

I returned his smile. "I may be mistaken, but in a castle occupied by an earl and countess, I would think there are far more sources of precious items than the modest rooms of a lady's maid. Think of the silver downstairs, the antiques, and priceless paintings. The countess must have beautiful jewelry. A thief could have a field day."

"What are you doing up here?" a sharp voice said from the open French doors.

George and I turned to see the housekeeper, Mrs. Powter, hands on hips and a frown on her face.

"This is a private home, not a public museum. Guests are not at liberty to wander anywhere they feel like. I'll thank you to leave this place at once and return to your rooms." She grabbed the doorknob and pointed to the hall. "Out! Now! If you please."

"We were looking for Mrs. Beckwith's apartment," I said as George and I exited the room. "Is this where she lived?"

"I do not have to satisfy your curiosity. This is not a tourist attraction. Imagine! Invading the home of a poor woman who's no longer here to protect her privacy. Is nothing sacred? I've a mind to call the constabulary right now."

I was about to declare that a police officer was standing right in front of her, when I felt George squeeze my arm. He shook his head slightly, and I held my tongue.

"Our apologies, madam," he said. "We were out of place. We'll leave straightaway."

"Indeed, you will. And don't think I won't let His Lordship know how some of his guests repay his hospitality." She followed us as we made our way back toward the stairwell. "You may find yourselves escorted outside tomorrow. I warned Her Ladyship of this very thing."

"What's that?" I asked.

"Of what comes of inviting strangers into the sanctity of your home. A New Year's Eve ball! A waste of staff time, and never mind squandering funds that could be set aside for other, more important things."

We reached the stairwell, and Mrs. Powter stopped at the door, watching as we descended the stairs. "I'm going to tell Mr. Gordon to count the silver before you leave."

Chapter Six

It was still dark when I awoke on the morning of New Year's Eve. In December, the sun doesn't show its face in the Cotswolds until after eight. Accustomed to being an early riser, I was showered and dressed by seven thirty and eager to get the day started. A sheet of paper that had been slipped under the door overnight promised light refreshments in the library for those who came downstairs before the morning meal was scheduled to be served. The paper offered a rough map of the castle and the surrounding property. Even though it was late in the season, fly-fishing was permitted on the lake for those who had brought their own tackle. Guests were invited to visit the stable but not to ride. And for hardy souls who enjoyed a good hike, a portion of the 102-mile Cotswold Way abutted the property, although the leaflet cautioned that signage—a wooden post with an acorn symbol—was not always easy to find.

George's door was open when I went into the hall. He was pacing in his room, his cell phone pressed to his ear. "The superintendent knows that I'm on holiday. We agreed I was to be called back only for an emergency." He covered the lower part of the phone with his hand. "I'll meet you downstairs," he whispered.

"If I'm not there, I may have taken a walk to the stable." I waved the leaflet at him.

He nodded. "I'm confident Morris can handle that on his own," he said into the phone. "Ask Atkinson to lend a hand, and while you're at it, pass along my congratulations on his becoming a father. Eight puppies, you said? Very impressive for a first litter. All right, I'll hold, but I can assure you I won't change my mind."

I walked down the corridor to the broad central staircase we'd climbed the day before. Mrs. Powter was not about, and I breathed a sigh of relief that the redheaded housekeeper was not there to scold me again for wandering around places in which I had no business being. I'd been astonished that she would speak so curtly to us since we were guests of the earl and countess, but I couldn't blame her for being upset. She was right. George and I had trespassed in a part of the castle not open to visitors. If I found someone strolling around the second floor of my home uninvited, I would be offended, too. That my motives were pure—well, at least not harmful—wasn't really an excuse. She was being protective of the family. I only hoped that she hadn't kept her promise to inform the earl of how rudely his guests had behaved. At least I had the excuse of George being a chief inspector for Scotland Yard, although he'd kept me from revealing that fact when Mrs. Powter came upon us in Flavia Beckwith's apartment. I wasn't sure why, but perhaps he wanted to save her embarrassment.

The library was on the ground floor to the right of the staircase. I knocked before entering but hadn't needed to. No one was inside, although a fire crackled in the hearth, and a round table in the center of the room held two pots, one for coffee and the other for tea, platters of buttered toast and croissants, both plain and chocolate, and small dishes with an assortment of jams. I poured a cup of tea, cut a plain croissant in half, and picked up one of the newspapers that had been neatly folded on the desk in front of a floor-to-ceiling bookcase.

"Anything of interest there?" said a voice behind me. "There isn't usually."

I turned to see the earl cross the room, take a piece of toast, and slather on jam. He poured himself a cup of tea. He was a nice-looking man, dressed this morning in heavy corduroy slacks and a white cable-knit sweater. Apart from an air of confidence, there was nothing in his appearance or manner to suggest he was a member of the aristocracy. He looked simply like a well-fed, middle-aged gentleman dressed for a weekend in the country.

"Good morning, Lord Norrance." I cleared my throat and read the headline to him. "It says 'Badger Cull Protesters Picket Local Farmer.' What's that about?"

"Big controversy," he replied, taking a bite of toast and waiting to reply further until he'd swallowed. "The National Farmers Union are trying to protect their members' cows from bovine tuberculosis, a disease carried by badgers. The government permitted the farmers to conduct a cull earlier this year. Brought their numbers down considerably. Apparently, one of my neighbors is still out hunting, and the animal society people are expressing their disgruntlement."

"Don't badgers hibernate in the winter?"

"I believe not."

"The article says two protesters from the Somerset Badger Patrol were arrested for aggravated trespass and theft after they climbed over a barbed wire fence and into a pasture."

"Hope you don't see my daughter's name among them."

"No. It names Archer Estwich and Maura Prenty."

The earl gave a soft snort and took a sip of tea.

"Is Archer Estwich related to your cook?" I took a sip from my own cup and polished off my half croissant.

"Her son. Didn't know he was an animal lover. Didn't think he cared about anything other than his hair and what time the pub closes."

"If you don't mind my asking," I said, smiling, "on which side of the badger controversy do you come down?"

"I think it's a sad but necessary measure," he said, finishing his toast and dusting the crumbs off his fingers. "It worked in Ireland. They lowered their bovine TB numbers over there. My complaint about badgers is that their holes can trip up my horses. Hasn't happened yet, but I live in fear." He took another taste of tea, making a slurping noise.

"Could the badgers give your horses tuberculosis?"

"Never heard of a case, so I doubt it. Problem seems to be with cattle. Are you interested in horses?"

"I have a niece who was a jockey," I said, not that my response answered his question.

"Then you might like to see our stables. I'm going over there now. You're welcome to join me."

"Thank you. I'd be delighted." It was fortunate I'd already told George that was where I might be.

The earl cocked his head at the newspaper. "Anything in there about yesterday's incident?"

"You mean the death of Mrs. Beckwith?"

He nodded.

I looked through the pages and shook my head. "Nothing."

"Good! Let's go before all the others come downstairs and we get waylaid." He grabbed a chocolate croissant from the tray, wrapped it in a napkin, tucked it in his pocket, and smiled at me. "Don't tell my wife."

I followed him out of the library and down the hall, trotting to keep up with his pace. He made a sharp turn and opened a door into a mudroom, where barn jackets and canvas coats of various sizes hung on pegs, and a dozen pairs of rubber boots were lined up on the floor.

"Grab yourself a pair of Wellies," he said. "The grass is wet, and you certainly don't want to get anything from the barn on your shoes."

I slipped off my shoes, picked a pair of boots that looked to be the right size, and put them on. The earl handed me a jacket, shrugged himself into a green canvas coat, and we took off, crossing the rear garden. A pair of black dogs with curly coats barked at us and loped over, tails wagging.

"Good morning, boys," the earl said, addressing the dogs.

"I thought I heard a dog bark yesterday afternoon. Are these yours?" The dogs moved in between us and brushed against my leg. I put a hand down to pet a soft head, and a wet nose poked into my palm.

"They live in the gardener's cottage, but they belong to the estate. Angus must be around somewhere. My father was a fancier of water spaniels. He bred them, but I haven't carried on that tradition. Don't have time to be an expert on so many things."

Angus came around the corner of the building, pushing a

wheelbarrow. He whistled, and the dogs raced over to him. "Morning, my lord. Sorry, didn't see you there. Thought the boys were annoying a guest."

"They weren't annoying us," I said. "They were just being friendly."

"What are you up to this morning, Angus?"

The gardener pulled from the wheelbarrow a tool I recognized as a lopper and held it up. "Going to give the fruit trees a trim before the snow comes in and it's difficult to get to them."

"See to it that you do a more thorough job than the last time."

"I know how to trim trees."

"That's debatable," the earl said. "Just be quick about it. And remember, there will be many more guests arriving later who will need help with their luggage."

"I'll be ready," Angus grumbled.

"See that you are."

"He's a surly bugger, that one," the earl said as we watched the husky servant lumber away. "If he hadn't come along with the countess, I'd have given him the boot a long time ago."

The dogs remained behind when the earl and I slipped out a garden gate and took a path winding through a small orchard, and then made our way downhill toward the stables, a group of three stone buildings at the edge of a meadow.

"I'm sorry that George and I were the bearers of such bad news yesterday," I said. "It must have been very difficult losing someone who'd worked for the family for so long, especially for your wife."

"She'll get over it. I've already sent for a girl from the village to help out until we hire someone. One of Clover's nieces, but not Maura, the one named in the newspaper, thank goodness."

Clearly my host was not upset by the loss of Mrs. Beckwith, who could be replaced so easily with a "girl from the village." I found it distressing, even a little shocking, that the family members didn't mourn the death of their former governess and recent lady's maid. Mrs. Beckwith was indeed a "poor old thing," as Jemma had called her, if she devoted her life to people who barely raised an eyebrow at her passing. Then again, Jemma had mentioned that the earl and Mrs. Beckwith were not on the best of terms. I wondered why.

We walked between two of the buildings, the area paved with bricks, and entered the open door of a stable. The sounds and smells of the horses assaulted me. A half dozen equine heads turned in our direction. There was soft whinnying and the clop of restless hooves on the straw bedding. The sweet aroma of oats and straw mixed with less-pleasing odors as we neared a stable hand mucking out a stall. When he saw us, the young man—he couldn't have been more than sixteen—pulled off his red ball cap, and leaned on his pitchfork, waiting for the earl to approach.

"Morning, Your Lordship."

"Where's Colin?" the earl asked.

"Believe he went into town."

"What for?"

The young man shrugged. "Jus' said he had to make arrangements. Didn't say for what."

"When do you expect him back?"

"Not certain, m'lord."

The earl heaved a sigh. "All right. Saddle up Todoro for me, will you, when you're done with that?" He waved at the pitchfork.

"Yes, m'lord."

The earl guided me to one of the stalls where a bay-colored horse with a white star between her eyes moved slowly, her belly clearly distended. "This is our prize mare, Lamia. Brought her all the way from Kentucky. Her sire was a derby winner."

"Is she about to foal?" I asked, hoping there was nothing else wrong with her.

"Any day now. We expect great things from her." He reached out to caress the mare's neck, but she backed away, snorting. "Just like a woman," he said, laughing. He moved down the stalls. "This one's Aramis. He's Kip's if he ever gets his a—" He stopped, editing what he was about to say. "If he ever gets down here to exercise him. Our trainer will take him out, but it's better for a horse to know who his master is."

"Is Colin the trainer?"

"You know Colin?"

"No. I just heard you ask for him."

"Of course. Yes, he's our trainer. Fine young man. Been around horses all his life. Started as a groom, a stable lad, just like Ian, there." He waved a hand in the stable boy's direction. "I sent Colin to work with one of the most famous trainers in Britain, up near Balmoral Castle, the queen's Scottish home. Man used to work for the royal family there. Wasn't happy being sent away—Colin, that is. Thought he knew all there was to know about horses. But now I think he appreciates the opportunity. Gave him a profession. He can work anywhere in the world. In fact, I had an impressive offer for his services just yesterday from a peer in Cardiff."

If Colin was the young man Ruby said Jemma came home to see every weekend, the earl's daughter would not be happy with that piece of news. I wondered if the nobility still thought they could direct the lives of all the people who worked for them, sending them to another aristocratic house when their service was no longer needed or desired. Maybe the earl suspected that his daughter was infatuated with the trainer and wanted to quash it in the best way he knew, by getting Colin a better job far away.

"Yes, Colin is a first-rate trainer," he said proudly. "Knows every one of these beasts, all their peculiarities and preferences. That's what's required in a good stable."

I hesitated to voice what I was thinking—that if a good stable required a good trainer, why would he consider sending Colin away? Instead, I asked, "Which horse is your daughter's favorite?"

"That would be Elektra, this one here," he said, walking to a stall with a black mare inside. "Jemma babies her, puts up with her skittishness, but she's too high-strung for me."

"The horse, you mean."

"What? Oh, yes. Very droll, you are. Jemma's a bit high-strung herself, but an excellent horsewoman, the best rider of my children. Sits a horse like a man, a natural in the saddle. Wish my sons were. . . ." He trailed off. "Well, every man has his strong points. Speaking of strong points, has Rupert laid out his scheme to you?"

I felt my stomach fall. "No," I said lightly. "We were introduced at tea yesterday, but I haven't spoken with him since."

"Well, he'd better get on his horse if he expects anything to come of your visit here, no pun intended."

I was reluctant to pursue the topic any further, but thought the earl might find my lack of curiosity odd, so I said, "Griffin Semple told me that Rupert wants to be a film producer."

" 'Wants to be' is the operative term. So far he's nothing more than a dilettante. Starts one thing, drops it, goes on to another." His lips formed a tight line. Then he sighed. "I understand *you* have experience with filmmaking."

"Only peripherally," I said. "Some of my mystery books were optioned by Hollywood and a few were made into films, but my involvement was only as a script adviser. I know nothing about the production process itself, and much less about the financing, distribution, and marketing ends of the business."

"It sounds as if you know more than you think. I don't go to the cinema myself, so Rupert's ambitions are foreign to me, but he insists his mates from university have all the expertise needed to make any project successful. He claims that with the right 'property,' as he calls it, sponsors will shower them with money."

I turned away so the earl couldn't see my smile. In my experience, Rupert was very naive if he expected investors to fund the moviemaking fantasies of rank amateurs. But far be it for me to discourage him—or his father. Stranger things have happened—especially in the entertainment industry.

"You think he's a fool, don't you?" Lord Norrance said, disgust in his voice.

"No. I wouldn't say that. Having big dreams isn't foolish. If it were, there would never be great things accomplished in the world. I would say, however, that Rupert is very optimistic, and he'll need to work twice as hard as the next person and be dedicated and persistent if he wants to fulfill his dreams."

"I have two do-nothing sons. I should disinherit them both and leave the whole lot to Jemma, but she'd never thank me for it. An estate like this is more than a full-time job; it's a lifetime commitment." He stopped, perhaps embarrassed that he'd revealed so much of his thinking to a virtual stranger. We were both thankful when we heard a cough behind us.

"Beggin' your pardon, Your Lordship, but here's Todoro ready for you."

"Good. You don't ride, do you, Mrs. Fletcher?"

"No, I don't." I could see relief plainly written on the earl's face.

"Well, then you must excuse me." He took the reins from Ian and invited me to walk outside. "They'll be serving breakfast up at the house by now. Thank you for telling me about your film experience. When Rupert finally gets around to discussing his plans with you, I hope you'll set him straight."

"I'll tell him exactly what I told you."

The earl put his boot into Ian's cupped hands and vaulted into the saddle. He took up the reins and pulled the horse's head toward the meadow. "I suppose that will have to do."

Chapter Seven

"There you are," George said when I found him in the dining room sitting next to Elmore Jackcliff, the artist we'd met at afternoon tea the day before.

"I was down at the stable." I took a seat across from the men. "Lord Norrance showed me around himself."

"Ah, that's what you were telling me when I was on my mobile," George said. "Wasn't certain."

"Very fond of 'is 'orses, is Norrance," Jackcliff said, his Cockney accent clearly marking him as a nonaristocrat. " 'Opes to build up a racing string, as I understand it. Not that 'e tells me 'imself. I'm Lady Norrance's pet, not his."

"Have you known Lady Norrance a long time?" I asked.

"She was a student of mine in 'er younger days—Marielle Dillard, before she married up. Daughter of a baronet, Sir Martin Dillard. Rather lower on the nobility scale than she is now." He examined his fingernails and made a show of polishing them on the sleeve of his woolen jacket. "Still above the rank of a commoner such as the likes of us." He laughed. "She's the earl's second wife, you know."

"We didn't know," I said.

"Very nice of 'er to keep me on, and to invite me to the party," he said, taking a pad from his pocket and scribbling on the paper with a marker. "I'm painting 'er portrait in oils. Giving us a chance to renew our friendship. O' course, His Lordship only agreed, I am informed, because I'm charging them peanuts. But I figure I got the best of the bargain."

"How's that?" George asked.

"She's my intro to the aristocracy, don't you see? All those nice toffs I get to chat up today and tonight. Might get one or two commissions out of it, maybe more. Who knows? Kip's wife, Poppy, already wants her portrait painted. She's going to be the next countess—and can't wait. All this is worth my renting a tux for the occasion."

"Well, then you both benefit, you and the countess," I said.

"Elmore's being modest," George put in. "He's got a gallery in Notting Hill, and probably has his own dress suit." He eyed the painter. "I read about you in the *Times*. You're not exactly a starving artist living in a garret."

"Don't let my secrets out now," he said, elbowing George. "I was that once. And these posh types like to think they've discovered a new talent and are supporting the arts."

As he spoke, his Cockney accent softened, and I realized that Elmore Jackcliff liked to create a portrait of himself in words. It made me wonder how much of what he said could be believed.

"Does the countess still paint?" I asked.

"She dabbles, but she's more into gardening now. The castle has a beautiful conservatory. That's her doing. Have you seen it yet? Lots of exotic plants and potted palms. Bit of a jungle, but *très chic*."

"We were there yesterday," I said, watching George's face for a sign as to whether I should say why. Jackcliff and several other guests had entered the drawing room after the discussion about Mrs. Beckwith had ended. Since George and I had left the room when the police arrived, I didn't know if the subject of her death had come up again over tea.

"You're talking about the room off the enclosed garden?" George asked.

"Yes, stunning space, isn't it? She came into the marriage with quite a bit of her own money, and that was her first great project." He cocked his head, looking down at his pad. From my vantage point, I couldn't see what he was writing. "There's the 'secret garden,' too, as she likes to call the outside one. Brought old Angus along with her to the castle to set it up. He was her father's gardener. He can't stand the earl, but he's totally devoted to *her*."

"I believe he's the one who carried up our luggage yesterday," I said.

Elmore laughed again. "So, he's filling in as footman, too, is he? The earl must be short of cash again."

"Or simply short of staff," I said, thinking Lady Norrance would not appreciate that the man whose patronage she provided would sneer at the family so casually.

"Did you happen to know Mrs. Beckwith, who was Lady Norrance's maid?" I asked.

"The lovely Flavia? Always did like blondes. Yes. I heard about her unfortunate demise."

"Did you know her well?"

"No one knew Flavia well, except perhaps the earl."

"What do you mean?"

"You'll have to ask Marielle for the details—Lady Norrance, that is. They were this close"—he held up two fingers—"at one point anyway."

George pushed himself back from the table and slapped his thighs. "Well, I'm well fed and ready for a walk. What say, lass? Are you up for a stroll into the village? You're welcome to join us, of course, Jackcliff."

"No. No. You two run along. I like to be inside when it's cold outside, a carryover from my garret days. Besides, I'm sure I can find someone—perhaps less well-read and not a chief inspector—to amuse with my tales." He tore off the top sheet of paper on his pad and handed it to me across the table. It was a sketch of my face with a palm tree in the background.

"How nice," I said. "Thank you."

"A souvenir of your visit," Jackcliff said. He clapped George on the shoulder and gave me a wide smile. "See you two tonight at the grand event."

"Did you straighten everything out with Scotland Yard?" I asked George when we'd left the dining room.

"I did," he said, looking at his watch, "but I have to ring up a colleague whose shift doesn't start until one o'clock. I hope I don't miss him. Will you remind me?" He shook his head. "I must be getting old. My memory is not what it was."

I rolled my eyes. "Whose is these days? Age doesn't have exclusive claim on poor memory. I've heard young people complain about forgetting names, promises, or appointments. At the risk of sounding like a fuddy-duddy, I think our lives are far too busy to keep track of everything we want to do—at least mine is, and clearly yours as well."

"You could never be accused of being a fuddy-duddy, whatever that is."

"I hope you're right. But, in any case, between our two brains, I'm sure one of us will remember you need to make a call at one." I took his arm and lowered my voice. "By the way, did you really want to walk into town, or were you just using that as an excuse to get away from our artist friend?"

George gave a bark of laughter. "He is quite full of himself, isn't he?"

"Lady Norrance would be horrified if she overheard what he was saying about her and the earl. How can someone who considers himself to be so close to her be so indiscreet?"

"It's a shame, but the countess should be careful of the friends she allows into her inner circle. People like Jackcliff, who stand to gain from the acquaintance, are more interested in raising their own reputations regardless of the cost to hers."

"After this morning, I didn't imagine I would feel sorry for the countess, but now I do."

"What transpired this morning?"

I filled George in on my conversation with the earl, and his expectation that his wife would get over her maid's death because he'd hired a replacement.

"That's one cold gentleman," George said, tsking.

"Cold and more than a little arrogant. While he was perfectly pleasant to me, I noticed that the only ones he wished 'good morning' were the dogs."

Chapter Eight

Chipping Minster was a good two miles from Castorbrook Castle. George and I had dressed for the season, but after walking a mile, we were pulling off our scarves and opening our jackets, and by the time we reached the village, our bodies were warm, our cheeks rosy, and we'd worked up a hearty appetite. At least I had. The half croissant I'd eaten before I accompanied the earl to his stables was long gone, and my empty stomach demanded to be fed.

"Shall we stop at the Muddy Badger?" George asked. "Don't know what kind of kitchen they have."

"I'll be happy as long as it serves food."

The pub, which was part of the inn, was on the edge of town, and with its warm yellow Cotswold stone walls and thatched roof, it looked as if it had been built to pose for a picture postcard. On the stone walk outside the front door was a water bowl for visiting dogs; there was also a ring on a post to tether a horse. Inside, twinkling lights dangled from the beams on the low ceiling, causing George to duck his head.

Wooden benches took up two walls, round and square tables in front of them, most of them empty. Christmas wreaths hung in every window, the corners of which had been spray-painted with fake snow. We took seats as far away from the large fireplace as we could get. George piled our outerwear on the chair next to his.

"Specials are on the chalkboard," the barmaid called out from behind the corner of the bar where she was drying mugs. "I'll be right with you."

"What would you like, Jessica? You never had a proper breakfast."

"Right now, the ploughman's pie is appealing." I squinted at the sign. "But I'm so hungry, my eyes may be bigger than my stomach." The menu promised two wedges of cheese, sliced apple, veggies, and a dish of chutney along with the meat pie.

"You go right ahead. I'll help you with whatever you can't finish."

"It's a deal."

We placed our orders with the barmaid, George opting for a short lager and I for tea to accompany our meal. Our drinks arrived first.

"It's good to get out in the fresh air." I took in a deep breath, hummed it out, and warmed my hands on the mug of tea. "I miss getting regular exercise when I travel."

"You did yourself well this morning. And if we walk back to the castle, you'll have clocked nearly six and a half kilometers today."

I laughed. "That's four miles, but it sounds more impressive in kilometers. Oh, I forgot to ask. Do you know when Detective Sergeant Mardling is coming back?"

"I spoke to Nigel this morning. He said he expects both officers back this afternoon and that the detective sergeant told him he might have to stay late."

"I'll bet Nigel wasn't happy about that. Is he hoping that you'll keep the detective sergeant busy so the staff can concentrate on the ball?"

"He didn't come right out and ask, but I got the impression that he would be grateful if that were the case. He said he could free up one or two of the staff for questioning early on, should they be needed, but he was adamant that after four o'clock, no one would be available until the next day."

"I think Detective Sergeant Mardling will understand, don't you?"

"If not, I'll give him bad marks for community relations."

While we waited for our food, a young man in a plaid cap and tweed jacket walked in and took a stool at the bar.

"Mornin', Colin Stanhope," the barmaid said. "Not working today?"

"Good day, Doreen. I'd rather watch you work."

"None of your sass, now, young man. What'll you be having?"

"A pint and a plate of bangers and mash, please."

"Unless I'm very much mistaken," I whispered to George, cocking my head at the newcomer, "I think that young man may be the horse trainer up at the castle."

"Why do you say that?"

"The earl was asking for Colin this morning, but he was told Colin had gone into the village."

"Not exactly an unusual name over here," George replied in a low voice. "Might be a different Colin."

"What're you doing in town today?" Doreen asked as she placed a glass under the tap to fill with beer. When her first pull yielded more foam than beer, she poured it out and started again. "Isn't there a holiday ball up at the castle tonight with bigwigs arriving all day?"

"No one's arriving by horse, so I guess they don't need me just yet."

I raised my eyebrows at George as if to say, "See? I was right."

"I would've thought the earl would want you making the barns spick-and-span and showing off his racing stock to the guests." Doreen slid Colin's glass across the bar.

"Ian is cleaning up. I have time. Got some business to do first."

"What business, other than monkey business, would such a young man as you be up to?"

"I'm not so young; I wouldn't be unwilling to take you for a whirl."

"And I'm not so old to be saying no to you," she shot back, grinning.

Doreen took a tray from a kitchen helper in a white apron and hustled over to our table. "Here you are, madam, sir." She placed a wooden board, beautifully arranged, between us. "You have pickled onion there, homemade bread. This cheese is Stilton, and this is a local one, double Gloucester. Here's cut apple, grapes, cucumber, and tomato." She pronounced it "tomahto." "And, of course, the ploughman's pie."

"What kind of chutney is this?" George asked, pointing his fork at what looked like a cup of dark jam.

"Rhubarb and sultana today. Our cook makes it herself." She hesitated. "Hope you don't mind my asking, but are you in town for the ball?"

"We are," I said, "and if I eat even half of this, I'll never fit into my gown."

"At least try the lamb and pork pie. Best in the region. See those plaques and medals on the shelf behind the bar? Except for the darts trophy, they were all won by our cook and her sister. We're right proud of them."

"As you should be," George said.

"Let me know if there's anything more you need."

Colin had swiveled around on his stool to watch Doreen's presentation of our lunch. He was a handsome man, older than he appeared at first. I judged him to be near thirty. Fine lines radiated out from the corner of his green eyes and bracketed his mouth. His complexion was ruddy, testament to the time he spent outdoors working with the horses. I caught his eye and smiled at him. He pulled at the peak of his cap in acknowledgment and turned back to his beer.

I cut the lamb and pork pie in half, and George and I began to eat, taking our time and quietly eavesdropping on the conversation at the bar.

"How many are you expecting at the castle tonight, Colin?"

"Don't know."

"If I could, I would've taken one of the serving positions up there, just to see everyone all dressed up in their finery. And the fireworks."

"Why didn't you do it?"

"Why? Well, isn't it New Year's Eve down here in the village, too? This place will be full to the brim tonight. We had to hire on extras ourselves."

"I'd rather be here at midnight myself."

"There's plenty of years you can see the New Year come in

from that seat," she said. "Lord and Lady Norrance never held a ball before since I've been here. You're lucky to be there to see it."

He shrugged.

"If I were working up at the castle the day of a New Year's ball, I wouldn't be wearing such a long face as yours."

"Lost my aunt yesterday, Doreen."

"Your mother's sister?"

He nodded.

"Oh, I am that sorry, Colin. I didn't know. She was a nice, quiet lady, was Mrs. Beckwith. What did she pass from?"

"Don't know yet. Probably heart. They found her in the garden."

"Oh, that's awful. And how is your mother taking her loss?"

"Me mam is taking it in stride. The two of them didn't talk much recently, but I can see that she's upset. Her sister was younger, so I think it scares her a bit."

"Does a bad heart run in the family?"

"Don't know." He paused before adding, "Certainly hope not."

"Oh, goodness, I didn't mean to suggest you might have it, too," Doreen said.

Colin must have smiled at her, because she hit his arm with her towel. "Oh, you." She slid a plate in front of him. "Here's your dinner. It's my treat today."

Colin shook his head. "Oh, no. That's not necessary."

"I'll decide what's necessary. And don't argue with a barmaid, or you might not get your glass refilled."

"Oh, Griff, look who's here!" said a voice from a door next to the bar. Ruby Miller-Carlisle and Griffin Semple, my British publisher, waved as they headed straight for our table. "You're on to lunch, and we haven't even had our breakfast yet," Ruby said, sitting down next to me and pulling an empty round table close to ours.

"Just got up," Griffin added, moving our coats and dropping into the chair next to George. He stretched and rubbed his eyes. "We're staying upstairs. Nice rooms, but having a pub downstairs was too much of a draw for Ruby. We closed the bar last night."

"It's all right to sleep in today," Ruby said. "We needed our beauty sleep if we're to stay up for the fireworks and dance until the wee hours. Are you excited, Jessica? I am. I may call you Jessica, right?"

"Yes, of course," I said. "I'm looking forward to this evening, but I don't know how much after midnight I'll last. I'm not accustomed to dancing till dawn."

"Oh, but you must. It'll be divine. Did you know some people are coming in costume? That will make it even more exciting. I can't wait. Do you mind if I pinch one of your grapes? They look delish."

"Help yourself. I think George and I have eaten all we can hold."

Ruby and Griffin finished off our grapes, as well as the cheese and bread, and then they ordered their breakfast. Although I found their youth and enthusiasm entertaining, I was sorry not to have the opportunity to hear more of Colin's conversation with Doreen. Had Ruby and Griffin not joined us, I would have called Colin over to express our condolences and let him know we'd been the ones to find his aunt. But while Ruby was telling a story about Rupert's wife, Adela, having been mistaken for a popular singer with a similar name, Colin slipped off his stool and left the pub. I glanced at George, who shrugged his shoulders as if to say, "What can you do?"

I now knew that Colin was related to Mrs. Beckwith, and I planned to revisit the stables when we returned to Castorbrook Castle. I would offer my sympathies and hope to draw him out. Perhaps he could shed some light on why his aunt and the earl didn't get along. I wondered if he was aware that someone had turned her bedroom upside down. Could he guess what that person might have been looking for? And could he tell me the source of the red dye on Mrs. Beckwith's fingers?

Chapter Nine

As soon as we were able, George and I excused ourselves and left Ruby and Griffin working on a ploughman's breakfast. We strolled down the village High Street arm in arm, admiring the holiday decorations that were still up and peeking in shop windows that advertised big New Year sales. There was a crispness to the air that I relished. Had I been in Maine, I would have said it smelled like it was going to snow. But I didn't know if the same atmospheric conditions heralded the white stuff in England.

I'd spent Christmas in New York City with old friends, and had flown to London two days later. George had arranged to take his vacation the week after the holiday, and, thanks to his seniority, was able to tack on a few extra days after the New Year. We hadn't seen each other for some time, and I had thought it might be awkward at first until we had gotten reacquainted. But I was surprised and grateful to find that we slipped into a comfortable camaraderie that, while affectionate, was accompanied by a clear understanding that our relationship could not move forward as long as there was an ocean between us—and there was always going to be an ocean between us. Even so, our mutual enjoyment of each other's company was wonderful, and if there was a pang of regret mixed in, it only made our time together more precious.

"Did Father Christmas treat you well this year?" George asked as we looked over a tray of holiday socks that had been set outside a clothing store.

"Yes, indeed. *Someone* gave me a lovely tartan shawl," I said, holding up a corner of the scarf. "Thank you again."

"You're very welcome again. And thank you again for the leather fishing belt."

"Made in Maine," I said, laughing. "I couldn't resist when I saw the silver trout on it. We'll have to go fishing together one day."

"I think I would enjoy that."

"I did buy myself a present when I was in New York City."

"And what did you get?"

"A book called *Police Procedure and Investigation*."

"I would have thought you knew all that by now."

"There's always more to learn. Plus, I love having my own library of reference books. The Internet is wonderful, but it doesn't match the feeling of paging through a book and finding something you didn't even realize you needed. I hope that experience never goes away."

As George and I walked, I scanned the faces of the people on the street; I was hoping to see Colin Stanhope again. Of course, even if I caught sight of him, I wasn't sure what George and I could say. It would've been so much easier in the pub where Colin had spoken about his aunt. But the arrival of Ruby and

Griffin had scuttled my chance to introduce myself. While it was unlikely I'd come across him in the crowd of shoppers, nevertheless I paused at each store window, peering inside in hopes of spotting a plaid cap and tweed jacket.

"I know the holiday displays are appealing, lass, but why are you so interested in a shop that sells cleaning supplies?" George asked. "Are you planning to Hoover your room at the castle?"

"What?" I looked down at the window display of vacuum cleaners and brooms. I'd been so intent upon checking the customers inside the store that I hadn't noticed what it sold. "Caught in the act." I grimaced.

"You're hoping to see the horse trainer again, aren't you?"

"I'm just disappointed I didn't get the opportunity to express our sympathies."

"And ask a few questions."

"And ask a few questions," I echoed. I looked at my watch. "Isn't there a call you need to make? It's almost one."

A puff of air escaped George's lips. "Thanks for reminding me." He looked around and frowned. "We should have stayed at the pub. Now, where can I make the call without standing in the middle of the street like those distracted pedestrians on their mobiles, who drive me crazy in London?"

"Let's walk a little farther." I saw a break in the storefronts up ahead and pointed. "Maybe there's another pub or park on the next street."

We reached the corner and turned down a brick-paved lane, more of a mews, really, with attached carriage houses on either side. At the end of the block, the lane broadened into a street with stone-fronted private homes, some of them converted into stores and businesses. The first one we came to had an ANTIQUES sign and looked vaguely familiar. In front was a stone bench. Away from the crowd of shoppers on High Street and far enough from the front door of the store to avoid being overheard, it was perfect for George's telephone appointment.

"When you're finished, look for me there." I cocked my head toward the antiques shop.

He nodded and began dialing.

An old brass sleigh bell sounded when I opened the shop door and stepped inside. The room was crammed with furniture and cabinets holding a variety of household items, some of it artfully displayed to reflect the season, including a collection of wooden nutcrackers grouped together. Chandeliers hung from the ceiling, and every available wall space was taken by gilt-framed paintings. Table lamps minus their shades stood on top of one cabinet, the shelves of which held porcelain figurines of dogs, horses, sheep, hunters, shepherdesses, and pipers dancing on painted grass. Upholstered chairs of differing vintage were pulled up to a mahogany drop-leaf table set for a holiday dinner party with a plaid runner down the center. My gaze lingered on a small Wedgwood bowl, but it was chipped. Sitting on a silver tray next to it was a four-piece tea service.

"That's not sterling," an elderly woman said when I picked up the coffeepot. She stood at the entrance to a hallway. "The good stuff is in the back room. Can't keep it up here. Too many tourists like to pocket a souvenir."

"I'm a tourist," I said, putting down the pot, "but I promise I have no designs on your silver plate."

"Didn't think you did," she replied. "I can always pick out the good ones. You have an honest face."

"Thank you, Mrs.—?"

"Mrs. Fortunato, but you can call me Hazel. And you are?"

"Mrs. Fletcher, but please call me Jessica."

"Are you looking for something in particular, Jessica?"

"To be honest, I'm not. My friend is making a phone call outside, and I just came in to browse."

"You're welcome to browse. That's how I make most of my sales anyway. They always find something."

"Have you owned this store a long time, Hazel?"

"Nigh on fifteen years." She paused, giving me a wry smile. "You thought I was going to say something like forty years, didn't you? After all, my youth is long behind me. But no, I only opened the shop after Mr. Fortunato died." She fingered a gold locket on a chain around her neck.

"Was your husband an antiques dealer?"

"He was a farrier. I think you'd call him a blacksmith in the States. You are American, am I correct?"

"Yes. I'm from Maine."

"Never heard of it, but I picked out your accent right away."

"Is there a lot of work for farriers in Chipping Minster?"

"Work enough. Those that have the big houses, lots of 'em have horses. And the farmers almost all have a horse or two even if what they raise are cattle or sheep."

"That must have kept your husband busy."

"Most of what he did was shoeing, and a little bit of veterinary surgery when it was called for, but we were able to raise our children and make a nice home. And I had time to the visit the charity shops. That's how I started my collections."

"So you turned a hobby into a business," I said. "Very clever."

"Well, you have to make your way somehow," she said, but she seemed pleased with the compliment.

"By any chance, did your husband work for the Earl of Norrance?"

"Worked for him and his father before him." She tilted her head to the side. "Are you and your friend invited to the ball tonight?"

"Yes. George and I arrived yesterday. We're staying up at the castle."

"If my husband were still alive, we would have received an invitation. I'm sure of it. But with Mr. Fortunato gone so many years now, I guess they've forgotten about the family left behind." She paused, perhaps reflecting on her disappointment at not being included. "His Lordship is a bit severe, but his wife is a kind lady, don't you think?"

"I've only just met her, but she seemed very welcoming," I said, choosing my words carefully. I wondered if Hazel knew Mrs. Beckwith, but I hesitated to ask. If she hadn't learned of the woman's death, I didn't want to be the one to deliver that news.

She clicked her tongue.

I waited, hoping she would bring up Flavia. When she remained silent, lost in her own thoughts, I decided to take another tack as I perused items on the table. "I visited the earl's stables this morning. I understand he's planning to breed horses for the racetrack."

"He has big ambitions, that man. His father raised spaniels, a little more modest. But my cousin's grandson has a job in the stables, so I'm glad of the work for his sake."

"Would that be Colin?" I asked.

"Oh, no. Colin is Emmie Stanhope's son. Ian is my cousin's daughter's boy." Hazel turned around and beckoned to me. "If you don't mind, come into the back where I can sit down, Jessica. My hips begin to ache when I stand too long."

I followed her down the hall to a small kitchen, where the shelves were stacked with more silver, presumably sterling, and a variety of china. Matching cups and saucers were prettily displayed with small vases of flowers. Even the old woodstove held an assortment of antiquated cooking utensils.

"Nice to have a bit of company," Hazel said. "It's been quiet today. Everyone getting ready for the New Year, I guess. May not look like it, but I can make a decent cup of tea in here if you'd like one."

"I just finished lunch, but you go ahead." I removed my jacket and hung it on the back of one of two chairs not occupied by tablecloths, draped with aprons, or piled high with brand-new souvenir dish towels advertising Chipping Minster. *Ah,* I thought, taking a seat, *that's why the shop looked familiar*. I'd seen its picture on one of those dish towels in Mrs. Beckwith's apartment.

Hazel plugged in an electric teakettle and took the other empty chair. She wrung her hands, then dropped them in her lap, sighing. "Did anyone up at the castle happen to mention something about sad news—I mean, did you hear anything about a mishap? Perhaps not. You wouldn't know her, of course. But someone I knew . . ." She trailed off.

I stifled a sigh of my own and reached out to put a hand on top of hers. "Are you talking about Flavia Beckwith?"

"Flavia! Did you know Flavia?"

"No. I never met her."

"Oh, but how? Of course, they must have been speaking of her. Please tell me what they said."

"Was she a good friend of yours?"

A small smile played on Hazel's lips, and her eyes grew moist. "We were the best of friends. She was ever so smart, a university graduate, always reading. We would often have our tea together and sometimes dinner if she wasn't needed at the castle. She would tell me about the books she was reading, and I would show her something from the shop and explain the history and why it was valuable."

"I'm so sorry for your loss."

"It's not easy for women alone, you know. It gets lonely sometimes. Friends are so important. She was a lot younger and far more educated than I am, but she was no snob. Anything she taught me, she made it sound like we were discovering it together. Those children were lucky to have her in their lives."

"The children of Lord and Lady Norrance?"

She nodded.

I didn't dare share how disrespectfully the Grant children had spoken about Mrs. Beckwith, if they acknowledged her at all. Rupert had referred to her as "the old girl," and Jemma had called her a "poor old thing." Kip, the earl's heir, hadn't uttered one word about the death of his former governess. And their parents hadn't expressed any sorrow either, at least not in front of George and me. Instead, I asked another question. "Had your friend been ill lately?"

"Goodness, no. She was the picture of health. Perhaps a little too thin." Hazel looked down at her own round middle. "She felt the cold keenly."

I almost told her that I had found Mrs. Beckwith's body, but I thought better of it. The information would only make her even unhappier.

"Flavia was planning to take a trip to Spain," Hazel said, rising slowly from her chair and going to unplug the electric teakettle. She poured water into a strainer of tea set over a cup. "Much warmer there. Said she'd saved up a bit of money and might use it to travel."

"It's sad that she didn't get that opportunity. Was she a widow, too?" I wondered if perhaps a former husband had died recently and mentioned her in his will.

"Never met him if there was a Mr. Beckwith," she said, sitting again. "She didn't speak of him. She was a very private person in her way."

"When did you two first meet?"

"Oh, let me see. Must be at least twenty or twenty-five years now. I didn't know her when she was first hired on when the earl's first countess was expecting, but of course that job fell through."

"Why was that?"

"Flavia was to have been the infant's nurse, but the countess and her babe died in childbirth."

"Oh, my. You don't expect to hear about a woman dying in childbirth in a modern country like England. And the baby, too. How awful!"

"Well, it was a terrible tragedy."

"Of course. What did your friend do?"

"Went to live with her sister up north. Didn't come back until His Lordship was remarried with another child on the way. Then they both moved here, Emmie and Flavia, and Emmie's son, Colin. That's when we became friends."

"Were the sisters close?"

"They used to be. Had a falling out a month or so ago. Flavia wouldn't tell me what it was about, but I know it grated on her. I feel terrible for Emmie. It's awful to lose someone when you haven't made it up with them, isn't it?"

The sleigh bell in the front room sounded, and a masculine voice I recognized called out. "Halloo, anybody here?"

"That's my friend," I told Hazel. I went to the hall and called out, "We're in the back, George."

"This is cozy," he said, coming into the kitchen.

I introduced George to Hazel, and she offered him tea.

"Wish we had the time," he said. He looked at me. "You and I have to meet Detective Sergeant Mardling in an hour. If we hurry, we can walk. Otherwise, we'll have to call for a taxi."

"Given a choice, I vote for walking," I said, gathering my things. "I need to work off that lunch."

Hazel thanked me for keeping her company, and she gave me one of the souvenir dish towels as a remembrance.

"I'm sure I'll see you again," I said, winking at her. "I haven't finished browsing yet."

Chapter Ten

With the prospect of meeting with Detective Sergeant Mardling on our minds, our walk back to the castle wasn't as leisurely as the one we'd taken into town. Dodging the postholiday shoppers, George took long strides down High Street. I had to move quickly to keep up with him. He was setting a swift pace, until I tugged on his sleeve to remind him that I was not a gazelle and needed a breather now and then.

"Sorry, Jessica." George slowed to a walk, but in no time, his long legs had picked up speed again.

I couldn't afford a blister with the heels I planned to wear with my evening gown. Thank goodness I'd packed a good pair of walking shoes, but I didn't want to press my luck by jogging in them.

"If you take it a little easier, I'll be able to keep up with you," I said as we reached the outskirts of town and entered the country road that led back to Castorbrook.

"My apologies, Jessica." George took my arm and ambled to

the middle of the road, making an effort to match his steps to mine. "I wasn't thinking, or sorry to say, I was, but not about you."

"Is something bothering you, George?"

"Not bothering me exactly, but—"

"But what?"

"I'm concerned about the timing of the inquest. I trust Mardling has enough sense not to barrel about like a wild bull and will tread carefully around the staff, not to mention the earl and his countess."

"They need to understand that he has a job to do as well. I can't imagine that a few minutes for an interview will throw off the whole evening affair."

"Perhaps not. I only hope that he can manage with just a few minutes." George pursed his lips and shook his head. "He struck me as a bit plodding yesterday."

I could feel myself rising to Mardling's defense and suppressed that reaction right away. There was something about the inhabitants of Castorbrook Castle and the death of Mrs. Beckwith that made me testy, and this time I couldn't blame my feelings on hunger.

George and I had such limited time together. I wanted our interactions to be happy and fun-filled; it was the whole reason I had agreed to the New Year invitation to begin with. Yet, ever since we'd discovered Flavia's body, I'd been irritable and on edge, arguing with his conclusions and doubting my own. Was our relationship not what I'd hoped it to be? Was I overthinking what should be a simple, pleasant vacation in each other's company? Was I simply coming down with the flu?

The growl of an engine captured our attention. Behind us, a

man on a motorcycle impatiently revved his machine until we stepped to the side of the road to let him pass. George gave him a mock bow and waved him on. The driver made a rude gesture and roared ahead. *Another one impatient and short-tempered today,* I thought. I looked up at the overcast sky. Some people attribute their mood swings to rising or falling barometric pressure. *I wonder if it's going to snow.*

The narrow road snaked uphill and down between grassy meadows bordered by low stone walls. George and I found a gait that was midway between his lope and my stroll, and we continued companionably down the lane, hands held. To our left, cows grazed in the field, and off in the distance a farmer walked the stone wall perpendicular to the road, a rifle cradled in his arms. I nudged George and pointed my chin at the farmer. We watched as he raised his rifle and took two shots.

"Must be after rabbits," George said.

"I think he's probably hunting badgers."

"Beg pardon." George looked at me curiously.

"There was an article in the local newspaper. Lord Norrance and I were discussing it this morning. Badgers can carry tuberculosis, which the cattle catch."

"Oh, yes. I remember reading about that, but it was several months back. The animal rights people raised quite a hue and cry when the cull was authorized."

"Apparently the controversy continues. One of the earl's neighbors is still killing badgers on his property. Two people were arrested trying to stop him."

"Ah. You must have the right of it, then. I never connected the hunter with badgers."

As we rounded a corner, the land rose up and a line of trees hindered our view, but they didn't block the sound of more gunshots. A short way ahead, the motorcyclist stood in the middle of the road, his vehicle propped against a stone wall. The man was pacing back and forth, cursing loudly.

"Are you all right?" George called out as we approached him.

"I was until that idiot farmer, Melton, took a shot at me." He dragged off his helmet and ran his fingers through a thatch of dark hair.

"Stay here," George instructed us. "I'm going to look for the hunter." He climbed over the stone wall and clambered up the hill, shouting. "Halloo! Farmer Melton. Hold your fire."

"Your friend a copper?"

"Scotland Yard inspector."

"Good! Get him to arrest that bloke. Will save us all a lot of trouble, not to mention lives."

"I'm sure the farmer wasn't aiming at you," I said.

"And I'm just as sure he was," he shouted back.

A brawny fellow with tattoos showing through the open collar of his leather jacket, he was about the same age as the earl's sons, I guessed.

"You seem to be in one piece," I said. "Did a bullet strike your motorbike?"

"Came close."

"How do you know?"

"I heard it whiz by. Struck that tree over there. See the broken branch?"

"From the speed you were going earlier, I would imagine you'd have been a quarter mile away from any branches hit by a bullet, even if you felt the breeze as it whizzed by. Were you stopped here?"

He kicked the dirt on the road. "I was waiting for a friend to meet me."

I looked around. There was nothing but road and stone wall and grassy fields on either side. "Your friend was to meet you here? In the middle of nowhere? There're no houses, no town, not even a signpost. How would your friend know where to stop?" I imitated his low voice. " 'Meet me at the seventh tree past the large rock.' "

He couldn't hold back a chuckle, then looked at me in confusion. "Are you a copper, too?"

"No," I said, extending my hand. "I'm Jessica Fletcher, a guest at Castorbrook Castle."

He paused, looking at my hand before accepting it. "Archer Estwich. I'm working the ball tonight."

"You're Clover's son?"

"You know my mother?"

"We've met, but I doubt she'd remember me. Was it Maura Prenty who was to meet you here?"

"How do you know all this?" He shook his head as if trying to knock some water from his ear.

"I read about you in the newspaper."

"Oh, no! Did my mother see it?"

"I don't know, but Lord Norrance did."

A stream of air escaped his lips. "I don't care about him."

"You're working for him tonight."

"Yeah, because my mother asked me. Otherwise I wouldn't give the earl the time of day."

"Why not?"

"Didn't you hear what he did? He demoted her. My mother. She's been a cook up at the big house for twenty years, and the countess goes and hires a fancy dandy French chef, but they want her to stay on just the same, but for less money, of course, the cheap bas—"

"I get the picture."

"Pleads poverty all the time, does the lord. Selling off land left and right to people who have no care for animals. Then what does he do with the money? Puts on a big show and hires a Michelin chef. And who suffers? My mother and probably others on the staff who've seen their salaries cut back."

"If you feel so strongly, why did you agree to work at the ball tonight?"

"Well, it's my mother's show, too. Can't let her down. We could use the extra bread. Besides, I'm hoping someone will hire away that Frenchie and the Grants will have to come begging on their knees for her to take over again." He smirked. "I'd be happy to see that."

George came over the hill with the farmer walking in front of him. Melton's gun was open and hanging over his arm, the muzzle facing the ground. Archer looked up sharply.

"It's not loaded," George said.

"I didn't shoot at anybody," Melton said, stepping on the wall and jumping onto the road with George following.

"Mr. Estwich here said a bullet whizzed by him and lodged in that tree." I pointed to the broken branch.

The farmer spat on the road. "I was aiming at the ground. If a bullet bounced off a rock, I didn't know it."

It didn't look to me as if he meant to apologize.

"Melton is through with shooting for the day," George said. "He understands he needs to be more judicious when using a firearm, or the authorities will come down on him. He's been cautioned."

"How many poor defenseless creatures did you kill today?" Archer asked.

"None," Melton replied.

"They're onto you, then. You don't credit them enough for brains and feelings."

"I credit them with carrying disease—that's what I credit them with."

"Then pay to vaccinate your cattle. Don't kill an innocent creature."

"You pay for it. Why you crazies want to protect useless rodents, I don't know."

"You don't know much. They're not rodents to begin with. They're related to otters and weasels. They lived on this land way before you brought your cattle here. They're a British institution, part of our culture and history."

"Yeah. Yeah. I've heard all the arguments. But if your mother wants her milk from healthy cows, she'll understand the need to get rid of these pests."

"You leave my mother out of this." Archer raised his fists and moved toward Melton.

George stepped between the two men. "That's enough of the animal rights debate for today, gentlemen. Melton, don't you have cows to milk?"

"I do."

"And you," George said, turning to Archer, "you were on your way somewhere, weren't you, son? You were driving fast enough."

Without another word, Melton climbed over the wall and trudged up the hill.

Archer put on his helmet and snapped the strap by his ear. "Sorry about the gesture earlier, Inspector."

George waved him off. "No harm. Just do us all a favor and stay away from Melton. I don't want to hear about any more bullets hitting rocks and then missing you."

Archer pulled his motorbike to a standing position. "Thanks, Inspector, Mrs. Fletcher. Maybe I'll see you later."

"Wait, Archer. What about your friend, the one you were supposed to meet here?" I asked.

"She knows where to find me. She's my cousin. Her sister's going to be working for the Grants, too." He climbed on his bike, revved the engine loud enough for the farmer to hear even though he'd already crested the hill, and drove off.

George looked at his watch. "We're going to be late for Mardling."

"He'll still be there when we arrive." I took his arm.

George patted my hand. "I'm looking forward to toasting the New Year with you."

"It's going to be fun."

"That it will, lass. I'm sure this kerfuffle will be our last misadventure for the day."

But George was wrong. There were more misadventures to come.

Chapter Eleven

My mind was full of badgers, or, more precisely, the arguments for and against eliminating them. I hate to see any animal mistreated or killed for no reason. Here, the farmers claimed a very good reason: to keep their cows healthy. But if there was an alternative—and apparently there was, a vaccination for the cattle—then why kill an innocent animal going about its daily living? Of course, the reason always comes down to money. The cost and inconvenience of vaccination was placed on the balance scale against the ease and economic practicality of shooting a badger, or worse, trapping and shooting a badger, and the decision was made.

I didn't know much about badgers. I remembered reading about them in *The Wind in the Willows* when I was a child. And a badger was the symbol of the Hufflepuff House in the Harry Potter books. It was probably used because badgers are known to be peaceful animals until threatened, when they surprise their enemy by the fierceness of their defense.

I haven't owned a pet in a long time. My travels get in the

way. It would be unfair to a cat or dog—any pet, really—to put up with my being gone for weeks at a stretch. But I count myself an animal lover all the same. My sympathies in this case were with the badgers, although I wasn't sure that Archer Estwich's approach to defending them by harassing the farmer was the right way to go about it.

These were the thoughts occupying my mind while we walked up the long drive to Castorbrook Castle and saw several police cars parked in the gravel circle in front.

"Subtlety is not Mardling's strong suit, I see," George commented as we skirted the pond and made our way to the front entrance, where a uniformed officer stood at attention.

"Where is Detective Sergeant Mardling?" George asked.

"I believe he's questioning the downstairs staff, sir."

George's expression was grim. "I told Nigel to ask Mardling to wait for us. Apparently, the detective thought it better to move ahead without interference. We'd better find him."

"Whether or not Mardling accommodates us is only a matter of courtesy. Remember, George, we're merely guests. You have no authority here."

"I can have that changed if necessary."

"Do you think that would be wise?"

"Let's see what he's up to before I answer that question."

It seemed to me that George had taken a dislike to Mardling, and I wondered if I'd been wrong when I assumed that he hadn't noticed what I'd perceived to be Mardling's mocking tone the first time we'd met him. Perhaps George had been aware that the local man felt threatened by the presence of a Scotland Yard chief inspector, and he decided to ignore his behavior in the interests of peace and cooperation. But my dear friend was not about to tolerate continued rudeness, and while I didn't blame him, we—really he—were on shaky ground when it came to jurisdiction. Even so, I was eager to find out what the coroner made of the death of Flavia Beckwith, if he was able to make a determination at all.

Mardling had begun his investigation in the kitchen, to the consternation of the staff cooking for the ball, if I read their expressions correctly.

The chef, wearing a tall toque on his head—the emblem of his rank in the kitchen—barked orders to Clover and two cooks assisting her, pulling out a fresh spoon to sample a dish and flinging it into the sink after the first swallow. Nigel was directing Angus, the gardener, who was thankfully in a clean uniform and white cotton gloves, on polishing the remaining silver flatware that had not already been set on a tray for delivery upstairs.

Every flat surface of the large room, a tribute to stainless steel and marble, was covered with stacks of baking trays in various steps of preparation. Platters of hors d'oeuvres partially cooked and ready to be reheated for serving were on shelves in one area, while other dishes awaiting finishing were being ferried from the walk-in refrigerator to the several ovens in service.

"Where is my scullery maid?" Chef Bergère shouted.

"The constable is questioning her," Clover replied.

"And the second kitchen maid?"

"I'm supposed to be next, Chef," said a sturdy young lady lolling by a closed door in the hallway. "He told me to wait here."

"How long does it take to ask a few questions? My langoustines will get overcooked." He shook a pan on the stovetop and pointed at Clover. "Be gentle with that caviar whilst you're putting it in the serving dish. Don't stir it—you'll break the eggs and ruin the taste and texture."

"As if I've never handled caviar before," she huffed.

"At a hundred pounds an ounce, it's worth more than you are."

"Who's taking care of afternoon tea?" Nigel called out. "We have an hour and a half to teatime."

"I have no time to fritter away on tea service."

"I'll do it," Clover said, untying her apron.

"No! I'll take care of it. You stay on the salmon mousse canapés." Bergère turned, his eyes roaming the kitchen. "Are the champagne cases on ice?"

"It's under control," Nigel replied. "Five cases are in the cooler, and three cases are stacked outside in the garden. You needn't bother yourself about my responsibilities, Chef."

"I'll require three bottles for my risotto, Mr. Gordon."

"And why am I just hearing about this now? I ordered the proper amount for serving, not for cooking."

"Then send someone into the village for three more bottles."

"Every merchant will be sold out. It's New Year's Eve, or did you forget?"

"Don't you have any spare champagne from the wine storage?"

"I'm not giving you Dom Pérignon to pour into rice. You'll have to make do with white wine." Nigel picked up a champagne glass and held it up to the light. "Who's responsible for washing these glasses?"

The young woman waiting her turn to see Mardling held up her hand. "I'll wash them again when he's done with me." She gestured to the closed door behind which Mardling was assumed to be questioning the scullery maid.

George and I carefully picked our way across the kitchen toward the closed door, trying to step out of the way as steaming pans were pulled from the oven and set out on the marble countertop. We reached the place where the second kitchen maid waited, just in time to come face-to-face with Mrs. Powter. The housekeeper ignored us, calling out, "Her Ladyship wants a cup of tea."

Nigel frowned. "Why didn't she ring the bell?"

"I don't have time to cater to her needs right now," Chef Bergère said. "Can't she wait until teatime?"

"I didn't ask. Would you like to go upstairs and put the question to her?"

Clover didn't wait for permission. She took a china teapot, cup, and saucer from a cabinet, rinsed the pot in boiling water, and set it upon a small silver tray. She prepared the countess's tea, adding a creamer and sugar bowl as well as a small plate of cookies to the grouping, and handed off the tray to Nigel. "Let's not lose all our senses of how this house is supposed to run."

"I'll tell Her Ladyship that you were pleased to prepare her tea." Nigel took the tray and made his exit.

"You do that," Clover called after him. "Some of us know which side our bread is buttered on." She stole a look at the chef and sniffed.

Mrs. Powter dusted her hands. "Then I may return to see to our guests." She eyed George and me. "Do you have a reason for being down here, or are you two playing tourist again?"

"May I introduce myself properly, Mrs. Powter. I am Chief Inspector George Sutherland of Scotland Yard. You had a death here yesterday."

Mrs. Powter paled.

"Yes, I see you remember. There's an inquest going on. Detective Sergeant Mardling is here." George gestured toward the closed door. "I believe he is expecting me."

"Begging your pardon, Chief Inspector. I didn't realize. Yes, of course. So sorry."

"We may wish to revisit Mrs. Beckwith's private chambers, assuming you have no objection, of course."

"No objection, sir." She gave a quick nod. "I'll return to my duties now, if I may."

"By all means, but please make sure Mrs. Beckwith's door is unlocked so we may bring Detective Sergeant Mardling to see her rooms."

"Yes, sir."

I had been half hiding behind George because, of course, I held no rank whatsoever, and I preferred not to give Mrs. Powter a reason to question my presence. But when she was gone, I stepped next to George as he knocked on the closed door and, without waiting for a reply, opened it.

Detective Sergeant Mardling and Constable Willoughby were leaning against a counter while the scullery maid, a girl who appeared to be about seventeen, sat primly in a chair and stared at a tape recorder on the table in front of her.

"Ah, Chief Inspector," Mardling said. "You'll forgive us, I hope, for starting without you. I have been led to believe that time is of the essence today because of the ball tonight, although I daresay we will still be on the premises when the event begins. And since I have not been given access to the host and hostess, I may decide to continue my inquiries until they are able to make themselves available."

"Beg your pardon for interrupting then," George said. "Please continue."

Mardling cleared his throat. "I think we may have finished with our inquiries of this young lady." He switched off the tape recorder. "You may go."

"I could tell you more stories about the Grant lads, if you like, sir."

"I will keep your offer under advisement. You may return to your duties, Miss Lambert."

Her mouth turned down. Her duties as scullery maid were to wash pots and pans, not half as appealing as being the center of attention of two officers encouraging her to pass along the local gossip. But she hopped out of her seat. "Shall I send Elsbeth in now?"

"No. I think we'll take a little break between witnesses." Mardling smiled and held the door open.

George waited until she left before asking, "Did the coroner's report hold anything to suggest the need for such a thorough inquest?"

"The preliminary report was inconclusive, but she had a heart defect."

George raised his eyebrows at me as if to say, "I told you so."

Mardling scooped up the tape recorder and handed it to Willoughby. "Tissue samples have been sent for toxicological analysis, but as you know, the results may take several weeks to come back."

"Did the coroner comment on the stain on Mrs. Beckwith's fingers?" I asked.

"He said he didn't know what caused it but hazarded a guess that she may have been cooking beetroot. His wife has complained of stains from handling the vegetable."

"I rather doubt she bothered to prepare fresh vegetables, from the limited cooking facilities available to her," George said.

"Oh?"

"Last evening, Mrs. Fletcher and I had the opportunity to visit Flavia Beckwith's apartment upstairs. In fact, we would like you to see her quarters yourself, if you have the time."

"It was certainly on my agenda." Mardling's face reddened. "We thought it best to get the staff interviews out of the way first."

"Very wise," George said.

Although his tone did not betray it, I was pleased that he was giving Mardling back a bit of his own medicine.

"Nevertheless, as lighting is limited on the staff floor, it might be a good idea to see her living space while daylight provides additional illumination. Would now be convenient?"

Mardling nodded to Willoughby, and the four of us made our way to the fourth floor.

The French doors to Mrs. Beckwith's apartment stood ajar. Mrs. Powter must have unlocked them as George requested. He pushed one door fully open and let the officers precede us into the room.

Her living room looked the same as it had the night before except that the Robert Louis Stevenson novel that had been left open on the sofa, and that George had been paging through, was gone. I didn't remember him putting it away, but my eyes scanned the bookcase to see that it had been replaced on the shelf. The books that had been shoved in haphazardly with their spines to the wall also had been removed and replaced correctly.

Mrs. Powter must have come back after she escorted us to the stairs. If she did . . . I had a terrible feeling George was not going to be happy.

"This is what we discovered here last night." George walked to the closed bedroom door and flung it open.

The two officers crowded into Mrs. Beckwith's bedroom. "Don't see what you thought was of great import in here," Mardling said. There was almost a note of triumph in his voice.

"What!" George pushed past Mardling and Willoughby. "Jessica! Come see this."

I hurried to the room, but I knew without looking what the view was going to be. Mrs. Beckwith's bedroom was pristine, the bed neatly made with decorative pillows leaning against the headboard. The dresser drawers had been closed, and I was certain everything in them was carefully folded.

"This room was a jumble last night," George said tightly, "linens everywhere, drawers poured out, nightstand toppled."

"There's no sign of disruption now."

"I think we need to have a discussion with the housekeeper," George said.

"Was she here last evening?"

"She was."

"And you didn't tell her not to disturb anything until the proper authorities arrived?"

"I didn't think it needed to be said."

"Apparently you were wrong."

"Apparently I was."

I felt humiliated and furious on George's behalf. He stared at his shoes, breathing hard with nostrils flaring; then he strode from the room and through the French doors into the hall. I was grateful that Mardling refrained from any more biting remarks. If he dug the knife in any further, I wouldn't have been surprised to see George explode.

I schooled my features to keep from showing my anger. "Excuse me for pointing this out, but despite its neat appearance now, this room had been ransacked when we saw it, most probably after someone learned of Mrs. Beckwith's death. Why Mrs. Powter presumed to clean it up when the staff had been informed that you would be conducting an inquest, Detective Sergeant Mardling, I can't begin to understand, unless she herself made the mess. If I were you, I would place her next on your list of interviewees."

"Are you telling me how to run my investigation, too, Mrs. Fletcher?"

"I'm telling you that to overlook an important piece of information would be irresponsible, but you do as you please." I nodded at Willoughby, left Mrs. Beckwith's quarters, and found George pacing in the hall.

"I had to leave, or I would have found myself giving him a pop on the jaw." George strode down the hall to the stairwell.

I followed him. "If you ask me, I think he was trying to irritate you on purpose."

George stopped and whirled around. "Worse than that, Jessica, he was right. Why didn't I identify myself to that imperious woman last night? Why did I let her chase us out of Beckwith's apartment like the trespassers she accused us of being?"

"You were being considerate of her feelings—and mine." I guided him to the stairs. "The fact is we didn't have any authorization to investigate Mrs. Beckwith's apartment. If anything, it was my insatiable curiosity—let's call it what it is, nosiness—

that's at fault, not you. I pushed you to do something that was not appropriate for us to do. That we found something possibly incriminating, or in any event irregular, was pure accident."

"But once we did find it, I should have asserted my authority and told Powter to stay away from what very well may be a crime scene. But I didn't. I let her chase us away like two dogs with our tails between our legs."

"George, you're exaggerating. But there's nothing we can do about it now. Let's allow Mardling to go his own way with this inquest. You yourself said the lady probably died of a heart attack or stroke magnified by exposure to the elements. Who knows why someone turned her room upside down? It probably doesn't matter."

We reached the third floor and stood outside our rooms. "We have a New Year's Eve ball to go to tonight," I said, resting my hand on George's arm. "It's going to be catered by a French chef with a Michelin star. There will be dancing to a jazz band, and the evening will be capped off by amazing fireworks, or so Ruby says. Let's leave Flavia Beckwith to rest in peace, and you and I get on with our lives."

He covered my hand with his. "I don't know what I did to deserve you, Jessica Fletcher, but I'm going to work very hard to convince you to stay by my side."

George ducked into his room, claiming the need for a rest before the evening activities, but I think he just wanted to be alone for a while. I paced in my own room for a few minutes before deciding that I was too agitated to stay still. I slipped out, closing my door softly in case George was trying to nap. I walked down the hall, pausing at the broad staircase, then decided to continue straight to see what was on the opposite side of the house from where we were staying. It didn't look any different. Closed doors lined the hallway, probably some of the nearly fifty bedrooms Nigel had said the castle contained. As they were on our side of the floor, the walls were covered with a patterned fabric in soft colors set into the rectangular spaces created by moldings. The moldings gave visual interest to the long corridor and served as additional frames to the many paintings on display. I stopped to admire a landscape that reflected the view from my room, and another that must have been painted in the walled garden on a summer day. Some paintings featured animals and still lifes, remarkable in their detail. That the Grant family had enough artwork to fill the walls of every room and every hall was impressive, even though I came upon a few blank areas where a darker patch on the wall fabric indicated that a piece of art may have been removed.

Up ahead, a shaft of sunlight from an open door contrasted with the muted illumination provided by wall sconces and picture lights attached to the tops of the frames. I walked a little faster, hoping to get a peek into another room in this fascinating castle. When I heard a murmur of voices, I slowed my steps. Was Mrs. Powter going to appear and accuse me of behaving like a tourist again? She would be right *again*, although she couldn't have assumed that guests would remain confined to their rooms when they weren't sharing a meal or attending an event with their hosts. The whole idea of inviting people to stay presumed they would enjoy the amenities the castle had to offer. Certainly enjoying the artwork would qualify.

I was rehearsing how I would answer the redheaded housekeeper, when I heard a man's voice. "Turn your head a bit to the left, my dear. I want to see that exquisite profile."

"Are you almost finished?" a woman asked. "I have to get ready for tea."

"You don't need a lot of time to look beautiful. You're lovely just the way you are. I hope the earl appreciates the treasure he has in you."

"You're a flatterer, Elmore, but I must admit I enjoy hearing your compliments, even if they're insincere."

"I only tell you the truth, Marielle. You're wasting your beauty on a man who only appreciates horseflesh. But I will show the world what a prize you are. You must let me exhibit this painting before you hide it away in this mausoleum."

"This mausoleum, as you call it, is going to make our fortune, and we'll be able to leave it to the next generation while we travel the world."

"You'll never pry the earl's hands from the wheel when it comes to Castorbrook."

"We'll see. Now I really must go."

"Aren't you going to give me my usual payment, my dear?"

Not wanting to be caught eavesdropping, I retreated halfway back down the hall and studied a painting of a pair of dogs in the English countryside, their noses pointing to a badger whose head peeked out from a hollow log. A horse and rider were in the background. A plaque on the painting credited the artist, Charles Towne.

I heard the rustle of fabric and looked up to see the countess hurrying toward me.

"You have such wonderful artwork here," I said.

"Thank you." She rushed past, turned at the staircase, and disappeared.

I waited a moment in case she had forgotten something and

might return, then continued my leisurely walk down the hall until I reached the bright splash of sunlight making a backward L across the floor and up the wall. I peeked inside. Jackcliff was swirling a paintbrush in a jar of liquid, which, by the smell of it, had to be turpentine. The room was the same size as both George's and mine, but with fewer pieces of furniture. A drop cloth was centered under a table spattered with paint. A large canvas leaned against an easel. From the door, I could see only the back of it. An armchair stood at an angle near the sunny window, and on the far side of the room was a chaise with several pillows. One had fallen to the floor. I knocked on the door frame. "May I come in?"

Elmore Jackcliff looked up, startled. "Yes, of course. Jessica, isn't it? You've discovered my private studio. Come in and admire my genius. You just missed my model." He waved at the painting I couldn't see.

"Would that be Lady Norrance? We passed each other in the hall."

"Did you?" Jackcliff turned aside, swiped a handkerchief across his lips, and stuffed it in a pocket. "Well, what do you think?" He concentrated on cleaning his brush.

I came around to the front of the canvas. "It's beautiful."

"Of course it's beautiful. The subject is beautiful. Do you consider it a fair likeness?"

The unfinished painting was mostly white with black lines sketching in a background of drapes and a chair. The figure of a woman stood in the center, her body angled slightly to the side, one hand on the back of the chair. She gazed over her shoulder toward the viewer. Only the head, torso, and one arm had been painted in detail. The rest of her was outlined in red. Four stripes of white paint covered where the artist had made corrections. A photograph of the countess in the same pose was taped to a corner of the picture, along with detailed sketches of her ring and her shoes affixed to the canvas below it.

While the real-life model was an attractive woman, the portrait revealed a glowing beauty that said more about the artist's view of her than what nature had created.

I turned to catch Jackcliff watching me closely. "Lady Norrance must be delighted with this. You're a wonderful artist."

He chuckled. "It's true." He wiped the brush dry with a dirty piece of cloth, tossed it in a red metal box that held other brushes and tubes of paint, and laid the cloth on top.

"George said you own a gallery in London. Do you sell your own paintings there?"

"Would that I could take 'ome enough from me own work," he said, the Cockney accent creeping back in. "No. I 'ave to offer the public a good variety to support my habit. But a commission like this one from the earl goes a long way to boosting my reputation and my ego."

I wondered if the earl had really given him the commission or if the countess was the one to insist her portrait be painted by her former teacher.

Jackcliff reached out and pinched my chin, turning my head from side to side to scrutinize my face. "Interesting features. I think you'd make a good subject for a painting."

I laughed and took a step toward the door to escape his touch. "I don't think I'm going to be around long enough for you to paint my portrait."

"You don't have to be." He came forward again, invading my personal space. "You can see, I also work from photographs. It's not as much fun as having a real flesh-and-blood person in front of you." His hand stroked up and down my arm. "A face like yours must photograph well. You'd be surprised how many people are willing to spring for a painting of themselves if they don't have to spend time sitting. You and I could find a pose that suits you, don't you think?"

"What I think is that I've interrupted your work." I backed out of the room.

He followed, leaning on the frame of the door. "I don't mind stopping work for you."

"It's kind of you to say, but I've taken up enough of your time today. Thank you for letting me see your painting."

"No trouble at all. I love visitors, especially pretty ones who admire my work." His lips tilted up, but the smile didn't reach his eyes. "I hope to see you later this evening." He reached for the door and closed it.

I stood for a moment, analyzing what had just happened. Was Jackcliff making a play for me? Probably not. It wasn't that I didn't think I could be considered attractive, but this was such a sudden interest. Why? More likely, he was trying to distract me. Maybe there was something he didn't want me to see. Or maybe he realized that his portrait of Lady Norrance revealed more than he had intended. Were they lovers? Or was the infatuation one-sided?

Or was I making up stories again?

Chapter Twelve

There was palpable tension in Castorbrook Castle on the afternoon leading up to the New Year's Eve ball. The staff, aware of the importance of the evening, was hurrying down hallways and up and down stairs readying the ballroom, freshening flower arrangements in the public spaces, filling the candelabra, and setting the individual tables for eight in the state dining room. Chef Bergère's elaborate dinner would take place at ten o'clock, with dessert to be served following the midnight fireworks display.

Afternoon tea for the family, its in-house guests, and other visitors—too many to seat comfortably in the drawing room—was being served in the gallery. It was a long, narrow room that led to the ballroom and was lined on either side with small groupings of tufted sofas, chairs, and small tables already set with gold-edged teacups and saucers. Nigel Gordon and two assistants, all attired in swallowtail tuxedos, carried in three-tiered serving platters of scones, pastries, and small sandwiches meant to fortify the guests and keep them satisfied until the hors d'oeuvres were served at the ball that evening.

I had come down to tea by myself. George was expecting a phone call and would join me shortly. I chose a love seat near the gallery entrance, so he would not have to look far, and enjoyed watching the parade of guests as they entered the elegant hall. Elmore Jackcliff had brought his sketch pad and was entertaining those around him by doing quick drawings of whoever caught his eye. The recipients of his artwork seemed to be charmed and accepted his business card. Jackcliff would likely leave Castorbrook Castle with the promise of commissions, just as he'd intended. I spotted the earl's man of business, Lionel Fitzwalter, whom I'd met only briefly at tea the day before. He and Lord Norrance seemed to be in a serious discussion until the countess pulled her husband away. Jemma was not wearing riding clothes this time, and Kip, her elder brother, wandered around, looking bored.

"Ah, Mrs. Fletcher. I've been hoping to have the opportunity to catch you alone. Is this a convenient time?"

"Certainly, Mr. Grant," I said, smiling at the earl's younger son, Rupert. "Please sit down."

"The earl told me of his conversation with you this morning at the stable," he said, pulling an armchair close to me and leaning forward, his knees practically touching mine. "Accomplished as he is, I can't always count on my father to present my views properly, or accurately relay your side of the discussion, for that matter. I am eager to hear what was said, from the horse's mouth, so to speak." He gave me a bright smile.

I laughed. "I'm afraid this horse didn't have a lot to say."

"I beg your pardon, Mrs. Fletcher. I meant no offense."

"And I took none. Your father merely said you were interested in producing movies, information I'd already learned from Griffin Semple."

"My father's not too keen on the idea."

"So I gathered."

"You didn't tell him it was a bad idea, did you?"

"I'm hardly an expert on your skills, or on filmmaking in general. No, I simply told him that to be successful in a field in which you have limited experience, you would have to work twice as hard as the next person and be dedicated and persistent. I believe those were my words."

"He doesn't believe I can do it."

"Well, what's more important is: Do *you* think you can do it?"

Rupert frowned. "I wouldn't be pursuing the idea if I didn't think I was capable of making a success of it," he said stiffly. "My friends and I—rather, my associates in the industry—have put together a business plan and are in the process of acquiring properties to develop."

"A start-up business also requires a considerable amount of financing," I said.

"That shouldn't be a problem. As the son of a peer, I have access to quite a number of potential investors."

It occurred to me that if Rupert inherited nothing else from his father, he already possessed some of the earl's arrogance.

"That's very impressive. Have any of your associates in the industry had experience in film production before?" I asked.

"Not directly, but we are all cinema enthusiasts. I have a collection of all the Hollywood black-and-white classics. I've taken a number of university courses in the subject, as have the others, and, as a matter of fact, I'm working on a screenplay right now."

"Congratulations. Then you certainly don't need any help from me."

"Well, um, I thought that while my script is still in its formative stage, we might move forward with something more complete. Griffin says several of your books have been made into films. I thought you might have another one you'd like to see brought to the big screen. I can promise you a nice return once the film is made and we've secured the international distribution. We would even allow you to provide the screenplay if you've a mind to try your hand in a different medium."

"How generous of you," I said, thinking the opposite, "but I prefer to stick with writing books. That's the medium I'm most comfortable with."

As we'd been talking, Rupert's wife, one of the young ladies I'd seen at tea the day before, came up behind him and put her hands on his shoulders.

He turned his head to glance up at her. "Not now, Adela. I'm having a business meeting."

"So sorry to interrupt." She gave me a small smile, before looking down at her husband again. "Your mother is asking for you, Rupert, and I didn't know what to tell her."

"Tell her I'm speaking with a very important business associate. Can't you find out what she wants?"

"I'll try, but she's not in the best of humor."

"Use your charm."

Adela pouted and walked off.

"Now, where were we?" Rupert asked, leaning toward me again.

"I was telling you my preferred medium is writing books."

"Well, I suppose we could have someone else do the screenplay. Which of your works would you like to offer for screen treatment?"

"None of them."

"Not one? I thought all authors wanted to see their books made into movies."

"Not this author."

"Are you sure?"

"Quite sure."

He sat back. "Well, I must say I'm very disappointed in you. I went to a great deal of trouble to have you invited to the ball, and for you and your friend to be our guests."

"And it was very kind of you. Was my cooperation in your venture supposed to be the payment for the invitation? If so, Griffin didn't alert me."

"No. No. Of course not. I'm just . . . frustrated. Nothing seems to be going right."

"I'm sorry to disappoint you. What will you do now?"

"I don't know."

"No plan B?"

"No. I don't have a plan B," he said with disgust. "My father has threatened to disinherit me if I don't come up with some profession to pursue. Not that *he* ever had one. He inherited everything."

"Have you ever offered to assist him with the management of Castorbrook? This place must be a business all in itself."

"And do what? Sit with a ledger all day, having him give me orders? No thanks!"

"There must be other opportunities on an estate this large."

He gave a snort. "Maybe he'd like me to take over the training of the horses. He's always praising our trainer. Between my father and Jemma, you'd think Colin hung the moon." He put his hands together as if in prayer. "I see myself working in the arts. I think that's where I belong. But he has no use for art. Just ask my mother." He looked down at his intertwined fingers. "I have these great ideas. I just need someone to give me a break."

"Well, I certainly wish you all the best," I said, feeling a little sorry for him. "If film production is the field you really want, I'm sure you'll find a way to pursue it."

"I hope you're right, Mrs. Fletcher," he said, standing. "My apologies if I came on too strong."

"No need for apologies. We just don't have the same goals, that's all."

George waved from the door and joined us. He shook Rupert's hand, and the young man left.

"Did you let him down easy?" he said, settling next to me on the love seat.

"I certainly let him down. I don't know how easy it was."

As the tea service wound down, guests began drifting from the room. Some tried to poke their heads into the ballroom but were shooed away by Angus Hartwhistle, who was guarding the door, allowing entry only to a piano tuner carrying a large case with his name, profession, and telephone number in white letters on the side. Through the room's tall windows I spotted other guests, bundled up, strolling Castorbrook's grounds, some stopping to watch workers setting up the fireworks displays out on the broad lawn.

As the gallery emptied out, George and I were once again left alone with the members of Lord Norrance's family, who were halfway down the room from where we sat finishing our tea. Nigel and his helpers were collecting the dishes and serving pieces when I saw Clover's son, Archer, enter the gallery carrying a long ladder. Trailing him, a large carton in her arms, was Elsbeth, the young maid we'd seen in the kitchen waiting to be interviewed by Detective Sergeant Mardling.

"What are you doing coming through here with that?" Lady Norrance demanded, gesturing at the ladder.

"Beg pardon, my lady," Archer said. "The ladder didn't fit through the other hallway. We tried." He turned to look behind him. As he did, he swung the back end of the ladder into Elsbeth, knocking her down. She dropped the carton, the side of which split open. Dozens of candles spilled onto the floor and rolled across the room, making walking hazardous for anyone in the vicinity.

"You idiot," the countess screamed. "Look what you've done. You're not supposed to be here to begin with."

Archer stood frozen in place, perhaps afraid he would knock over someone else with the ladder if he tried to move.

Nigel and his helpers stopped clearing the dishes and rushed to help pick up the candles, some of which kept rolling as they chased them across the floor. George and I hurried to help.

"It was an accident, Marielle," the earl said to his wife. "They'll clean it up."

"Those are beeswax, James. You may not care, but I do. They cost the world, and now they'll be ruined." She looked at Elsbeth, who was a heap on the floor. "Any broken candles will come out of your salary, young lady."

Rupert and Kip were convulsed in laughter, their wives giggling behind their hands.

"It's like a comedy of errors," Rupert said, wiping his eyes. "I've got to include this scene in my screenplay."

"Most diverting sight I've seen today," Kip said.

Only Jemma was not amused. "It's not funny, you know."

"You two," the countess shouted, pointing at George and me. "Don't touch those candles."

George and I straightened.

"Why not, Mother?" Jemma asked. "They won't break them."

"They're not staff. I won't have guests doing the job of staff." She turned to her husband. "Help me out of here, James." She held out her hand to the earl who guided her to the door to the ballroom, pointing out any errant candles in her path. The Grant children and their spouses followed, all of them stifling laughter, except Jemma.

"Did you see her expression when the ladder swung into her?" Rupert said, hooting.

Angus pulled the door closed behind them.

Nigel helped Elsbeth to stand. "Are you all right?"

"Yes, sir," she replied, but her hands were shaking as she reached down to collect some of the candles that were piled at her feet. "I'm so sorry, Mr. Gordon."

"Not your fault. Come sit over here," he said, steering her to a chair. "We'll get it tidied up in no time."

George and I looked at each other, wondering what to do.

"Thank you, very kind, but no need to help, Inspector, Mrs. Fletcher," Nigel said. "We're on top of it."

George and I backed away from the scene, careful not to trip on a stray candle.

"How awful," I whispered to him as we left the gallery. "That girl could have been hurt, and all Lady Norrance cared about were her candles."

"The countess is clearly under a lot of pressure today," he replied. "Let's give her the benefit of the doubt. I'm sure she'll see things differently when she's had a chance to calm down."

"I hope so," I said.

Chapter Thirteen

Nigel Gordon stood in the broad gallery leading to the ballroom in Castorbrook Castle and announced the guests. "Miss Ruby Miller-Carlisle. Mr. Griffin Semple."

George and I were in line, waiting to be announced to our host and hostess and their family before entering the ballroom. From this short distance, I could hear the strains of lively music floating from the room, and felt a shiver of excitement.

Even though we were not on their usual invitation list, I was determined that George and I would enjoy ourselves and not let the family's false expectations spoil our evening. Griffin had been right when he suggested that staying in Castorbrook Castle might provide fodder for my next book. I was already using the desk in my room and the stationery provided to make notes on the layout of the great house and my impression of its occupants.

"I can't even try to be blasé about this," I said to George as I straightened his bow tie.

"I hope I told you how beautiful you look this evening."

"You did and I thank you, sir. You're looking especially well yourself."

George was wearing a Prince Charlie fitted jacket over a kilt in the Sutherland dress tartan, a black-and-white plaid with narrow red stripes running through it. I wore a pale blue gown—George said it matched my eyes—with a beaded top. All around us the finery rivaled any red-carpet event I'd ever seen on television.

"Mrs. Jessica Fletcher and Chief Inspector George Sutherland."

George and I stepped up to greet our hosts. A photographer moved in to snap our picture.

The earl was handsome in his tuxedo, pearl gray waistcoat, and white gloves. "Thank you for coming," he said, shaking my hand and then George's.

The countess was a picture of elegant simplicity in a column of white satin accented by a red sash that ran across her shoulders and tied behind her back. For jewelry, she wore only ruby earrings and a large domed ring with a fleur-de-lis pattern in diamonds that was fitted over her long white kid gloves. She took my hand in both of hers. "You must excuse that little scene at tea this afternoon," she said with a pert smile. "How embarrassing to have you witness that."

"It's forgotten," I said, thinking that the one who deserved an apology was poor Elsbeth, who'd been really shaken, first by her fall, and then by being the victim of the countess's wrath. I didn't say that, of course. Instead, I thanked Lady Norrance for inviting George and me to the ball and for having us as her houseguests.

"Not at all," she replied, waving a hand in the air. She turned to George. "But *you* could do us a great favor."

"At your service, my lady."

"Try to keep that odious Mardling fellow under control, won't you? It's provoking that James even allowed him to be here," she said, flashing a raised eyebrow at her husband. "I don't want that man pushing his nose into our affairs and disturbing the guests."

"I'll do my very best," George replied.

After greeting the other family members in the reception line, we stepped inside the great ballroom, together with some one hundred forty close friends and relations of Lord and Lady Norrance. The spacious room sparkled like a fairyland with crystal chandeliers and sconces. In the corners, tall Christmas trees, reaching nearly to the ceiling, were decorated in gold and white, with their delicate lace snowflakes and sparkling glass ornaments hanging from branches that were also host to flickering crystal birds.

Unlike the other public rooms, which were painted or papered in dark colors, the walls here were a pale robin's egg blue with gold latticework panels set in the coffered ceiling. Ornate gold-framed mirrors, hung between the tall glass windows, reflected back the glittering lights and even more glittering guests. On the opposite wall, gold filigree screens—three panels of pointed arches—echoed the shapes of the windows. The screens were flanked by tall free-standing candelabra with more candles than I had ever seen in one place, apparently undamaged by their roll on the carpet after tea.

The space in front of the jazz band was already filled with couples dancing to the big-band classics. George and I slowly made our way through the room. All around us, guests chattered, greeting old friends, catching up with news, and gossiping about our hosts. Snippets of conversation reached our ears.

"I see Norrance is doing well," I overheard a guest say to his companion. "This bit of décor must've cost a pretty penny."

"Word is the high-end hotel chains are queued up to woo him," she replied. "They must be lining his pockets."

"Did you see the sapphire ring Kip's wife is wearing?" a young woman asked her escort. "Poppy is flaunting her jewelry like she's already the countess. I'm sure Marielle doesn't appreciate it. She hates to be outshone."

"Wanna bet the dowager passed down one of her baubles just to annoy her daughter-in-law? My father says the elder Lady Norrance never liked the earl's choice in wives."

"I must say this champagne is not the highest quality," a matronly woman told her escort. She took a full glass and placed her empty one on the tray held by a waiter whose back was to us.

"Probably saving the good stuff for themselves," the gentleman muttered.

The waiter, who turned out to be Archer Estwich, pivoted and extended the tray of tall glasses. "Would you and the inspector like some champagne?"

George shook his head, smiling.

"I thought it was pretty good quality myself when I sampled it in the kitchen." Archer winked at me.

"I'm all set for now," I said, laughing, "but we'll look for you a little later."

George and I drifted among the partygoers, keeping an eye out for Mardling and anyone else we might know. On the dance floor were Ruby and Griffin, she in a gray silk organza gown with a plunging neckline and skirt slit up to her thigh. When Griffin twirled her around and dipped her back, I was almost afraid to look, but her dress stayed in place with no "wardrobe malfunction" to embarrass her.

As Ruby had predicted, some of the guests were in costume, several of them attired in classic black-and-white harlequin checkerboard, and wearing half masks. I spotted Jemma dancing with one of them, and wondered if Colin had been invited to the ball, and if not, if she'd sneaked him past her parents by having him come in a costume.

With all the elegantly attired guests, it was not difficult to spot Dudley Mardling in a navy suit with his six-foot-tall assistant. They were standing off to the side, in front of one of the gold filigree screens. Willoughby, to her credit, wore a floor-length black dress rather than her uniform, but it was hard not to notice that she felt distinctly out of place, adjusting her shoulder straps and pulling at her long white gloves.

"Good evening, Detective Sergeant, Constable," George said when we approached them. "Is this duty part of the inquest?"

"Tough to get through all the staff interviews in one afternoon," Mardling said. "The earl and the countess still haven't accommodated our requests."

"You can't possibly think they'll talk with you during the ball," George said.

"No, of course not. We're just observing the scene. Lord Norrance gave his permission. Don't have a dress suit, but thought this would do better than a canvas coat and tweeds." He gestured at his clothes.

"We didn't want to stand out," Willoughby said, wincing.

"You look lovely," I told her.

She gave me a weak smile.

"Chief Inspector?" Mardling lowered his voice as he leaned

toward George. "Sorry to get off on the wrong foot this afternoon."

"No problem. You had the right of the situation."

"We did as you suggested. Questioned the housekeeper." He nodded at me. "She swore nothing had been amiss in the deceased's quarters. Said no one other than you two had been on the premises since the lady's death."

George's eyebrows rose in surprise.

"She's not trying to say we're responsible, is she?" I said.

Mardling coughed to clear his throat. "You know you've never shown us any identification."

"I beg your pardon," George said.

Willoughby jumped in. "Mrs. Powter suggested that you two might not be who you say you are." A blush rose in her cheeks. "She told us she overheard you plotting to steal the silver, artwork, and jewelry in the house."

"Good heavens!" I said. "I remember saying to George that whoever ransacked the room must have been looking for something; a common thief wouldn't bother with Mrs. Beckwith's modest possessions with a houseful of valuables downstairs." I held out my palms and looked around at the opulent surroundings. "At the risk of sounding flippant, that hardly qualifies as planning a burglary."

"It explains what she heard, however," Mardling said.

"I hope you looked us up and are reassured we are who we say we are," George said to him.

"Not to concern yourself, Chief Inspector. Called the Yard to confirm and also saw your photograph on the *Times* of London website."

"Did you check up on me, too?" I asked.

"*I* did," Willoughby put in. "Even ordered one of your books, one with your picture on the back."

I didn't know if I should thank her. Perhaps Mardling had told her to buy the book to provide his superiors with proof of my identity.

Willoughby stole a glance at *her* superior officer before continuing. "I spoke with Mrs. Powter. She claims that she never saw anything in a muddle upstairs, and if it had been, then someone else must have tidied it, because the last time she entered the room, it appeared as it is now."

"I find that very difficult to believe," I said, thinking that the housekeeper had a lot to account for.

"As do I," George added.

Mardling shrugged. "She could be lying. But why?"

"If she ransacked the room herself," I said, "it's unlikely she'd step forward to admit it."

"Why would she turn a room upside down and then clean it up?"

"Come now, Mardling," George said, dropping the man's title. "The occupant of the apartment is deceased. If the housekeeper knew or suspected that the dead woman had some money hidden somewhere, that could be motive enough."

"Or if she's not lying to defend herself," I added, "perhaps she's covering up to protect someone else."

"Do you happen to have anyone in mind?"

"I don't."

George heaved a sigh. "Difficult as this may be to believe, Detective Sergeant, given all we've been through, Mrs. Fletcher and I only arrived here yesterday afternoon. We're scheduled to leave the day after tomorrow. I'm afraid you're going to have to work on this investigation yourselves."

I squeezed George's hand. I had suggested we let Flavia Beckwith rest in peace and allow Mardling to go his own way with the inquest, but I hadn't been certain if George would take my advice.

Mardling coughed again. "Didn't mean to impose. Just thought you might have an opinion on the matter."

"I didn't believe that Mrs. Beckwith's death was suspicious to begin with," George said, glancing at me, then back to Mardling, "that is until I saw her bedroom last evening. Her demise may still be ascribed to natural causes, but you won't be able to confirm that until the coroner's tests are concluded."

"As you say, and that may not be for several weeks' time," Mardling said. "Since you and Mrs. Fletcher have told us what you observed, we've decided another interview with the housekeeper is in order. Is there anyone else in particular you recommend that we interview?"

"You know your business well enough, Detective Sergeant, Constable," George said, nodding at each of them. "You don't need us to advise you. We plan to spend the rest of the evening enjoying the festivities. Since you're here, you may as well do the same. I will give you one suggestion, however."

"What's that?"

"Don't conduct any police business during the ball. It's unlikely you could get anyone to focus on your questions, and it won't endear you to your hosts."

Chapter Fourteen

"Are you enjoying yourself?" George murmured in my ear some hours later.

"Very much," I said, leaning into him, as we moved together to the music of "All the Things You Are."

The band had switched from up-tempo classics like "Anything Goes" and "A Fine Romance" to a slow dance. I suspected they had changed their pace to try to discourage Kip Grant from leading the musicians. The earl's heir, who, having had quite a bit more than one too many, had plucked a hair ornament resembling a chopstick from some poor lady's chignon and proceeded to conduct the band, tapping out the beat on the microphone stand and singing off-key, although he surprised me by even knowing any of the lyrics in the first place.

Ruby had told me that the band was an abbreviated group that was usually part of a popular dance orchestra known for its attachment to the 1940s and 1950s songbooks, with a little Beatles thrown in for good measure. The bandleader had split its many musicians into quartets, quintets, and sextets to accommodate the increased demand for their services on New Year's Eve. The earl and his countess had rated a sextet: piano, string bass, saxophone, trumpet, guitar, and drums. The trumpeter, a woman, doubled on vocals.

Before Kip's impromptu session as a conductor, he had set his champagne glass on the side of the music rack of the Steinway grand piano, earning a scowl from the pianist, who then placed the glass on the floor next to several other glasses that people had unthinkingly left on his instrument.

"Are you sure you don't know any Pink?" Kip had asked. "No? How about Destiny's Child? Everybody knows 'Say My Name.' That's a classic. No? Only my father would pick such a supernannu—no—superannunated band. Super-nunu-ated. Something like that. You like that word? It means old."

"Easy for you to say," the trumpeter, a woman no older than forty, had responded, eliciting laughs from her fellow musicians.

Just then, Kip's wife, teetering on stiletto heels, had grabbed his arm to pull him away.

"Wait, Poppy. The band needs me."

"I want to eat. You can come back later. They're starting the dinner service."

Kip crooned along to "All the Things You Are" as his wife dragged him off.

George mouthed the rest of the chorus. " 'Someday my happy arms will hold you,' " he sang softly, " 'And someday I'll know that moment divine / When all the things you are, are mine.' "

"I didn't know you could sing," I said, smiling up into his face.

"I particularly like that lyric. It's rather apt, I think."

I don't normally blush, but I could feel my cheeks flushing.

"I'm embarrassing you?" George said, nuzzling my temple.

"A little," I said.

"Then let's abandon the dance floor and follow our hosts' eldest into dinner. Would you like that?"

"I'm actually quite hungry."

"And I know how your mood changes when you crave something to eat."

"Oh, it's not that bad," I said, but I stepped out of his embrace and we joined those leaving the ballroom on the way to the dining room on the floor above. Elmore Jackcliff, in a long black cape, was walking just behind us, arm in arm with one of the costumed guests. "We meet again." He wagged his eyebrows up and down, reminding me of Groucho Marx.

Waiting by the door, the earl's mother leaned on Rupert's arm while his wife, Adela, carried the old lady's pillow. We slowed our gait to allow them to walk ahead of us. Rupert gave me a tight smile and a nod as they started up the stairs to the main floor. Blocked from moving more quickly, I couldn't help overhearing their conversation.

"Are the hotel people here?" the dowager countess asked.

"I believe so," Rupert replied.

"How much are they offering?"

"I heard one bidder plans to invest three hundred fifty million pounds, but I don't know how much of that the earl gets to keep, and how much is plowed into renovations."

"I hope they put in a spa," Adela said. "I would love a spa."

"You wouldn't get to use it anyway," her husband responded. "Kip said they told him he could keep a suite for himself. I'm assuming Mother and Father could stay if they want, but no one else was mentioned. So I guess that leaves the rest of us out."

"Does that mean we'd have to move, Rupe?" Adela asked.

"Sounds like it, doesn't it?"

"But where would we go?" Adela's voice came dangerously close to a whine.

"At least we'd get some money out of it," Rupert said.

"Ridiculous!" Honora said. "Castorbrook has been in the family for generations. I won't have James selling it out from under us."

"I don't believe you can stop him, Grandmother. Mother's all for it. Lucky for you, the dower house isn't included in the deal, so your home isn't threatened."

"It is if my son isn't willing to use receipts from the castle to cover my expenses."

"I thought you were financially secure, Grandmother."

"My finances are not your concern, young man, but I will say I don't intend to move from my home of eighty-three years. And I certainly object to Castorbrook becoming a full-time hotel. Accommodating the wedding trade is bad enough."

"If there isn't a hotel buyer, he may have to sell to someone else," Rupert said as they reached the landing. "The castle is not earning its keep. The earl put together this event to show us at our best, to give prospective buyers an idea of what's possible with an infusion of cash."

Honora halted in her slow walk to the dining room. She fixed her grandson with a stern look and poked her index finger into his chest. "No hotel," she said in a low voice. "If you want to remain in my will, get some of your movie friends involved. You're always nattering on about how smart they are. Prove it! We've got to stop your father from selling to a hotel."

"Let me help you to your table, Grandmother."

"You understand what I said?"

"I understand."

"Well, well, well," Jackcliff whispered, leaning between our shoulders after the three Grants had moved on. "Intrigue in the Earl of Norrance's family."

Chapter Fifteen

Chef Bergère was the star at dinner, directing the service from the side of the dining room and racing back to the kitchen between courses. The menu, according to an engraved card at each place setting, included Devon crab dim sum with mustard velouté, coquilles Saint Jacques, duck breast with cherry and mango chutney, truffled langoustines with celeriac purée and champagne risotto, and a salad of sweet potato, chestnuts, and baby leeks, all accompanied by wines matched to the courses.

George and I shared a table with Ruby and Griffin, who greeted us like old friends; the earl's business adviser, Lionel Fitzwalter, and his wife, Birdie, a tiny woman who lived up to her name with her high voice and occasional head twitches; and Elmore Jackcliff and his costumed friend, an Italian lady whom he introduced as Zita Aldobruzzichelli. Her thick accent, augmented by several glasses of champagne, rendered it almost impossible to make out what she was saying, although she certainly was a cheerful dinner companion as she laughed at every comment Jackcliff made.

"Bergère's sure to get another star if he continues to cook like this," Griffin said, patting his lips with his napkin at the end of the meal.

"Do you think they'll create a restaurant for him here?" Ruby asked. She had draped a long chiffon scarf across the front of her dress, covering the plunging neckline, which had attracted many admiring gazes in the ballroom.

"Lionel would know more than I," Griffin replied, tilting his head toward Fitzwalter. "What are Lord Norrance's plans for Castorbrook, if I may be so bold as to ask? The rumor tonight is that the Corduvon hotel chain has the lead, as it were."

"I stayed in one of their hotels in Majorca once," Ruby put in. "It was right on the water, every room with a view and butler service. *Très élégant*."

"Call me a blinkered Englishman, but I don't think you can get any more *élégant* than Castorbrook. Look around you," Griffin told her. "What do you say, Fitzwalter?"

"Norrance will have to speak for himself," Fitzwalter replied, "but I like the chances of Platinum Places; they're a small exclusive consortium. And you can't count out the National Trust. They're in the mix, too."

"Will it be Corduvon or Platinum Places or National Trust? It sounds like names from an equestrian sport," Jackcliff said, amused. "How appropriate for a pinched peer hoping to put together a string of racehorses." He put two fists up to his eyes, mimicking binoculars, and intoned, "It's Corduvon and Platinum Places neck and neck, but moving up on the outside is National Trust. Here they come down the backstretch, and it looks like it's going to be—" He paused for effect, then continued. "Yes! It's Affronted Dowager by a nose."

Ms. Aldobruzzichelli's peal of laughter had heads turning in our direction.

"Is there no chance the family could keep Castorbrook as a private home instead of selling the estate?" I asked.

"I'm sure the family would much prefer that," Fitzwalter replied.

"Certainly the elder Lady Norrance would," Jackcliff said, winking at me.

"But twenty-first-century realities come into play with a structure of this age, not to mention the delicate condition of its furnishings and treasures," Fitzwalter continued.

"Have you seen the earl's collection of rare books?" Birdie asked.

"Books are only part of it, my dear," her husband said. "There are family portraits dating back centuries that are coveted by the National Portrait Gallery, French laces bought by one of the earl's ancestors from King George the Fourth when he was trying to settle his debts. Rare silk tapestries from India. The house is full of history and precious items that require repair and maintenance, not to mention whole-house alarm and sprinkler systems. And all this doesn't come for pennies."

"Perhaps they could sell off some of the goodies in order to keep the place," Ruby offered.

Fitzwalter shrugged but remained silent, perhaps aware that he shouldn't compromise the privacy of his client more than he already had.

Griffin had no such hesitation and jumped in. "My father sold quite a few of the earl's rare books and manuscripts in the past," he told her. "I've heard that parcels of land carved from the estate have been auctioned off for years. You can sell an acre here and a portrait there—eventually there will be nothing left to barter with. I don't blame the earl for looking to make a killing. I'd do the same thing myself if I had a jewel of an estate to bargain with."

"Well, we'll see." Fitzwalter folded his napkin and laid it next to his plate. He made a show of looking at his pocket watch. "The pyrotechnics begin in a half hour." He rose and helped his wife from her seat. "So nice to see you all and spend a pleasant dinner together."

"I'm ready!" Ruby jumped up, allowing her chiffon cover-up to fall to her elbows. She saw me eyeing her décolletage and leaned down to whisper, "Don't worry. I'm glued in." She pulled Griffin from his chair. "Can't wait to see the fireworks. How long is the show?"

"Twenty minutes, I hear," he replied.

Ruby smiled at George and me. "We'll see you downstairs."

Jackcliff stood as well. "Ready, my dear?" he asked Ms. Aldobruzzichelli.

"Ah, *fuochi d'artificio*," she said, and clapped her hands. "Very pretty, yes?"

"Let's go see."

She laughed as she took his hand.

"What do you think, Jessica?" George asked when we were alone at the table.

"I think we're very lucky to have had the opportunity to stay here before Castorbrook becomes an ultra-luxury hotel."

"I agree. My guess is the cost of a room here will be far more than anyone but the richest among us can afford."

"Too bad. It really is lovely. Let's go celebrate the New Year with the Grants while we can."

We followed the crowd slowly making its way out of the dining room, and we passed the table at which our hosts and their family still lingered. The earl stood, giving last-minute instructions to his staff. "You have the sweets table ready?" he asked Bergère.

"It will be rolled out at the fireworks' finale. It is exquisite, if I may say so myself."

"What's for pudding?" Kip asked, rolling his head. It didn't appear to me as if time and a four-course meal had sobered him up.

"You told me you weren't hungry," Poppy said. "That's why you didn't want dinner, you said."

"He's not hungry," Jemma put in. "He's just drunk." I noticed that her costumed companion from earlier in the evening was not dining with the family.

"Can always manage a bit of trifle," the heir said, slurring his words. "Is there trifle?"

"I'll send you some trifle if you'll go up to bed." The earl looked at him with annoyance. "You're embarrassing the family."

"Couldn't do that. Don't want to miss the show," Kip replied with a silly grin.

The earl turned back to the chef. "Make sure the tray of caviar and champagne for the countess and me is delivered prior to the countdown. We'll be at the north end of the room, near the gallery."

"It will be waiting, sir."

"Are you certain you want to bother?" the countess asked her husband.

He lifted her hand and kissed her fingers. "Some traditions should never be broken, my love," he said in a voice loud enough for those of us waiting to access the hall to hear.

Several people around me, who'd been eavesdropping on their conversation as I had, voiced their support with a chorus of appreciative murmurs.

The earl acknowledged them with a nod.

"You're very sweet, James," Lady Norrance said.

Downstairs, the lights were dimmed in the ballroom in anticipation of the midnight fireworks. The band alternated slow ballads with lively tunes, each time increasing the tempo until the mood of the crowd was at a feverish pitch. George and I wandered to the far end of the room where the amplified music was not as blaring. Chairs were set up facing the tall windows, and a large lighted clock had been rolled in to count down the year's remaining minutes. Waiters with trays circulated, offering more flutes of champagne to toast the New Year.

Lord and Lady Norrance took seats near us that were reserved for them, their private serving of caviar and champagne set out on a tray by Archer Estwich. The countess took a glass of champagne and handed the other to her husband. She leaned over the tray, picked up a mother-of-pearl spoon, and stirred the caviar, scooping a spoonful from the glass bowl sitting on ice. She tapped it onto a cracker and gave it to the earl, who popped it into his mouth. Kip reached to take the spoon, only to have his mother slap his hand.

"That's for your father, not you."

"But *you'll* have some."

"I may, but that doesn't mean you are entitled to your father's treat. Not after the way you've conducted yourself tonight."

Kip pouted and fell into a chair next to his wife. "Have I been that bad?"

"Don't ask. You don't really want to know."

Rupert took out his cell phone and snapped a photo of his inebriated brother. "I'm going to get paid plenty not to post this."

Adela laughed. She used her phone to shoot Rupert shooting Kip.

Poppy shifted in her seat to shield Kip from the camera. "Don't be rude. I don't take pictures of you when you're not looking your best."

"Oh, yes, you do," Adela said. "Last Easter, you posted one of me with my hair sticking up everywhere."

"That was funny. You have no sense of humor."

"You only have a sense of humor when someone else is the victim."

"I have to protect my image as the heir's wife. You don't need to worry about that."

"Put those damn things away!" The earl turned to his wife. "Everybody's obsessed with those mobiles. I hate them."

Lady Norrance held up a cracker with caviar for him. "I know, dear." She made another for herself and looked at the earl. Before she could take a bite, he grabbed her hand and brought it to his mouth, nibbling on her fingers as he ate the caviar.

"James, people are watching."

"Let them."

Ruby and Griffin walked by and stopped to thank the earl and countess for inviting them.

"Not at all." Lord Norrance's eyes widened as he took in Ruby's neckline. "We're happy to have Jemma's friends here." He looked around for his daughter. "Where is she, by the way?"

"Oh, we just saw her talking to a friend near the band."

The earl craned his neck to look down the ballroom, but the movement seemed to make him dizzy. He swayed and put out his hand. Griffin caught it and steadied him.

"I'm sure Jemma will be here any minute. How do you like my dress?" Ruby pirouetted in front of the earl.

"Very nice, Ruby. You look charming." He grimaced and put a hand to his forehead. "I suddenly feel a headache coming on."

"Where's my chair?" The dowager approached the family group. She wielded her cane as Nigel accompanied her. "And my pillow?"

"I've got your pillow," Adela said.

"Sit here, Mother." The earl held the back of his chair for her.

"What is that?" She frowned at the caviar platter. A puff of air escaped her lips. "Fish eggs! Take those things away."

"Not so fast," her son said when Nigel reached for the tray. "I'll have a little more." The earl took another spoonful of caviar, smacked his lips, and handed the tray to Nigel. "Have the rest of that delivered to my rooms. I'll finish it up later."

"Certainly, Your Lordship."

Kip hailed a waiter with a tray. "I need some champagne for the toast. Can't welcome the New Year without a toast."

"Kip, I think you've had enough," Poppy said.

"You can never have too much champagne." He took two glasses.

"Is one for me?"

Kip reared back. "No! Get your own."

Nigel returned moments later, bringing the earl a cordless microphone.

"That time already?" The earl, looking upset, glanced over to the giant clock.

"Nearly, sir. You asked me to give you the microphone at five minutes to."

"Yes. Yes. I'm ready."

After some painful electronic feedback that silenced both the band and the guests, Lord Norrance gave a welcome speech, his eye on the lighted clockface. "Lady Norrance and I are delighted to have you join us to usher in this New Year." He stopped to clear his throat. "Over the generations, Castorbrook has played host to other balls with five times our numbers here tonight, but we thought we'd keep this year's celebration small and intimate with you, the most important people in our lives. The forecast is for light snow tonight, so we may have some heavenly lighting to add to our performance." He doubled over with a fit of coughing.

There were several shouts of "Coming close" and "Watch the time."

Eyes watering and red-faced, the earl cleared his throat. "All right, everyone, time to count down with me . . . Ten, nine, eight, seven, six, five, four, three, two, one."

"Happy New Year!"

The earl raised his champagne, looked at his wife over the rim of the glass, and threw back the remnants.

All the while, the clock bonged twelve times, the round face flashing on and off. A whining scream could be heard from outside, ending with an explosion in the sky with a shower of sparkling lights in yellow, white, and red drifting down to oohs and ahs by the crowd. Many held up their cell phones to capture the colorful display outside the windows. Recorded music filled the ballroom timed to the flashes outside, each more spectacular and brilliant than the last, until the smell of smoke could be detected in the ballroom.

George put his arms around me. "Happy New Year, lass. I hope it's one of many to come."

I smiled. "I hope so, too, George." I turned my face up to his for a kiss, when the earl, choking, staggered backward into George's side, forcing us apart.

He keeled forward into his wife's arms. A piercing wail went up. "James! James! What is it?"

George rushed to help, using the Heimlich maneuver in case the earl had something lodged in his throat, but the man's body was shaking with a convulsion, and then he went limp. George helped Lady Norrance lower the earl to the marble floor as the fireworks outside lent an eerie glow to the peer's face. I knelt down next to them.

"What's happening?" The dowager raised her voice to be heard above the blasts and accompanying music.

Rupert pulled the pillow from behind his grandmother's back and gave it to George, who placed it under the earl's head. "I'm calling for a doctor." The earl's younger son narrowed his eyes at the cell phone screen.

"It was so sudden," Adela said. "He was just drinking his champagne."

"What's Father doing?" Kip pulled himself halfway out of his chair, leaning on his wife's shoulder.

"Shut up, Kip. Sit down before you fall down."

"James. James. Talk to me."

"Is he all right?" the dowager called.

"I can't see clearly to dial the number."

"What can I do, Inspector?" Nigel asked.

"Nothing." George put his fingers on the earl's neck, searching for a pulse. He looked over at me, and I saw the truth in his eyes.

"He's dead?" I whispered.

"Very much so."

Chapter Sixteen

You can never find a police officer when you need one, I thought, grimly searching the crowd for Mardling and Willoughby. I didn't fool myself into thinking I'd recognize the backs of their heads in the darkened room as I skirted along the lines of chairs and behind clumps of guests who'd risen to get a better view of the fireworks presentation. I hoped Willoughby's tall silhouette would catch my eye. But it was not to be. I reached the end of the room where the musicians were taking a break, laughing at some story. I retraced my steps, trying once more to spot the pair on my way back.

Some of the guests had gone outside to watch the fireworks. If Mardling and Willoughby were among them, I had no hope of finding them. I was not dressed for the weather, especially with snow expected.

While I'd been hunting for the officers, George and Nigel managed to wrestle one of the three-paneled filigree screens into place to shield the earl's body and family from the gaze of guests who might turn away from the fireworks and discover what was wrong.

George was rapping out instructions to Nigel when I slipped behind the screen.

"Make sure no one touches that tray of caviar he gave you," George said, "Good, you have gloves on. Don't touch anything with bare hands. Lock it away somewhere until I ask you to produce it."

"Yes, sir."

"Where's his champagne glass?"

"I believe it broke when he fell."

"Leave it where it is, then. Don't allow anyone to clean up."

George looked at me questioningly, and I shook my head. He turned back to the butler. "Get Angus and some of the other lads up here to stand guard. No one is allowed to come behind this screen unless I say so."

"Understood."

"Perhaps you should ask the chef to bring the dessert table back to the dining room," I said. "That way we can encourage people to go upstairs when the fireworks are over instead of lingering in the ballroom."

"Good idea, Jessica," George said.

"Right away, sir." Nigel beckoned to a waiter and passed along my suggestion with instructions to do it quickly. "Anything else?" he asked George.

"I've told Lady Norrance that the body may not be touched until the authorities investigate the scene. We can't know for certain, but it's possible the earl did not die from natural causes. She and her family are welcome to retire into a private chamber if they wish, but once you've escorted them there, they may not leave. They must wait until the officers have a chance to put questions to them."

While we'd been talking, the earl's wife, mother, and children had huddled together near the body of James William Edward Grant, seventh Earl of Norrance.

His mother sat stiffly in her chair, waving away any offers of a drink and demanding people leave her alone.

Jemma knelt on the floor by her mother's side and held her hand.

Rupert had attempted to conceal the body with his tuxedo jacket, but he managed only to cover the earl's face and upper chest. Lord Norrance's pearl gray waistcoat and white tuxedo shirt, part of which were visible, bore evidence of spilled champagne, the damp spots clear on the otherwise-pristine cloth. Rupert, in shirtsleeves, was hunched over in his chair, his head in his hands. Adela sat beside him, rubbing his back in slow circles.

Poppy sat next to Kip, whose head kept dipping as he struggled to stay awake. "Are you certain he's not just injured? Tell him to get up."

"He's dead, Kip. If you weren't so drunk, you'd understand what that means."

"I unnerstand."

"I'm not certain the family will follow my direction," Nigel told George. "They're accustomed to giving instructions *to* me, not taking them *from* me."

"I'll talk to them, and I'll send Mrs. Fletcher to accompany the family to ensure everyone stays in one place."

"Is there any room with a washroom attached or at least close by?" I asked. If I was going to be charged with keeping all of them together, I needed to think of what excuses someone might use to leave the room. *Where are Mardling and Willoughby? We could surely use their help right now.*

"There's a cloakroom across from the drawing room," Nigel said, interrupting my worried musing. "It has a loo."

"Perfect," George said. "We'll invite them to go to the drawing room. If the countess wishes to stay with her husband, I'll allow it, but I'm hoping to convince her to accompany her children and mother-in-law."

"I'll have a fire built in there now."

"Have some tea brought in for them, too. No alcohol for anyone, except if the countess or the dowager requests it, of course. Nothing but tea for the young earl."

I realized George was talking about Kip. With his father dead, he was now the eighth Earl of Norrance. And Poppy was the countess. I stole a glance at her. Unlike the others who appeared to be in some pain, she wore a serene expression as her husband sat next to her, sniffling. I couldn't decide if Kip was fighting tears or trying to summon them.

There was a big boom as the finale of the fireworks show began with multiple rockets rising into the sky in quick succession. A giant wheel of sparklers twirled, and the numbers spelling out the New Year burned so brightly, they were impossible to read. As the explosions grew louder, many of the guests covered their ears, but when the last spray had fizzled into the smoky air, a great round of applause rose from the ballroom.

"Happy New Year, ladies and gentlemen," the vocalist announced. "There is a slight change of plans. Please join us in the state dining room again for the sweets table. The chef has outdone himself with a chocolate surprise. Get your mobile cameras ready, because those goodies are going to go fast. We'll join you shortly as we continue the party upstairs."

The musicians began packing up their instruments to move

them to the new location—all except the pianist, who shrugged as he closed the fallboard of the Steinway.

The ballroom emptied out, and while many guests glanced curiously at the filigree screen, no one attempted to find out what was behind it.

"Shall I turn the lights back on, Chief Inspector?"

"Yes. Thank you, Nigel."

"Sorry, sir. No one is allowed behind there." Angus put his hands out to block a visitor.

"Police. Stand aside." Mardling pushed his way into the area behind the screen. Willoughby followed, nearly tripping on her hem.

George pulled them away from the family. "Where the devil were you?"

"Outside, watching the fireworks display."

"Without a coat?" I asked.

"We sat in the car with the heater on," Willoughby added.

George sighed. "Well, while you were gone, it appears as if someone may have poisoned the earl."

The chandeliers suddenly came on and flooded the room with light, startling everyone in the area. Members of the family came to attention, squinting at the unaccustomed illumination. Lady Norrance looked down at her husband's body and moaned. Jemma lifted her mother from her seat and guided her to another chair. "Come sit over here with Rupert and Adela."

Rupert stood and hugged his mother. "It was his night of triumph, Mother. He was never happier than when showing off Castorbrook."

The dowager raised her cane in the air. "But he was willing to sell it, the fool. I told him no son of mine should sell the family home. His father would have been horrified. It's our heritage, our responsibility to maintain for future generations."

"Hush, Grandmother. Not now."

"Don't you hush me, Rupert. I'll have my say whenever it pleases." She slumped back in her seat and grumbled, "Where's my pillow?"

Kip roused and sat up blinking. He turned to Poppy. "Is the party over?"

"It is."

"Did I miss the fireworks?"

Mardling walked over to the body and lifted the jacket. The earl's face was a bright pink as if he had been exercising, but his lips were blue. His eyes stared, unseeing, at the gold coffered ceiling. Mardling leaned down and sniffed. He draped the jacket back over the earl and returned to where George and I stood.

"You shouldn't touch his clothing," George said. "There's always the possibility of secondary contamination."

Mardling looked surprised. "Are you certain he was poisoned?"

"Do you take me for a fool?" George said impatiently. "If we assume heart attack and it turns out otherwise, we will have lost precious time. I'm not taking any chances. We're still in the golden hour."

Mardling took out his cell phone. "Do we need backup?"

"Do you have to ask? Absolutely. Start an action book. We need crime scene examiners, and enough officers to take a record of all the guests and staff. I'm putting you in charge of the kitchen. Cordon off the area. I want the names of everyone who had access to food and drink. Nothing is to be thrown out until it is checked."

"I'll have to check with my superiors." Mardling looked uncomfortable dealing with this demanding side of George.

"I'm afraid I'm pulling rank on you, Detective Sergeant, until we are clearer about the circumstances. If you need confirmation, here's the number of the Met's CID."

George had called the Criminal Investigation Division of the Metropolitan Police, the formal name for Scotland Yard. He'd been instructed to stay at the scene and oversee the investigation until someone from the CID could be assigned to the case.

"If we're dealing with murder, we have to move swiftly, Mardling."

Willoughby raised her hand tentatively. "May I go change, Chief Inspector? My uniform is in the car."

"Stay as you are until reinforcements arrive," George told her. "It may make it easier for you to mingle with the guests. Keep your ears open and make notes of anything said that may pertain to the case."

"Yes, sir."

The officers left and George looked at me. "Mardling is going to try my patience. He didn't want my interference, but he's going to have to bear it now."

"You said that he's a competent investigator. He just has a different style than you."

"He certainly does."

Nigel had gathered the family at the ballroom door that led to the gallery, where we'd had tea that afternoon. The deceased earl's mother gripped his sleeve.

Kip staggered after Poppy. "Why won't you let me hold your arm?"

"I've done enough for you tonight."

They made a sad procession, the Grant family, leaving behind their leader lying on the ballroom floor. Rupert glanced behind once, then put his arm around his mother's shoulder and walked her out.

"Will you be all right staying with the family in the drawing room?"

"Of course, George. Is there anything else I can do to help?"

"No, lass. Just having you nearby has a calming effect."

"I'm glad." I stood on tiptoe and gave him a soft kiss. "I never wished you happy New Year."

Chapter Seventeen

It was a somber group that waited in the drawing room for the police to arrive. Nigel had arranged for a fire to be lit, and the room was warm, at least in the area closest to the hearth. Lady Norrance had dropped into the chair that had been occupied by her mother-in-law at tea the day we arrived. The dowager countess frowned but didn't raise an objection. Before he exited the room, Nigel helped her to another seat, grabbing a pillow from a settee to tuck behind her back since the one that usually accompanied her was cushioning the head of her deceased son back in the ballroom.

The two young couples found places near each other and whispered together. Jemma sat on an ottoman at her mother's feet and laid her head on the countess's lap.

"Foolish, foolish man. What was he thinking?" Honora muttered. "Didn't take care of himself properly. I told him his eating would bring on a heart attack." No one challenged her. "Not supposed to lose a child. It's not in the natural order of things."

I sat in the same wing chair that had been my seat when

George and I were invited to take tea with the family, right after I'd discovered Mrs. Beckwith's body. Was it only two days ago? Now there had been another death. We still didn't know for sure if Flavia Beckwith had died of natural causes. But it was almost certain that the earl had not. Could the deaths be related?

When Mardling lifted the jacket covering the earl's face, I'd seen him lean down and inhale. I suppose if he recognized the scent of bitter almond, it would confirm for him that the earl had been poisoned. Cyanide gives off that aroma, but it's usually only detected in a body during an autopsy—if it's detected at all. Mardling hadn't sniffed at the earl's champagne glass or even his caviar, which Nigel had been instructed to take to Lord Norrance's room. In those, the bitter almond odor might come through if cyanide was present. More telling, however, was the earl's bright pink complexion, which was not the usual pallor of death. Cyanide, as well as other poisons, can turn blood cherry red. And his lips were blue, an indication of oxygen deprivation.

The famous author Agatha Christie was knowledgeable about cyanide poisoning and used it in several of her books. As a fan of hers and a mystery writer myself, I was familiar with the symptoms and signs. I was confident George was, too. Cyanide is one of the few poisons that can strike down a victim within minutes. Of course, without verification from a lab, we could be accused of speculating, even if our assumptions were based on known facts. I was acutely aware that I'd criticized George—at least to myself—for jumping to conclusions. Still, I couldn't fault him for now proceeding as if a crime had been committed. To my way of thinking, there had probably been two murders, in close succession.

Why someone would want to kill the Earl of Norrance was the

question. He'd been an affable host. I hadn't witnessed any angry exchanges beyond the usual gripes that can arise in a family whose members spend a lot of time together. The earl and his countess seemed content in their marriage. Admittedly, it was hard to know what went on in private, but in public they appeared devoted to each other. Rupert, the aspiring filmmaker, had complained that the earl had threatened to cut him off if he didn't find a job. If every father who made such a threat was killed, the world population would decline significantly. Kip could be accused of wanting to inherit the title and perhaps the estate, but he didn't strike me as someone with any ambition. If anything, he seemed to be the kind of young man who avoided responsibility, even as his wife appeared eager to assume it. Jemma might be angry that the earl was trying to come between her and her "good friend" Colin, but was it certain that the earl knew of their relationship? The dowager countess was determined to stop the sale of Castorbrook, but would she go so far as to have someone kill her son? That seemed to me unlikely. At least, I hoped so. If the earl had been murdered, as we believed, we couldn't dismiss those closest to him as suspects, but we might be better off looking outside the family for anyone with a grudge against him. I suspected there might be more than a few individuals.

There was a knock on the door and Nigel entered, carrying a tray of desserts. Behind him, Angus was bearing another tray with cups and saucers and pots of tea.

"Beg pardon, my lady. I thought you and the family might like to sample some of what the chef is serving." Nigel set down his tray on a table and gestured to Angus to do the same.

"Very kind of you, Nigel, but I'm afraid I have no appetite. Do our guests know what has occurred?"

"There was no general announcement, but I believe the officers who were here earlier have been informing people as they circulate among them. We asked the band to refrain from playing. I trust that meets with your approval."

"Thank you. I couldn't bear to hear music right now. What a dreadful way to greet the New Year. Oh, James." She caught herself before breaking down and waved off Angus's offer of a cup of tea.

"I'll have something," Rupert said, approaching the table. "May I make a plate for you, Grandmother?"

"Take away that poison. Fatty food is probably what killed your father. I blame your mother for hiring that French chef."

"A little bit of chocolate never hurt anyone, Grandmother, but if you'd rather not, I understand."

Kip stood, gripped the back of his chair to steady himself, and held out his arms by his side for balance as he tottered toward the dessert tray. "I'm really hungry now," he announced. But when he looked down on the rich desserts—the petits fours, cups of trifle and whipped cream, and squares of dense chocolate cake with spirals of spun sugar rising from each piece—his face turned green. He slapped a hand over his mouth and reached for the door. Angus held it open for him and followed Kip into the cloakroom across the hall.

Nigel filled two plates with samples from the dessert tray and delivered them to the young wives of Kip and Rupert. Then he did the same for me. I thanked him and set the dish aside. As attractive as the desserts were, I found I couldn't eat while I was sitting in the midst of a family in mourning. No one had asked why I was there. I wasn't even certain myself. George hadn't wanted any of the Grants to leave the room before the local authorities arrived to remove the body and take their statements of what they believed to have happened. But I could hardly put my hand up to keep a sick man from reaching the bathroom. Even though I could reason with the others and request that they remain in the drawing room, if any of them insisted on going somewhere else—to their private quarters, say—I would have been hard put to insist that they stay.

Rupert, standing next to the table, dipped a spoon into several of the delicacies and licked it off. He tossed the spoon on the tray, wiped his fingers on a napkin, and shook his head. "Delicious, I'm sure, but everything has a bitter taste right now."

"Not good for you anyway," his grandmother said.

"Did Father ever consult a physician?" he asked his mother.

"Why should he? He was the picture of health despite what your grandmother claims. He rode every day. Jemma can tell you. That's excellent exercise. He ate moderately." She gave her mother-in-law a severe glance. "I watched him carefully."

"Stress. Stress can kill you, too," Honora put in.

"If you wanted to reduce the stress on him, you could have stopped criticizing James for his efforts to put the estate on a strong financial footing."

"The estate, as you call it, has been in *my* family for three hundred years."

"And at the rate we were going, it could put you in the poorhouse in one. He did everything to try to maintain it for you—and for his children. How dare you criticize him for caring about our future."

The door to the drawing room burst open, and Elmore Jackcliff strode in, black cape streaming behind him. He threw himself at Marielle's feet and took her hands in his, practically pushing Jemma aside. "My dear, dear lady. I am so terribly sorry. We've just learned the news, and I had to come at once to express my deepest condolences."

"Thank you, Elmore. You are most kind."

He looked around the room at the others, a pained expression on his face. "He was such a vibrant soul, so generous and caring. It's a great loss, a great loss." He rose to his feet and bowed in front of Honora. "And you, dear Lady Norrance," he said, using her formal title. "My sincerest sympathies."

Honora looked up at him, horrified. "We are not receiving at the moment, Mr. Jackcliff."

"Of course. Of course. My humble apologies. I will return at the appropriate time."

He left as swiftly as he'd come, and there was a stunned pause, as if the air had left the room. Rupert was the first to speak. "He's a little odd, Mother, don't you think?"

"I know. I know." Marielle pushed her long gloves down her arm and removed them. "I'm sure he meant well. He was very fond of your father."

Rupert's eyes widened and his eyebrows rose toward the curl that dangled on his forehead. "He had a strange way of showing it, and Father had no patience for him at all."

"Perhaps, but that doesn't mean that Elmore didn't respect and admire him." Marielle stood, leaving her gloves on the chair, and approached the table with the desserts. She had removed her jewelry. Her gown was creased across the front from sitting, and she rubbed her bare arms up and down even though the room was very warm. "I think I'd like some tea now."

Rupert shrugged his shoulders and rolled his eyes at Adela and Poppy.

The door opened again and Angus poked his head in. "Begging your pardon, my lady, but I thought you'd want to know I took the young earl up to his room."

Marielle nodded. It was the first time anyone had acknowledged Kip's ascension to the title.

Poppy jumped up. "Kip needs me. I'm going upstairs."

"He was sleeping when I left him."

"Please sit down, Poppy," Marielle said. "There will be plenty of time to nurse Kip back to health. He will certainly need your patience and understanding in the morning. For the moment, however, we agreed to wait for the authorities, and I'd like for us to keep our word." She poured herself a cup of tea and returned to her seat. "Thank you, Angus. You may go."

Honora gave Poppy a baleful look. "The earls and countesses of Norrance have always kept their word."

Poppy looked as if she wanted to object, but in the face of two women with the title of Lady Norrance, she hesitated to stand her ground. I had a feeling it would not be long, however, before she exercised her power as the new countess.

The third time the door opened, I was relieved to see George, who entered with two men I didn't recognize. He introduced them as officers in the local constabulary.

Marielle put down her tea and stood to greet the men. "Chief Inspector, are the guests still here in the castle? Speaking for the family, I think we would all like to go up to our rooms as soon as reasonably possible, but we cannot neglect our duties as hosts."

"Most of the guests have already departed, my lady. Those staying in the castle have been directed to retire for the evening. Many of them indicated they plan to leave in the morning, and they asked if there would be an opportunity to express their condolences in person."

Marielle's shoulders slumped. She looked exhausted, and I imagined the long preparation for the ball and the wrenching events of the evening had taken their toll on her. "The children and I will make an effort to see as many of them off as possible."

"I'll be there, too." Honora pushed herself to a standing position and leaned on her cane. "Never let anyone say the family of the Earl of Norrance shirked its duty. Now, when may I be excused?"

"We will not ask your forbearance for much longer, Lady Norrance," George said, addressing Honora. "Thank you for accommodating us. These gentlemen would like to ask your family a few questions, if you will kindly follow them."

Honora pointed her cane at one of the officers. "Give me your arm."

He stepped forward, extended his arm, and escorted her out of the room.

The second officer invited Poppy, Adela, and Rupert to accompany him to the library.

"Are you questioning us separately?" Marielle asked.

"It simplifies things," George replied. "It makes it easier for each person to remember what happened without being distracted by what others believe they may have seen. In any case, I was hoping to speak with you privately, after which you will be free to retire."

"Does speaking with me privately include Mrs. Fletcher?"

"She can leave if you object to her presence."

Marielle waved a hand in front of her face. "It doesn't matter. She may stay. I have nothing to hide." She returned to her chair and sat, shaking her head. She heaved a sigh, her breath coming out in small bursts. She seemed to be working hard to remain composed.

George waited until the others had left the room to bring a chair close to the countess and sit in front of her. "I'm afraid I have some difficult news to impart to you, Lady Norrance," he said softly.

"How much more difficult can it be than seeing my husband, my sweet James, die in front of me? I only wish . . ."

"Yes?" George said, inclining his head.

"I wish I hadn't spoken so harshly to him today." She looked from George to me. "We argued. . . ." Her voice cracked, and the tears she had been holding back coursed down her face.

George reached into his pocket, pulled out a clean white handkerchief and handed it to her.

"Thank you," she said, sniffling. She patted her wet cheeks.

"Would you care to say what you argued about?"

"It was silly. He gave that local constable, Marder or somebody . . ."

"Detective Sergeant Mardling."

"Yes, Mardling. He gave him permission to attend the ball. I was furious."

"Why were you so angry?"

"You have to understand, Chief Inspector, this event has been planned for months. The guest list very carefully selected. There were people I would have liked to invite, wanted to invite, and James said no. We had to keep our numbers down. And then he allows that awful man and that ridiculous woman . . . Oh, what does it matter now? It's over, and all our designs were for naught."

"Perhaps you can carry them out without your husband," I put in.

She pressed George's handkerchief under her nose, then shook her head. "I don't know if I can proceed without James. He was my rock. He always took care of me. He always loved me, even when I was terrible to him." She leaned over, weeping into George's handkerchief.

George flashed me a look, and I gave him a grim smile. We waited quietly until Lady Norrance was able to collect herself.

"I'm so sorry. You must excuse me." She stood and crossed the room to the table that held the trays Nigel and Angus had brought in. She shook out a napkin, wiped her eyes, and dabbed at her nose. She glanced at her reflection in the mirror over the fireplace and tucked in a stray strand of hair that had come loose. "I won't cry anymore," she said.

"It's all right," George said, standing as she returned to her chair. "You have good reason to cry."

"No. No. I'll do my mourning in private. James would have wanted it that way." Lady Norrance sat up straight and cleared her throat. "You said you had difficult news for me." She wiped her eyes again. "I'm ready to hear it."

George sat down again. "Lady Norrance, I'm very sorry to say that we do not believe Lord Norrance died of natural causes."

"What do you mean?"

"We think someone may have poisoned him."

She gasped and raised the napkin to her mouth, then leaned forward, her words urgent. "How? When? Are you sure? My mother-in-law is convinced he had a heart attack. She blamed me for hiring Chef Bergère, said it was a diet of fatty foods that killed her son."

"He didn't die from a rich diet. We believe someone may have slipped poison into his caviar."

"But I had some, too. . . . No, James took it from me." She sat back and swallowed audibly, perhaps realizing how close to death she may have come herself. She looked up at George. "You're certain?"

"We have to wait for laboratory tests, of course. We need confirmation as to what kind of poison it was, but we are convinced that someone tried to kill him."

"And succeeded," she added, her voice hardening. "Who? Who would do such a thing?"

"That's what we need your help with, Lady Norrance. Did you see anyone tamper with the caviar?"

"No, I was the only one to serve it to him. My son wanted some, but I wouldn't let him have it. Oh, Kip!" She let a small moan escape her lips. "What if I'd . . . ? Could it have been meant for both of us? How could this happen?"

"It may have been tampered with in the kitchen. We have officers questioning the staff. We don't believe you were the intended victim, but you can assist us in the investigation."

"How?"

"We'd like you to provide the police with a list of people they should interview."

She blinked rapidly. "You mean a list of suspects? I have no idea who might have wanted us dead. How would I know that?"

I came forward in my seat to catch her eye. "You don't need to accuse anyone. Just think about the people you and your husband knew and interacted with. Perhaps there was someone who held a grudge against the earl for a decision he made. Someone he may have offended or bested in a business deal."

"He was a hard negotiator, of course. He always said you had to be in business—even though he was never raised to participate in business. He learned, however. He learned how to conduct himself when circumstances required it. And recent circumstances did require him to 'take up the cudgels' as he used to say." She gave me a wan smile at the memory.

"That's all the chief inspector needs," I said. "Who might have felt slighted or injured by any action or even any threat of action on his part—or yours, for that matter."

"I don't need this list tonight," George added. "Give yourself some time to think. Perhaps your children can help you come up with some names."

Marielle sighed. "All right. I'll think about it. Is that all? Am I free to go now?"

George stood and held out his hand to her. She took it and rose gracefully from her seat, leaning back to pick up her gloves. I stood as well.

"Mrs. Fletcher and I are very grateful for your time and co-operation."

"Not at all." She rapped her gloves against George's shoulder and speared him with a stern look. "Find him," she said. "Find the man who killed my husband."

Chapter Eighteen

There was a light layer of snow on the ground when I came downstairs on the morning of New Year's Day. The castle was eerily quiet. No light breakfast was set out in the library. The state dining room was deserted; the extra tables still wore the used linens from the evening before. A little hungry and more than a little curious, I found myself on the stairs that led down to the kitchen. With trepidation, I pushed open the door to find Clover Estwich, white apron in place, rolling out dough on the marble island, and whistling. She glanced up when she heard me enter. "There's coffee in the big pot over there if you don't mind serving yourself." She cocked her head at a large coffee urn on the counter.

"I don't mind at all. I'm Jessica Fletcher, by the way. We were never introduced the other day."

She squinted at me, then went back to her dough.

I thought perhaps she didn't remember. "The auxiliary larder where—"

"Knew you looked familiar." She shook her head. "Mr. Gordon has no sense sometimes; putting a body in my larder. Thank goodness he didn't do it again."

"Terrible, losing two people from Castorbrook so close together."

"Certainly unusual. Won't have these rolls ready for another half hour, I'm afraid. Sorry to make you wait, but we're a bit short on staff this morning."

"I'm surprised to see you here at all," I said, pouring myself a cup of coffee.

"Milk or cream's in the fridge. Sugar's over here."

"Thank you." I doctored my coffee and came around to the opposite side of the island from her. "You must have been working very late last night."

"Late and later, given the time the constables finally left. Never did finish our cleanup. But I'll nap after the breakfast service and catch up." She hummed as she punched down a ball of dough and covered it with a linen towel. "Trouble is, I don't know how many to bake for."

"The police said most of the guests are leaving this morning, but I imagine they'd appreciate a few of your cinnamon rolls before they take off."

"Well, they'll get them if they're still here when these come out of the oven." She sprinkled cinnamon and sugar over the rolled-out dough and dotted it with butter, adding pecans and raisins. Then she rolled up the dough into a long log, pinching the seam closed. "I suppose I can freeze any that are left over."

It was odd to see the cook going on about her business without any grief or apparent sorrow over the death of her employer. I wondered briefly if the kitchen workers had limited contact with the earl and his family, but I decided that couldn't be. With so few permanent staff at Castorbrook, the family would likely know the ones who served them well. And according to her son, Clover had been on staff many years. It occurred to me that Clover's demotion when Chef Bergère was hired may have resulted in hard feelings. Perhaps she wasn't sorry at all that the earl had died. Maybe she was secretly pleased. Could she have been the one to introduce poison into something the earl ate? I hoped not, but it wasn't beyond the realm of possibility.

"It was a beautiful event last night, Mrs. Estwich. Everyone raved about the food. You and the rest of the staff should be very proud of what you achieved. It's just such a shame that all your hard work was followed by a tragedy. You have my sincerest sympathies."

"I'm not the one needing sympathy."

"I just assumed you would be distressed at the death of your employer."

"Sorry for the family is what I am."

"They certainly have suffered a shocking loss. Did you happen to speak with the earl yesterday?"

She grunted as she took a sharp knife and sliced the log of dough into rounds. She arranged the spirals on a baking sheet, then speared me with a cold glare. "I don't know anything of what happened upstairs. I was here all night cleaning up after the Frenchie, if that's what you want to know. That's what I told the constables, and that's the truth." She set the pan aside to allow the dough to rise again, her movements quick.

"I didn't mean to offend you."

Archer backed through the open door with an armload of tablecloths. "Sorry I'm late, ma'am. I've got all the linens. Where do you want them?"

"You know where the laundry room is."

"Good morning, Archer."

"Good morning, Mrs. Fletcher. Beautiful day. Did you see it snowed?"

"I did."

Clover looked up sharply. "And how do you two know each other?"

"We met on the road from the village," her son replied. "Her and the chief inspector saved me from Farmer Melton's shotgun."

"Well, then thank you, Mrs. Fletcher." Clover looked me in the eyes for the first time.

"You're very welcome."

I hoped Archer's endorsement might soften his mother's attitude toward me, so I resumed our conversation. "At home I make these cinnamon buns, too, but my mother always taught me to melt the butter before putting it on the dough."

"You use a lot more butter that way. I was trying to cut back on the fat the family consumed to make their dishes a bit healthier. Of course, once the countess hired Bergère, all pretense at wholesome meals went out the window." She took the second ball of dough and began rolling it out, bearing down on the rolling pin to express her exasperation. "Plenty of money for exotic ingredients. More butter. More salt. More sugar. Of course, everyone loved his cooking, but I don't want to see what he did to their arteries."

"By the way, where is Chef Bergère this morning? Is today his day off?"

"He can take a day off whenever he wants. As of this morning, he's no longer employed by the Grants."

"Oh, my goodness! What happened?" I couldn't imagine that he'd been fired after his dinner was so highly praised.

Clover smirked down at the dough. "I would have loved to see him given the sack, but no such luck as that. The earl shot himself in the foot, so to speak. He brought in all these hotel bigwigs last night, and one of them walked off with the prize. Bergère is getting his own restaurant in one of the Platinum Places, or so he boasted to me last night. The Grants are stuck with me again."

"You're not afraid they'll bring in another French chef?"

"I can cook every bit as fancy as Bergère. I watched what he did, and there were no skills there that I don't have. I was the one who made most of the spun sugar frills that decorated the desserts. But if they want another toque in their kitchen, I've already talked to my sister about joining her at the Muddy Badger."

"I didn't realize the cook at the inn was your sister. You two have won quite a few awards." I remembered the barmaid at the pub pointing out their plaques and medals on the shelf.

"Ate there, did you?" Clover gave me a satisfied smile.

"We did, and the food was delicious." I decided to take advantage of her better spirits to probe a little about Mrs. Beckwith. "Do you mind if I ask you a question?"

She stiffened. "About the earl?"

"No. About the lady's maid, Flavia Beckwith."

Her shoulders relaxed as she prepared the second pan of cinnamon rolls. "Oh, her."

"You told the police that she never took her meals with the staff. I wondered why."

"Mrs. Beckwith considered herself above it all, as if she wasn't a working person like the rest of us on staff. She pretended to be part of the family, although I never saw them invite her to dine with them, at least when the earl was in residence."

"I understand they didn't get along, she and the earl. Do you know why?"

"They never took me into their confidence. But I can tell you that she was a queer bird, Mrs. Beckwith was, always fussing about her looks, and holding herself as if she was as deserving of the same respect as Lady Norrance. Never understood why the countess stood for it, but I imagine it's a lonely existence out here with children to raise and such a big house to run. Her Ladyship probably kept her on for the company."

"Did you work here when the children were little and Flavia was their governess?"

"Some governess! She let them run wild, spend all their days outside in the rain and mud while she sat with a book. Brought her nephew around to play with the Grant brats, and the four of them carried on until the earl finally put a stop to it by sending his children off to boarding school." She slid the first baking sheet of cinnamon rolls into the oven, turned on the timer, then covered the second pan with a towel and set it aside to rise. "Felt a bit sorry for Colin when his playmates left. He was a good boy, if spoiled. Moped around here for days until the earl gave him a talking to and put him to work in the stable."

"Didn't he go to school?"

"Oh, sure, the same one as my Archer and my sister's girls." Clover dropped her cooking utensils into the huge stainless steel sink, and began wiping flour off the marble countertop. "I imagine Mrs. Beckwith would have liked to see her nephew at Eton, but her hopes were dashed there. Maybe that's what started the bad blood, but they didn't associate much after that, her and the earl."

"But Lady Norrance kept her on?"

"She did. Who can understand the decisions of the nobility?"

Mrs. Powter pushed open the swinging door and, ignoring me, beckoned at Clover. "You'd better come at once."

"I have rolls in the oven, Ginger. I'm not going anywhere."

"The constables are questioning Archer again."

"So? They questioned him last night, too. Don't know that there's anything new he can tell them."

"I heard them say they searched his rooms and found a bag of rat killer. They want to know what he planned to use it for."

"Searched his rooms? Why?" Clover untied her apron and threw it on the island. "Where are they? And we don't have any rats, so don't be spreading any rumors."

Without being asked, I followed the cook out of the kitchen as she trotted behind the housekeeper, who charged down the hall. *Doesn't this woman ever walk at a normal pace?* I thought as I hurried to keep up with them. We heard Archer's angry voice before we rounded a corner to see him struggling with two policemen.

Clover ran forward and pulled at the arm of one of the officers. "Leave my son be."

"Madam, if you don't let go of my sleeve, I'll have to take you in for willfully obstructing a constable in the execution of his duties."

Clover dropped her hand, but she refused to back away. "I demand to know what you are doing with my son."

"We have reasonable grounds to bring him in."

"Reasonable? What's reasonable?" Archer tried to shrug off their grip, but the constables had his arms pinned behind his back as they pressed him against the wall.

"You already questioned him last night. Why do you need to take him to the station house for more questions?"

"We have our orders. Now will you come quietly?"

"I'll come quietly if you let go of my arms."

The officers took a step back but maintained their positions, flanking Clover's son so he couldn't make a break for it.

Archer shook his hands and rubbed his arms.

"Archer Rodney Estwich, you are—," one of the officers began.

"Will you let me talk? I already admitted to the judge that I stole the poison to keep Melton from killing the badgers. I paid my fine and was dismissed. You can't charge me again with the same crime."

"We're not charging you with the same crime."

"Then what do you call this?" Archer shouted, throwing his hands up.

"Don't add resisting arrest to the charges."

"What charges?" Clover and Archer said at the same time.

The constable replied, "Archer Rodney Estwich, I am arresting you on suspicion of murder."

"Murder? So someone killed Melton?" Archer shook his head. "Well, he certainly took enough innocent lives himself."

The officer continued. "You do not have to say anything. But it may harm your defense if you do not mention when questioned something which you later rely on in court. Anything you do say may be given in evidence."

"I didn't kill Farmer Melton. When did this happen? I was working here all day yesterday. Ask my mother. Ask Mrs. Powter."

"We're not arresting you for the murder of Farmer Melton.

We're arresting you for the murder of James William Edward Grant, seventh Earl of Norrance."

"What? I was told the earl had a heart attack."

"That's ridiculous," Clover shouted.

"Better contact your criminal solicitor, madam."

"I don't have a criminal solicitor."

"He had someone representing him the last time we arrested him."

Mrs. Powter turned her head and sniffed the air. "Something is burning."

"My cinnamon rolls!"

Chapter Nineteen

George and I stood outside the entrance to Castorbrook Castle, waiting for our driver, Ralph. Inside, Marielle, the Countess of Norrance, and her family accepted the condolences of their departing guests.

They stood in the same reception line as they had for the ball, only this time, Kip and Poppy were at the head of the line, an acknowledgment of their new roles as the Earl and Countess of Norrance, followed by Kip's mother, then his grandmother, brother, and sister-in-law. James William Edward Grant, eighth Earl of Norrance—Kip's full name—was very pale and shaky. Those who hadn't seen his inebriated behavior the previous evening must have thought the young earl's trembling fingers were a result of his great grief over the death of his father. Those who'd seen him drinking understood that the new Lord Norrance was terribly hungover.

Poppy kept a sharp eye on her husband, nudging his side when he shut his eyes and swayed on his feet. I gathered that she was not about to let him miss this first responsibility in their newly elevated status.

"Ralph's on his way," George said to me. He shaded his eyes to peer down the driveway. "We can't remain here without transportation. I've asked him to stay on a few days, and he's agreed. I've arranged to put him up at the inn. We've worked out a fair compensation."

"I thought Scotland Yard was sending someone to take over the case," I said.

"It may be a while. The holiday schedules have the assignments all bollixed up, and no one else is available at the moment. You don't mind terribly, do you, Jessica?"

"I don't mind at all, George, but I'm not certain our recently bereaved hostess will be enthusiastic about having some of her guests linger."

"Given the investigation into the nature of her husband's death, I would think she may appreciate having the security of a Scotland Yard official on hand."

"Since an arrest has already been made, she may wonder why it's needed at all."

George smiled. "Do I detect a note of skepticism on your part, Mrs. Fletcher?"

"You do, indeed, Chief Inspector Sutherland."

I had told George about Archer's arrest that morning. And while I couldn't swear that Clover's son was not the perpetrator—after all, he had both motive (his mother's demotion) and opportunity (his service as a waiter during the ball), not to mention the suspected poison in his possession—his arrest struck me as too neat. That thinking wasn't exactly scientific, I know, but my instincts, coupled with my past experience with murder cases, kept telling me that Archer was not a killer. I couldn't cite familiarity with his character. We'd met briefly only once before the earl died—on our way from town back to the castle—not counting the few words that passed between us during the ball as he served champagne. I certainly had no proof of Archer's innocence, and the police believed they had plenty to prove his guilt. But their evidence was circumstantial at best. And this may sound like foolish reasoning, but my intuition argued that a man who would defend badgers and who would go out of his way, at his own peril, to protect a hunted animal, was unlikely to be a killer. Of course, history is full of stories of violent killers who loved their mothers or who related to four-legged furry creatures far better than to their fellow human beings. But there it is: Illogical or not, I did not believe Archer had murdered the earl.

Nor did I believe that the countess had been the target. Not that I knew who had murdered her husband. But there were others whose motives might be called into question.

The earl had been arrogant with a prickly personality. For one, he had a strange relationship with Flavia Beckwith, who lived under his roof for all these years but from whom he withheld any friendly interaction. Whom else might he have insulted? Who else might have seen him as an enemy?

Possibly Elmore Jackcliff, his wife's former teacher. Despite flowery expressions of sympathy, Jackcliff carried as much disdain for his patron as the earl did for him.

And what of Flavia's nephew, Colin, whose close friendship with the earl's daughter may have motivated Lord Norrance's plans to banish him to Wales?

Other staff members besides Clover might be holding on to resentments as well: Nigel, the butler; Angus, the gardener; even the waspish Mrs. Powter. The earl's penny-pinching dealings with his employees while he mounted an extravagant ball to impress investors could have aroused long-simmering anger against him. Yes, Archer was a bird in the hand, but there were more than a few other birds in the bush.

"There he is." George put up his hand to wave at the London taxi making its way down the long drive and around the lake before drawing up in front of Castorbrook Castle.

"George, Jessica, happy New Year to you," Ralph said. He came around to the other side of the cab and held the door for us.

"Happy New Year to you, too, Ralph. How was your celebration?" I climbed into the backseat and George followed.

"It was a pretty quiet party, compared to yours." Ralph shut the door behind us and settled himself behind the wheel. "The wife and I watched the Thames fireworks on the telly at the cousin's house. We toasted each other with a pint of lager and were off to bed an hour after midnight. I would've been happy to skip the fireworks, I was that tired, but the cousin likes to show off his big-screen television. We had to ooh and ahh through it all. Kay said it was a small price to pay to enjoy their hospitality in the country."

"Sounds like a nice cozy evening," I said.

"Yours was a lot less quiet and a lot more exciting, it seems." Ralph picked up a newspaper from the seat next to him and passed it back to George.

"It's in the news already?" I said.

"Special edition," George noted.

I leaned into him so we both could read the front-page story. Archer's arrest wasn't in it, of course; that was too recent. And while the reporter hinted that there may have been questions about the earl's untimely death, there was nothing to suggest a murder had been committed. Most of the story covered the ball, photos of the society guests in their finery, including one of the host and hostess in the reception line, and the tragic loss at the end of what had been a spectacular evening. There were quotes from notables around the country praising the Earl of Norrance and his service in the House of Lords. I imagine the reporter must have had to awaken many of his sources to get appropriate reactions by his deadline.

"So we're off to the constabulary?" Ralph asked.

"Yes, but we're going to drop Jessica in town first." George turned to me. "You're sure you don't mind?"

"I would love to be a fly on the wall while you talk with the coroner, but I understand that I don't have any official reason to be there."

"It's not like the States here, Jessica. Civilians aren't invited into the precincts unless they're being questioned about a crime." George looked uncomfortable. "I just don't want any questions about our relationship to surface in the press the way they did when you and I were in Bermuda."

"It's all right, George. You don't have to explain."

A while back, George had been part of a Scotland Yard investigative team assisting the Bermuda police looking into Jack the Ripper copycat murders. I had been vacationing in the British territory at the same time. When my host's niece had been killed in a similar fashion, the island paparazzi had photographed George and me sitting close together and discussing the case. Unfortunately, the newspapers had made a big deal of our association, suggesting that George was spending time with his "girlfriend" instead of investigating the crimes, while the Bermuda government footed the bill for his services. It was a humiliating period for him, and it threatened to tarnish his reputation with his superiors back home in London, not to mention the local officials on the island, who were already disdainful of the visiting detectives.

"You can drop me off at Chipping Minster Antiques," I told Ralph. "I'll show you where it is when we get into town."

I'd called ahead to the proprietor, Hazel Fortunato, to make sure her shop was open. New Year's Day was a national holiday after all. When I'd left her shop the day before, I'd promised a return visit and the purchase of a souvenir. I didn't think at the time that I would be back so soon, but I was looking forward to seeing her again.

"Perhaps I'll discover something new about her friend Flavia Beckwith," I'd told George when I first learned that his appointment didn't include me. I'd put on a cheerful face, not wanting to admit that being left out of his meeting with Mardling and the coroner stung more than a little.

Ralph pulled his London taxi into a parking spot close to the curb in front of the antiques shop. He hopped out to open the door for me.

"I'll ring you up when we're about to leave," George said.

"Take notes," I said, teasing. "I'll expect a full report later on."

"Will do." George smiled and gave me a mock salute.

I watched from the curb as Ralph's taxi pulled away, rolled down the street, and turned at the next corner. Another car immediately slipped into the spot Ralph had vacated, and a dark-haired woman got out. She pulled two shopping bags from the trunk and bustled up the walkway.

Sighing, I turned toward the shop. The lady walking in front of me bumped her leg against one of the bags that she carried and had to catch herself before she tripped. The paper on the side began to tear, but I didn't think she was aware of it.

"Ma'am" I called, "your bag is . . ." I was too late. The contents of her shopping bag spilled onto the path leading to the door. Silver forks, spoons, and knives clattered onto the stone, along with several books and an iron doorstop. No wonder the bag had split. A silver cup without a handle rolled into the brown grass and came to rest at the edge of a patch of snow.

"Good heavens," I said, rushing forward. "Let me help you." I leaned over to pick up the cup.

"I knew these old carrier bags wouldn't hold," she said, disgusted. She set down the other one, catching it before it fell over. "Stupid me."

"Don't blame yourself. That could happen to anyone." I knelt down and picked up one of the books.

"You're very kind. Look, would you mind terribly waiting here while I get a box from the shop? I'll only be a minute."

"I don't mind at all," I said, standing.

She ran the rest of the way to the door and disappeared inside. I looked down at the book in my hand. It was an old edition of Shakespeare's tragedies. I flipped open the cover and was startled to see a bookplate reading THIS BOOK BELONGS TO with "Flavia Beckwith" added in looping script.

The door to the shop opened, and the woman came down the step, holding a cardboard carton. Hazel followed with a second empty box.

"Hello there, Jessica," Hazel called, waving. "Your timing was good. This is my friend Emmie."

"Nice to meet you, Jessica. Thank you so much for minding my goods." Emmie set down the carton and began throwing her scattered items in it. "I'd have hated to leave this silver sitting on the path for anyone to pick up."

I looked up the street and chuckled. "There don't seem to be any people around who would've walked off with it."

Emmie's gaze followed mine, and she shook her head. "You can see how observant I am these days."

"That's all right, Emmie. Jessica didn't mind guarding your things, did you, Jessica?"

"Not at all," I replied. I put the silver cup and the book into the box, took the other box from Hazel, and placed Emmie's second shopping bag inside. "Just to make sure this one doesn't tear, too," I said.

"Brilliant!" Emmie said. "I never would've thought of that."

"I've got this one," I said, lifting the box with the bag. "Can you handle the other?"

"No problem," Emmie said. "You're a lifesaver. Come on, Hazel. I can use a cup of your tea now."

"I already turned on the kettle."

Hazel's sleigh bell jingled as the three of us crowded into her store. She used the toe of her shoe to push aside a doll's carriage and pulled out two of the chairs from the side of the mahogany table decorated with the holiday displays. "Just set the boxes down here. We can put the stuff away later, after we have our tea." She shivered. "Brrr. This weather is not good for old bones."

"Tell me about it," Emmie said. She followed Hazel down the hall, shrugging off her coat as she went.

I trailed after them.

"I really appreciate your opening for me today," Emmie told Hazel. She dumped her coat over a pile of dish cloths and sank into a chair.

"Was the shop supposed to be closed?" I asked, taking a seat next to her.

Hazel took down three cups and saucers, and placed them on the counter. "When I knew Emmie was coming in," she said to me, "I figured I'd stay open for you, too."

Emmie leaned forward and gripped Hazel's hand. "You're such a good friend." Her eyes filled with tears.

"Now, don't fuss over me. Let me fuss over you. You're the one suffering."

"But you miss her, too."

I looked from Hazel to Emmie and back.

"This is Flavia's sister, Emmie Stanhope," Hazel said. "I didn't formally introduce you."

"Did you know my sister?" Emmie asked.

"Not really," I replied.

"Emmie, this is Jessica Fletcher, who's visiting from America and came for the Norrance ball last night. We met yesterday." She poured hot water into a teapot. "Jessica, there's a box of biscuits on that shelf behind you. Would you please put them on this plate?" She held out a rose-patterned saucer.

Standing, I took down the cookies, arranged them on the plate she'd given me, and placed the dish on the small table.

"Jessica Fletcher," Emmie whispered. "Why do I know your name?"

"I'm a mystery writer," I said. "Perhaps you've heard about my books?"

"That's not it," Emmie said, looking at me curiously.

"Well, that's interesting, Jessica. You didn't tell me that yesterday." Hazel placed the three cups and saucers on the table. "Here's our tea." She pulled up a third chair for herself. "Now," she said, wiggling her hips from side to side to get comfortable. "Tell me what you've brought in, Emmie."

Emmie tore her gaze away from me and looked at her friend. "Oh, Hazel. I know it's crazy to want to get these things out of the house so quickly. I just feel like I'm surrounded by Flavia's belongings and I'm choking on them."

"You don't have to explain. Death creates its own strange needs. If you feel better, clearing out Flavia's things, I'm happy to help you dispose of them. It's not every friend can do that for you."

Emmie looked back to me. "My sister . . ."

"Yes. I know. I'm so sorry for your loss."

She leaned against the back of the chair. The air whooshed out of her as if she were a balloon with a slow leak. "It's funny. When we were children, I always looked after her. She was a sickly girl."

"I didn't know that," Hazel put in.

"Oh, yes. She was always catching something. She hated to go outside. Every day she wore three jumpers, even while I was threatening to throw open the windows because it was that hot in our room."

"Well, she grew to a healthy adult," Hazel said, sipping her tea.

"I thought so, too," Emmie said, "but the police report said the coroner found a defect in her heart, and that's what caused her death. I imagine it may have contributed to her illnesses as a girl." The cup of tea was halfway to her mouth when she gasped and looked over at me. "You were the one who found her, weren't you? I knew I'd heard that name somewhere."

Hazel's eyes were accusing. "How could you not say anything yesterday?" she asked.

"I didn't want to cause you more pain, Hazel. You were so upset about Flavia's death. She was your close friend. I didn't know her at all. It was simply an accident that I found her. And it was too late for me to do anything to help. I thought if I told you, it would just make it worse for you."

"Well, I don't know that you were right."

"I'm sorry that you're upset. I was trying to be sensitive."

"Where? Where did you find her? Tell me," Emmie demanded. "How did it happen?"

"We had just arrived and been shown to our rooms. I was looking out the window and noticed a purple cloth on the ground. I couldn't tell what it was, but when the wind blew it aside, I saw your sister's leg. I assumed she was hurt and unable to get up. I ran to get my friend George, and we raced downstairs to try to find her. I reached her first."

"She was already dead?" Emmie whispered.

I nodded.

"Could you tell how long?"

"I'm not a doctor, but it looked to me as if she'd been gone for some time."

Emmie covered her face with her hands.

"Emmie, dear, there's nothing anyone could have done," Hazel said.

"I know." She raised her head. "I just wish we'd made up before it happened. I loved her, but she was so stubborn, spoiled, wouldn't listen to reason. She was always that way." Emmie's grief was mixed with anger.

"Would it help to talk about it?" Hazel asked.

"Oh, it's all the fault of that idiot earl. Did you see that he died last night?"

"No!"

"It was in the morning paper: 'Magnificent Ball Ends in Tragedy.' That was the headline. Everyone's talking about it in the village." Emmie pulled a tissue from her pocket and blew her nose.

Hazel clicked her tongue. "Clearly, I must get out more."

"I can't say I'm sorry about the earl. He was a dreadful man."

I had been keeping quiet, caught between guilt at not being honest with these ladies about my suspicions concerning Flavia's death, and fearing that if I said anything and I turned out to be wrong, I would have caused them unnecessary distress. But if anyone could clear up why Lord Norrance and Mrs. Beckwith weren't on speaking terms, it was her sister. "If the earl was so awful," I said, "why did your sister stay on at Castorbrook?"

"Money. He had it. She wanted it. I told her we didn't need his hush money. We do fine as we are. But she wanted to punish him."

"Why?" Hazel asked.

Emmie started. She seemed to realize she was about to divulge family secrets. She shrugged. "Oh, it's a long story. You don't want to hear it. It's in the past. And anyway, Flavia is dead. The earl is dead. Don't they say, 'When you're dead, all debts are paid'?"

Chapter Twenty

George reached into his pocket. "I have a present for you."

"You do?"

"Yes. I think you're going to like it."

We were sitting side by side at a corner table having lunch at the Muddy Badger. Our taxi driver, Ralph, had declined our offer to join us, and was standing at the bar with a mug of cider—"I never take alcohol when I'm on duty"—entertaining his new friends in Chipping Minster.

George handed me a sealed envelope.

"May I look at it now?"

"Look at it, but don't read the whole thing. Your dish will get cold."

I broke the seal of the envelope and pulled out the sheaf of papers just far enough to identify the contents. It was the coroner's report on Flavia Beckwith. "Oh, George! Thank you so much." I flung an arm around his neck to give him a quick hug.

George chuckled. "No one would believe it if I told them you got excited about a coroner's report. They would understand it if I gave you a piece of jewelry, perhaps a ring. . . ."

"Don't you dare give me a ring," I said, laughing to cover my embarrassment. I hoped George wasn't offended. He didn't appear to be. I tucked the envelope in my shoulder bag to examine later, and picked up my fork.

The luncheon special at the pub was something called "toad in the hole," a kind of potpie with sausages baked in Yorkshire pudding. It was served with red-onion marmalade and a side dish of roasted vegetables. Hearty fare for a cold winter afternoon, but I'm not sure how good it was for my health. I thought of Clover, who took pains to serve nutritious meals to the Earl of Norrance and his family. In a sense, her concern for their well-being had backfired on her when the countess elected to hire a French chef to prepare meals for the family and guests.

It would be ironic if Clover turned out to be the one who poisoned the earl while her son stood accused of the crime. Archer was being held in jail despite his mother's efforts to hire a criminal solicitor to bail him out. George had stopped in to see the prisoner after his meeting with Mardling and the coroner. Archer had been morose but philosophical, and George had commented to him about his acceptance of his condition.

"Naught I can do about it now," he'd told George. "But since I know I'm innocent, I figure the constables will release me at some point."

"I'm not sure I'd trust in the local lads as much as he does," George told me.

"If they stop the investigation on the assumption they have the murderer in hand," I'd said, "he'll be in a lot of trouble. But if they follow up on other possibilities, he should be all right."

* * *

George had met Maura Prenty at the jail. She'd come to see her cousin Archer. Maura, I remembered reading, had been arrested along with Archer for trespassing on Farmer Melton's property to protest the killing of badgers. At the jail, she carried in a basket of food from her mother, the Muddy Badger's award-winning cook, whose cuisine I was eating now. The police had argued the propriety of allowing such a gift and had run the basket through a metal scanner, but Maura, or her mother, had been smart enough to pack plastic forks and spoons in the basket in anticipation of the examination.

"This is delicious," I said, scooping up a bit of the creamy Yorkshire pudding. It tasted like something midway between a bread pudding and a popover. "How's your dish?"

George looked down at his grilled fish. "It's good, but I think I'm missing out on something special you have there."

"You're welcome to share my meal," I said. "It's far too much for me to finish."

"I think I'll just take a bite from this end." George cut himself a taste from an untouched corner of my dish. "That's quite good."

I smiled. The scene reminded me of many meals Frank Fletcher and I had shared over the years we were married. When we were newlyweds, Frank loved simple food—meat, potatoes, a salad—and that was what he would order when we went out to a restaurant. Yet he always wanted a taste of the more exotic dishes I was eager to try, and I would sample his meal in return. As our time together grew, Frank's palate became more sophisticated, and he wanted us to order different dishes so he could experience more than one. We would tease each other and say we were members of the "flying forks brigade." I missed that easy camaraderie, that innate understanding of each other's likes and dislikes, that . . . not just acceptance of, but appreciation for who each of us was. I missed Frank.

I had been a widow for a long time. Good friends had filled in the gaps, inviting me to celebrate important occasions with them, including me in family events, keeping me from being lonesome. But I'd never met anyone who intrigued me as Frank Fletcher had, or admired my skills and put consideration for me ahead of his own needs—until George. He was his own person with a life and a history and a profession that was complete, as I liked to think I was, too. We found we had so many interests in common, viewed things from a similar point of view, even shared the same sense of humor. George respected my instincts, my need to analyze, my attraction to knotty puzzles. And I admired his honesty, his sensitivity, his principled approach to life, and it certainly didn't hurt that he's a very handsome man.

Yet, there we were with an ocean between us, with me in Maine and George in London, and neither of us willing to give up the lives we'd built, and leave friends and family behind to start a new adventure in a new country with a new love. It was a challenge, one we hadn't been able to overcome. But we couldn't deny the pull. For now, we would take trips into each other's territories to spend precious time together. As for the future, it was unknowable.

"Does Detective Sergeant Mardling think his men have arrested the right man?" I asked.

"I got the impression he was pleased to have a subject in hand, but he did say his team is continuing the investigation."

"But are they only looking to bolster their case against Archer, or are they developing other suspects as well?"

"Good question. I wish I knew for certain. Mardling has always resented my intrusion. Nevertheless, I told him that their evidence was unlikely to result in a conviction and that there was more work to do. I advised him to cast a wider net. For Archer's sake, I hope that happens quickly. We're going to have a case meeting tomorrow with the other investigators and the chief constable. I'll press them on that issue. But I'm a little at a disadvantage."

"Why?"

George rubbed his jaw and grimaced. "I'm afraid I'm viewed as a placeholder until someone else is assigned to supervise. The Yard want an officer from the Homicide and Serious Crime Command to serve as liaison to the local constabulary. However, the divisional CID in Cheltenham is expecting to serve in this role. It's only because Norrance was a peer and spent a good deal of his time in London that the Met's higher-ups think the Yard should be involved in the case."

"But don't you investigate homicide? I thought that was your specialty."

"It has been. It is. But different departments cover different geographical locations. My work is in London; we have to tread a bit carefully here not to step on toes."

"A jurisdictional dispute?" I asked.

"I'd rather not refer to it as a dispute, but who's in charge does come into question."

"I would think that since you were a witness to the crime, or at least to the results of the crime, and since you're currently staying at Castorbrook, it would give you an advantage in investigating the case."

George smiled ruefully. "It does. But unfortunately not officially. However, no one else has shown up at the door yet, and until they do, we can continue to wander the halls."

"So long as we keep out of Mrs. Powter's way," I added, folding my napkin and placing it next to my plate. "Actually, I think we're overdue for a conversation with that lady."

"I agree, but while we're in town, I wonder if it would make sense to try to catch up with Mr. Fitzwalter before we head back to the castle," George said.

"The earl's business adviser. What's on your mind?"

"See if you follow my reasoning. As you well know, Jessica, people kill other people for a reason. They have a motive." He smiled, pointing a finger at me in a friendly gesture. "I can see you are about to argue that some murders occur in a fit of rage without a motive per se."

I smiled. "You know me well."

"That is the exception. But even then, something lies behind their rage, and in many cases it involves money. I'm sure that you've picked up on the fact, as I have, that the earl was grappling with financial problems."

"It was obvious," I agreed, "and there's no doubt that Lord Norrance's negotiations with hotel chains didn't sit well with others in his family, particularly his mother."

"She certainly defines transparency," he said, laughing. "The oldest member of the Grant clan doesn't hesitate to make her feelings known."

"An advantage of age," I said.

"Refreshing, that sort of candor."

George waved over Doreen, the barmaid. "We wondered whether you know a gentleman named Fitzwalter," he said.

"Lionel Fitzwalter," I added.

"Of course," the waitress said. "He comes in often for lunch. A nice gent, always polite. What do you need to know?"

"Does he have an office nearby?" George asked.

"He does. Don't know if it's open today, being as it's a holiday, but his office is in the Colligan Building, across the street and 'round the next corner. He moved here from London a few years ago, him and his wife, Birdie. Lovely lady."

"Yes, we met her at the New Year's Eve ball," I said.

Doreen scrunched up her face and wrapped her arms about herself as though a sudden cold breeze had blown through. "Ah, the ball. Terrible thing what happened to the earl, isn't it?"

"Yes, terrible," I said.

"He wasn't the most beloved chap in town, but no one deserves to die as he did, especially not while ringing in the New Year."

"I suppose we can't always pick our time to go," George said. "Thank you for the information, and for the fine lunch."

As we got up to leave, Ralph vacated his spot at the bar and came to us.

"Stay where you are, Ralph," George said. "We're just walking around the block. We'll pop back in when we'd like a ride back to the castle."

"Whatever you say," Ralph said. "I'm feeling really comfortable in this place. Lovely way to spend an afternoon."

The Colligan Building seemed out of character in the quaint village of Chipping Minster. The architect had designed a modern two-story white structure that clashed with the older buildings and homes on either side of it. We stepped into the foyer and read the list of tenants. Fitzwalter Financial Management was on the second floor. We went up the stairs, and George tried the door. It was locked. "Well, it's a holiday," he said.

I pressed the buzzer anyway. "Just in case," I said.

We'd already turned toward the stairs when a voice came from a speaker mounted over the door. "Who's there?"

"It's Jessica Fletcher and Chief Inspector Sutherland," I said. "Sorry to disturb you, but we were hoping to steal a little bit of your time."

"Can you wait, please?"

A moment later, the door opened, and Fitzwalter gave us a wan smile.

"Sorry to barge in like this, Mr. Fitzwalter," George said, "but we were in town and—"

"Not a problem," Fitzwalter said, "not a problem at all. Please come in. And it's Lionel. We were dinner companions after all, were we not?"

His office was nicely appointed, although the furniture was of another era, not the sort of modern design I had expected in such a contemporary building. George and I took the chairs that sat on the other side of the large walnut desk from our host.

"You're lucky to catch me here today, but I thought I'd better get a head start on work. It's going to be a busy week. Tea?" he asked. "Or perhaps you would prefer coffee." He directed that suggestion at me.

"Neither, thank you," I said. "We've just come from lunch at the Muddy Badger."

"Great food there," Fitzwalter said. I hadn't noticed when we'd dined together at the ball how large a man he was, in sharp contrast to his aptly named wife, Birdie. It wasn't so much that he was heavy, just broad in the way football linebackers are. His general shape was rectangular.

"If I remember correctly, you're with the Yard, right, George?"

"Yes, but I came to Castorbrook with Jessica purely as an invited guest. Because I happen to be here, I've become involved in the earl's death, at least until a replacement has been appointed."

"Frankly," Fitzwalter said, "I'm still having trouble believing it."

"Everyone was shocked," I said, "except, I suppose, for whoever killed him."

"Is that the official finding?" Fitzwalter asked. "I suppose that's a foolish question since I hear an arrest has been made."

"It's actually not a foolish question," George said. "The official finding will have to wait until the coroner completes his examination. But one look at the earl's body leaves little doubt that he was poisoned."

Fitzwalter closed his eyes and gave a pained grunt. "And what kind of evidence do they have against the lad charged with the murder? Do you know him? Chipping Minster is a small village. The fellow is the nephew of the cook where you had your midday meal." He shook his head and sighed. "Hard to take in that we have a murderer in our midst. Birdie and I came out to the countryside to get away from this kind of violence. Can't believe it followed us to Chipping Minster. Makes me wonder if I should look over my shoulder when I walk home."

Crime can happen anywhere in the world, I thought, but didn't say. My own hometown of Cabot Cove was as peaceful and safe-seeming as Chipping Minster, yet we'd certainly seen our share of crime. Even so, I never hesitated to walk around our village, or ride my bike on less traveled roads. You always should be alert to your surroundings, of course, but that doesn't mean you need to skulk around, jumping at every little noise. It would make for a very uncomfortable life.

"The constables may have been a little precipitate," George said. "Archer Estwich has been accused, it's true. But his guilt is not confirmed—at least in my mind."

"But they must have arrested him on some evidence," Fitzwalter said.

"Archer was the last one to serve the earl," I said.

"The police believe either the earl's champagne or caviar may have been tainted," George added. "And investigators found rat poison in Estwich's room where he and his mum live in town."

"Hardly seems sufficient evidence to make an arrest," said Fitzwalter.

"There's some talk of his having resented the earl's treatment of his mother, who is the cook at the castle," I offered, "but I doubt his anger rose to the level of committing murder. There's also a very large difference between the ingredients of most rat poisons and that which killed the earl. Rat poisons usually contain anticoagulants. We believe the earl died of cyanide poisoning."

"I'm impressed with your knowledge of poisons, Jessica."

"Jessica writes crime novels under the name J. B. Fletcher," George explained. "She's a devoted student of murder and the means employed to commit murder."

"Quite a team," Fitzwalter said, "a Scotland Yard chief inspector and the writer of crime novels. But you're obviously here to discuss some aspect of my relationship with the Earl of Norrance."

George nodded. "Because you were the earl's business affairs manager, Lionel, you must know what financial pressures the earl labored under—and the circumstances and/or persons that put him under that pressure."

"We know that the earl was exploring the possibility of selling Castorbrook Castle to a hotel chain," I added. "You and Griffin talked about it over dinner. Had a decision been made?"

"You both know quite a bit, considering you're newcomers to the earl's family and life. I'll cut to the chase. As the earl's business affairs manager, I, of course, am intimately familiar with every aspect of his financial life. Yes, he was under considerable financial pressure and had been for quite a while."

"Trying to keep up the castle?" I asked.

Fitzwalter laughed. "Yes, of course. Castorbrook is a bottomless money pit, always something in need of repair or renovation. Renting it out for photo shoots or weddings brings in some money but hardly enough to cover all the expenses. And there was his irrational love affair with horse racing. Cost him a bloody fortune, and it was money that he didn't have."

"You mean the racehorses that he was planning to breed?" I asked.

"Those, too. A filly he bought in Kentucky cost him sixty-two thousand pounds. But, no, I'm talking about wagering on horse races. Of course, there were always those infernal second-mortgage companies willing to lend him money to cover his bets at exorbitant interest rates."

This was a side of the earl that neither George nor I was aware of.

" 'Second mortgage companies'?" I said.

"A polite name for loan sharks," George explained.

"Are you suggesting that the Earl of Norrance owed money to loan sharks?" I asked. "Organized crime?" I had difficulty keeping the shock out of my voice.

"Criminal, yes," Fitzwalter said, "but not quite as pervasive as your Mafia in the States. What do you call them, Inspector?"

"British firms," George said, "is the general name for organized crime groups. The White British are so called to differentiate between them and the organized crime groups that involve immigrants from the Middle East, Asia, and Africa. They specialize in white-collar crime, including loan-sharking. They operate quite effectively and under the radar around the racetracks in Epson, Brighton, Lewes, and elsewhere."

"Was he behind in his payments to these groups?" I asked.

"Quite a bit, I fear," his business affairs manager said.

Neither George nor I commented, but I knew we were thinking the same thing—that the Earl of Norrance could have been killed by someone from one of these so-called "second mortgage" groups who'd attended the New Year's Eve ball. This added a whole new dimension to the investigation.

"What about the townspeople?" George asked. "Did the earl owe anyone in town a sufficient amount of money to justify taking revenge on him?"

"He owed a number of companies in the area, mostly tradesmen, the fishmonger, the wine purveyor, but those were relatively small bills. I could cover most of those when some funds came in. There would be the occasional delay, however. I did my best for them, but I know some of those merchants were not pleased."

"The earl must have had a will," I said. "Were you responsible for that, too?"

"His solicitor in the City is the one who handled Norrance's will. Kip, as elder legitimate son, inherits the title automatically, but the disposition of the estate is at the earl's discretion. I believe the largest portion will be left in the hands of Lady Norrance to direct, since a good deal of it came with her in marriage. Norrance gambled with his own money, but rarely touched hers.

So that at least is something. Parts of the estate have already been distributed, of course. The dower house that Honora occupies is hers in full. The stables and stock will likely go to Jemma. I don't recall what, if anything, he planned to leave Rupert. He was quite adamant that the lad find a profession. Of course, if the sale to a hotel chain goes through, Rupert stands to gain a portion of the proceeds. His mother would see to that."

"Do you know if he would have provided any bequests for staff?"

"I should be surprised if he didn't."

"What about the lady's maid who recently died?" I asked.

"She was in an interesting situation. Flavia Beckwith earned considerably more than other staff members and received large bonuses. I asked the earl about it on a few occasions, but he was never specific, would only say her length of service merited the greater amount. I didn't pursue it. After all, it was his money. Have I answered all your questions?"

"One more if you don't mind," George said.

"Ask away, Chief Inspector. If there's anything I can tell you that will help bring the earl's killer to justice, I'll feel good, very good indeed, about having provided it."

"The competition between hotel groups to gain the rights to Castorbrook Castle. I take it that you've been smack in the middle of those negotiations."

"I have, indeed."

"There's a great deal at stake for the winner," George said. "Would having the earl out of the way make it easier for one of the chains to prevail, perhaps because that chain had gone behind the earl's back and was dealing with a family member, someone more amenable to its offer?"

"I'll have to give that some thought, George. As far as I know, only the earl was involved with those negotiations. Can't imagine which one of his children would know enough to venture an opinion, much less involve themselves in other details. I can't come up with an answer off the top of my head, but I'll mull over the matter."

I doubted that any of the earl's children were sophisticated enough to try to undermine the negotiations their father was undertaking. But two other family members possibly were. Honora had already expressed her staunch opposition to relying on a hotel buyout to rescue the Grant family finances. And there was also the new countess to consider. Poppy was an unknown quantity. Clearly, she was more detached than her husband, sister-in-law, and brother-in-law. Was she also more conniving?

As we said our good-byes, I tossed out one further question. "Lionel, you're obviously someone who knows the earl's family quite well. Apart from the usual sort of conflicts present in every family, was there any rancor between the earl and any member of the family over money?"

"If you mean did any family member disagree with the proposal to sell the castle to a hotel chain?" His laugh was meant to convey that I'd asked a silly question. "There was plenty of discord about that, Jessica, plenty, indeed. Please feel free to stop by anytime. And I'll ring you up, George, if I have any brilliant insights in the next few days."

"The earl appears to have been in far deeper debt than we presumed," George said as we walked back to the Muddy Badger to collect Ralph and return to the castle.

"And Archer's arrest notwithstanding, there could be a very long list of suspects if Detective Sergeant Mardling takes the time to look a little harder."

Chapter Twenty-one

"Would you be interested to know that there was quite a bit of talk at the bar about the earl's murder?" Ralph asked us when we were in his taxi on our way back to Castorbrook.

"We are *very* interested," I said. "What was said? Did they know about the arrest of Archer Estwich?"

Ralph twisted around in his seat to look at us. "They know and they're not happy about it."

"Please keep your eyes on the road," I said. "We can hear you fine."

Ralph faced forward but tilted his head so his voice would carry to the backseat. "Estwich seems to be a popular fellow, especially with the ladies."

"Do they believe he committed the crime?" George asked.

"The barmaid, Doreen, said that Archer, despite his rough exterior, was as gentle as a lamb and would never have harmed the earl unless he saw him abusing a small animal. Since there weren't any small animals at the ball, she said, the bobbies must have gotten the wrong man."

"From the little I know of Archer, I would have to agree," I said.

George leaned forward. "Did they mention anything about the earl himself?" he asked.

"Well, there was one bloke who raised his mug, saying if Estwich offed the earl, he did the neighborhood a favor."

"Oh, dear, why would he say that?" I asked.

"Apparently the earl was late in paying his debts, causing some financial hardship on local establishments that supplied the castle with goods."

"We're aware of that," George said.

"But did you know he also took advantage of people who couldn't defend themselves?"

"That last part's news," George said.

"Haven't lost my police interview skills, have I, Chief Inspector?" Ralph said.

"We're impressed," George replied. "How did Norrance take advantage?"

"There's a small group of immigrant workers who have moved to the edge of town. Lord Norrance hired them to work in his gardens last summer, but he neglected to pay them. There's some suspicion that His Lordship knew they were illegals who couldn't report their victimization to the constabulary without jeopardizing their residency."

"Sounds like he doesn't have a particularly praiseworthy reputation, doesn't it?" George said to me.

"I'm sorry to hear it. I knew he was arrogant and extravagant, but I didn't suspect he was dishonest as well."

"If you want to know a man's true character," Ralph said, "see how he treats those he considers his inferiors."

"Did you learn that in your police training?" I asked.

"Nope! I read that in one of the Harry Potter books."

Ralph passed by a satellite truck outside the gates to the estate. "Uh-oh. Fleet Street is already here," he said, referring to the nickname for London's national press. In years past, many of the nation's newspapers had offices at that London location, and the street name came to represent the industry.

"I would have been surprised if the press hadn't picked up the story," I said.

"Fortunately, the murder of a peer is not an everyday occurrence," George said. "I'm glad to see the constabulary has some law enforcement on duty here to keep the reporters and the curious out." He nodded toward two police cars positioned on either side of the gates.

George rolled down his window and held up his Scotland Yard ID so the officers could see it.

They waved us through.

Ralph drove up to the front entrance, where two more police cars were stationed along with several other vehicles, one of which bore a sign: CHIPPING MINSTER VETERINARY CENTRE.

"Who might that be for?" Ralph asked.

"The Grants have dogs and horses," I said. "I hope everything is okay."

"I'll call you later to arrange for tomorrow," George told Ralph as we exited the cab.

Nigel was in the front hall when we entered the castle. "We saw the vet's car outside," I told him. "Is everything all right?"

"Dr. Ford has just arrived. The trainer called him in. Lady

Jemma accompanied him down to the stable. I was told that the late earl's prize mare is about to foal."

"Lamia?" I said.

"I believe that's correct."

"You know the horse's name?" George asked.

"The earl talked about her when I visited the stable. Lamia's sire was a Kentucky Derby winner. He said he was expecting her to do great things for his racing stock." I looked at Nigel. "Do you think they'd object if I went down to watch the birth?"

"I don't know, Mrs. Fletcher, but I'm sure they will tell you if they want you to leave."

"George, what do you think? Would you like to come with me to the stables?"

"Would you mind terribly if I said no?" George asked, wincing. "Childbirth or equine birth . . . It's not that it's not of interest. It's just that, well, there are some processes I'd prefer not to observe up close."

"But you won't mind if I go?" I asked.

"Not at all. I've got calls to make. We can meet up later, and you can give me all the details."

"Highly edited, of course."

"I would appreciate that."

I found my way to the mudroom that Lord Norrance and I had used. I selected a warm-looking barn jacket large enough to cover the jacket I was already wearing, stepped out of my shoes, slid my feet into a pair of Wellington boots, shouldered my bag, and walked outside. The dogs, running loose around the flower beds in the rear garden, barked a greeting and trotted over to sniff me. I gave them each a head rub before slipping sideways through the garden gate to keep them from following me. The afternoon sun was low as I strode through the orchard and then down the hill toward the stone barns.

I wondered why the veterinarian had left his car up at the castle when the stable was so far away. I could see a gravel area to the side of the first building. A pickup truck, its bed piled high with hay, was parked there, along with a horse trailer.

There was a light on in the barn that I'd visited with Lord Norrance. I entered, but no one was around other than the resident horses, which, after a curious glance as I walked down the aisle, ignored my presence. Lamia's stall was empty, however. *I hope nothing has gone wrong.*

I turned around. The light was dim in the second building across the brick courtyard, but through a glass partition on the door, I could make out three people leaning against the wooden boards and peering into a stall. I walked softly into the second barn and waved. Jemma looked up. She moved away from the stall and met me at the door.

"Is it all right if I watch the foaling?" I asked.

"You have to be very quiet. The mare is struggling a bit. We don't want to upset her further."

Colin and another man, who I assumed was Dr. Ford, glanced up at me when I accompanied Jemma to the stall. Dr. Ford was wearing blue scrubs.

"This is Mrs. Fletcher," she whispered to the men. "She's a guest up at the castle." I thought Colin might have recognized me from the Muddy Badger, but he didn't say anything.

The mare was standing in a stall, knee-deep in straw, shifting her weight from one side to the other and blowing noisily. Her coat was dark with sweat.

"You checked her udder?" Dr. Ford asked.

"Before I called you," Colin replied. "There was a drop of milk there."

"Has her water broken?"

"Don't believe so."

"What else have you done?"

"Cleaned out this stall, put in fresh straw. Washed down her udder."

"Did you wash her belly as well?"

"No, sir. Are you thinking she may require a cesarean?"

"Let's hope not," Dr. Ford said.

I was surprised to hear that a horse might need a C-section to birth a foal. "Does that happen often?" I asked quietly.

"Often enough," Dr. Ford replied. "I'd prefer to have her in the dispensary for any procedure, but we've done them in a barn before."

"Will that put her in danger?" Jemma asked.

"More of a problem for the foal than the mare," he replied. "But let's think positively. If we're careful, they'll both come out all right."

"She's already been laboring for fifteen minutes," Colin said, looking at his watch. "We should have seen the foal by now."

"Does it happen that fast?" I asked.

"Oh, yes," Dr. Ford replied. "Fifteen, seventeen minutes, up to a half hour. That's average. It's not like a human labor."

Dr. Ford walked to the end of the stall and leaned over to see the back end of the horse. Colin had bound up Lamia's tail in a white bandage. "There's your problem," he said. "It's a red bag delivery. Are your hands clean?"

"Yes, sir," Colin replied.

"Then come with me." He snapped on a pair of surgical gloves.

All three entered the stall. Lamia backed into a corner, her eyes wide. Jemma took her bridle and crooned softly to her, leading her forward while Dr. Ford and Colin worked on the opposite end. I couldn't see what they were doing, but there was a whoosh that sounded as if someone had emptied a bucket of water into the straw.

"She's trying to lie down now, Dr. Ford," Jemma said. "Is that okay?"

"Yes, let her go down. Don't try to keep her standing. The placenta has separated. She needs to get the foal out quickly."

With an audible grunt, Lamia sank to her knees in the straw and leaned to the side, stretching out her legs. While Jemma squatted next to the mare's head, Dr. Ford and Colin began to pull the foal out. I saw the small hooves first, followed by a dark brown nose, and, in no time, the foal slipped out, shivering and blinking in the faint light. Jemma stood and stepped out of the way, and Lamia raised her head, put her nose to her foal, and nuzzled the new arrival.

"Give her a bit of time to be a proper mother, and don't wipe down the foal," Dr. Ford told Colin. "Cleaning her foal is an important part of the mare-foal bonding process."

Jemma tried to look over Dr. Ford's shoulder. "What do we have?" she asked.

"A colt," the vet replied.

Jemma and Colin grinned at each other. Then Jemma's face crumpled and she started to cry. I knew she was thinking about her father. "This is the start of the Norrance racing string," she said.

Dr. Ford smiled at her. "You two will do fine, carrying on with the stock."

"That we will," Colin said.

"Congratulations!" I whispered when Jemma came out of the stall.

"Thanks," she said, smiling through her tears.

Bearing witness as the prize mare Lamia gave birth to her foal was a tense but exciting experience, to say nothing of life-affirming. Dr. Ford, Colin, and Jemma had worked smoothly as a team as they aided Lamia to deliver her colt. If the earl had been right, the newborn would one day go on to become a prize-winning, money-generating racehorse. This gangly little foal, already trying to pull himself up on his spindly legs, had no idea of what was expected of him. Would he be able to live up to those expectations? The earl was no longer alive to confirm that his purchase of Lamia from a breeder in Kentucky had been a wise investment. It had been a costly one. Fitzwalter had said the earl paid sixty-two thousand pounds for her. That was more than one hundred thousand dollars. Between the earl's gambling and spending, would there be sufficient funds for his heirs to carry out his dreams of breeding racehorses in the Norrance stables?

The veterinarian examined the youngster briefly. "I'll come back tomorrow to check them both. Let's allow them some private time together." He followed Colin out of the stall.

"Well done, my friends," Dr. Ford said, stripping off his rubber gloves and dropping them in a satchel that he'd left next to the stall. He slapped Colin on the back and shook Jemma's hand. "He's a fine-looking foal, healthy as can be. He'll be tearing up racetracks across the UK in no time. His mother is looking good, too, not the worse for wear."

"Have to be grateful surgery wasn't required," Colin said.

"Much better this way, but you've got to keep your eyes on them both." He gave Colin a list of instructions regarding the mare and her colt.

"I can't wait until he's old enough to ride," Jemma said, leaning over the gate and smiling at the newest horse in the barn.

"You've never met a horse you didn't want to ride," Colin said to Jemma while washing his hands in a bucket of clean water, then drying them on one of many towels brought to the stable in anticipation of the birth. "It's a shame that your dad isn't here to enjoy it."

"I know," Jemma said, her attention still focused on the newborn colt. "He would have been so pleased."

"Sorry to learn about the earl," Dr. Ford told her. "Rumor has it that your father might have been poisoned. Did I hear that right?"

"That's what has tongues wagging around the village," Colin said, putting his arm around Jemma's shoulder. "If you ask me, the constable in charge of investigating is a bit of a bumbler."

"Mardling's a good man," the veterinarian said in defense. "Of course he hasn't had to poke into many murders, a good thing for us here in the Cotswolds. But I hear there's a Scotland Yard fellow staying at the castle who must have seen plenty."

"That would be Mrs. Fletcher's friend," Jemma said, suddenly seeming to remember that I was still there.

"How are you, Mrs. Fletcher?" Colin asked, realizing that I was standing silently in the shadows.

"Me? I'm just fine," I replied, "although I admit that I'm still in awe at the miracle I've just seen. Does he look like he has the makings of a champion racehorse?"

"Never know at this stage," the veterinarian replied, "but I'd say he's a fine specimen. Wouldn't be surprised if he became a champ. Well, I'd better get back home. It's gotten dark—not fond of these shortened winter days—and the missus will be getting supper ready. Please give your mother my condolences," he said to Jemma. "Hope she'll be pleased about this new life we've brought into this questionable world." He closed up his leather bag. "Pleasure meeting you, Mrs. Fletcher. Now, if someone can drive me back to my car . . ."

Jemma didn't seem eager to leave the stable, but she held up her hand.

"The police wouldn't let me through the back entrance," Dr. Ford said to me. "Had to come through the front where the constables could use their radio to confirm my legitimacy to pass."

"I wondered why you hadn't driven to the barn directly," I said.

"I'm sorry you were inconvenienced, Dr. Ford, but as I told you, we're trying to keep the reporters out," Jemma said.

"Not such an inconvenience. Always appreciate the company of a beautiful young lady, especially one so knowledgeable about horses."

"I'd offer you a ride, too, Mrs. Fletcher," she said, "but the pickup truck only has two seats."

"Think nothing of it," I said. "I'll enjoy the walk back. You run along. Nice to meet you, Dr. Ford. Congratulations to all on this new addition to the family."

"Are you going back up to the castle?" I asked Colin after the veterinarian and Jemma had departed.

"Afraid not, Mrs. Fletcher. I'll be here in the stable the better part of the night to make sure nothing goes amiss."

"It was a fascinating experience. I'm so glad I got to see it."

"Maybe you can use it in one of your books," Colin said through a laugh.

"How do you know that I'm a writer?"

"Me mam called me. Said she met you today, that you were the one to find my aunt in the garden."

"I did. There have been a lot of losses here at Castorbrook. I'm sorry about your aunt."

"Me, too. She was a kind lady. Used to take me with her to play with the Grant lads and Jemma when we were little."

"Then you've known Jemma a long time."

"Yeah, she's like a little sister to me. We're very close."

"Did the earl and countess approve of your friendship?"

Colin snorted. "Not hardly. The earl sent me up to Scotland to get me out of the way. But it worked out for me anyway."

"How so?"

"I got to apprentice with a famous trainer there, Aaron Elgard. Mr. Elgard used to work for the royal family. Balmoral is the queen's Scottish home. Jemma was jealous that I got to go and she didn't. Ended up being a great education. I'm grateful for it."

"Maybe that was his plan all along. Maybe the earl was trying to help you."

Colin raised his eyebrows at me. "Maybe. Maybe not. Maybe he didn't like his daughter associating with a stable hand. But it's too late now."

"What do you mean?"

"Well, he's dead, isn't he?"

"Are you happy about that?"

"What an odd question. If you think I had something to do with it, you're wrong. I wasn't even at the ball."

"Weren't you? I thought perhaps you were one of the costumed guests."

"Well, well, you thought wrong." He turned his head, his eyes looking anywhere but at me.

I had a feeling he was lying.

"I hope you're not carrying that tale to the constables," he said, frowning.

"If it's not true, you have nothing to worry about."

While we'd been talking, Lamia had gotten to her feet and was cleaning her foal. The colt was also standing, although he wasn't very steady on his legs. He tottered toward the mare and poked his nose around her underside until he found the milk.

Colin's frown turned into a smile. "Nice picture that, huh?" He seemed relieved to change the subject.

"Very. I'd better get going," I said, slinging the strap on my purse over my shoulder. "The night's not going to get any lighter, and it's not going to get warmer."

Colin looked outside. "It's quite dark now. You'll be all right getting back to the castle on your own?"

"Heavens, yes. It isn't very far. You can see it from here."

"Just be careful walking through the orchard. The trail is narrow, and at night—"

"Don't give it a second thought," I said. "You take care of this fine-looking foal. Don't worry about me. And thank you for allowing me to be here during this wonderful event."

The earl had said Colin was a fine young man, I thought when I walked from the stable into the Cotswold darkness. But Colin believed his employer distrusted him, at least where Jemma was concerned. Was Ruby right when she said the relationship between Jemma and Colin was like a fairy tale of the princess and the groom? Now I wasn't so sure. It seemed unlikely that Colin would have a motive to kill the earl if there was no romantic relationship between him and Jemma for the earl to come between. And it didn't sound like Colin was planning to leave Castorbrook to go off to work somewhere else. Perhaps the earl hadn't had an opportunity to tell him about the offer from the peer in Wales. But if he had told him, would that news have upset Colin enough to act to safeguard his position on the estate?

While I'd been in the confines of the stable, I hadn't been aware that a wind had blown up. The current of air took what was an already chilly January night and dropped the temperature even lower—or at least it felt as if it had, with the wind chill factor. I'd dressed appropriately for the season, but I clutched the collar of my borrowed barn jacket tightly around my throat as I headed back in the direction of Castorbrook Castle.

I was not really looking forward to getting there. A festive atmosphere was out of the question. Where the scene on this first day of the New Year should have been celebratory, I was returning to a house in mourning. I wondered whether George and I would be expected to meet with the family again or whether Lady Norrance had even left her room all day after bidding most of her guests good-bye. Whether we dined with the family or found ourselves alone for dinner, it promised to be an awkward evening. Death has a way of casting a pall over things.

I looked in the direction of the castle, its lights visible in the distance. I shuddered. Maybe it hadn't been such a good idea to walk back by myself. Colin could have called for someone to drive down and provide a lift, but he was busy enough without having to worry about me. Or maybe if I'd waited long enough, Jemma would have returned with the truck.

As I proceeded toward the castle—and warmth—it started to sleet; the ice crystals blown sideways by the wind felt like tiny daggers pricking my face. I thought of Cabot Cove as I trudged forward, past the three stone buildings that comprised the stables, and started up the steep hill that I'd come down only a day earlier with our host, the earl. We have severe winters back home, with lots of heavy snow and biting winds that come off the water, so this weather was not unfamiliar. Yet there was something different about winter in the Cotswolds, a feel, almost a discernible scent in the heavy gray air.

I shivered as I started up the hill. While I consider myself to be in pretty good shape for my age—riding a bicycle around Cabot Cove keeps my legs toned—it was a lot tougher going uphill than it had been the first time. I'd made that return trip in the daylight, in dry weather, eager to find George and tell him about my conversation with Lord Norrance. This time I was aware only of the vertical pitch of the hill, how slippery it was underfoot, and how difficult it was to see through the sleet and snow and into the dark orchard ahead. The cold wind managed to creep under my jackets and chill my body. I paused to catch my breath at the top of the hill—panting out little white clouds in the freezing air—before continuing on to the head of the trail that wound its way through the now-dormant orchard. As I recalled from having accompanied the earl, the trail wasn't marked, which shouldn't pose a problem, not with the castle's lights as my beacon. I entered the path and slowly made my way, being careful not to lose my footing on the dead leaves. Although the center of the trail was solid, it sloped off on either side, a prescription for someone to misstep and twist an ankle—or worse.

The sleet pasted wet strands of hair to my face. I swiped my hand across my forehead. A snap as if a branch had broken sounded behind me. I whirled around. What was that? I held my breath for a few seconds to listen. Funny how even the sound of your own breathing can interfere with your hearing.

I turned back toward the castle when I heard it again. Another branch snapped. I gasped at the sound of heavy breathing, and of leaves or bushes being rustled. Had the dogs gotten out of the garden? They would have barked at seeing me, wouldn't they have? Was someone stalking me?

"Hello?" I said into the darkness. "Is that you, Colin?" Had he been upset with my questions? Was he trying to scare me off? He'd warned me about the orchard. "Colin?"

There was no response.

I moved ahead again, picking up my pace. Now the sound was more distinct. I *was* being followed. I glanced over my shoulder, but the lights of the castle were not strong enough to illuminate whoever or whatever was behind me. I couldn't see any movement through the darkness. Only the silhouettes of the trees nearest me were visible. My mind conjured up terrifying scenarios. Did they have bears in the Cotswolds? But if they did, wouldn't they be hibernating? Badgers didn't hibernate. Was I too close to their den? Did they chase people who ventured near their tunnels? Did they bite? I stumbled and turned to face Castorbrook, wondering whether I could outrun my pursuer. I started to trot, hugging my shoulder bag to my side. If attacked, I could use it as a shield. But for how long? I quickened my pace. I was almost running when a husky male voice shouted, "Stop right there!"

I froze.

"Don't you move," he said.

I peered into the gloom and saw Angus, the castle's rough-hewn gardener, approaching. A howl went up from the dogs that accompanied him. They trotted up to me and circled where I stood, their pants loud in the silent night.

"Hello, boys," I said softly, imitating the earl's greeting to them the day before. One of the dogs nudged my leg. It didn't feel like an aggressive move. Angus whistled and they raced back to him. But it was what the gardener was carrying that suddenly riveted my attention. It was a very large and menacing shotgun, and it was pointed directly at me.

Chapter Twenty-two

"Oh, my goodness, Angus," I said, "you scared the life out of me."

He jutted his large head forward to better see me. "Do I know you?" he said.

"Yes," I said, breathing a sigh of relief. "I'm Jessica Fletcher." I don't know why I felt compelled to add, "I'm a guest of the Grants, along with Scotland Yard Chief Inspector Sutherland." But I did. "You met us when we arrived, remember?"

"You shouldn't be walking around out here at night," he said, shifting the shotgun from one arm to the other.

"I was down at the stable where Lamia gave birth and—"

"I already know about that," he said gruffly. "You see any of those newspaper people around?"

"Newspaper people? No."

"Bunch of leeches, bloodsuckers, that's what they are, snooping where they don't belong and tryin' to dig up dirt on Her Ladyship's family."

"I knew that the press was covering the earl's death, but—"

He interrupted me again. "I won't stand still and see the countess, fine lady that she is, made a mockery of by those bloody Murdoch people."

"Murdoch people?"

"The tabloids. Dirt peddlers—that's what they are. Ought to be a law against them, but you can't expect anything smart to come out of what the politicians do, that's for certain."

"Is that why you're out here tonight, Angus, to run off any members of the press?"

"And they'll feel a round of buckshot in their rear parts, pardon the expression, if they don't get off the estate. I suggest that you get yourself back to the castle, Mrs. Fletcher, before somebody mistakes you for one of those bloodsucking leeches."

That somebody meaning you.

"Thank you for the advice, Angus," I said, trying to keep my voice steady as the cold and wind penetrated my clothing and set me to shaking again.

He turned from me without another word, the dogs flanking him, and disappeared into the darkness.

By the time I reached the castle, I was thoroughly chilled. My legs ached as I wearily entered the mudroom, where I sank down on the bench to change out of my borrowed boots and shrug off the barn jacket that had failed to insulate me from the icy weather. The castle hallway was empty, but the door to the drawing room was open. I went directly to the hearth, where I stood in front of a freshly stoked, roaring fire, rubbing my hands together and over my upper arms.

"Mrs. Fletcher," Nigel said, startling me.

"Oh, hello, Nigel."

"May I get you something—tea, brandy, something to warm

you up? This is not a night to be walking about. We're getting a spot of snow."

"So we are. Would it be too much of an imposition to have tea delivered to my room?"

"Of course not, madam. I'll see to it immediately."

Sufficiently warmed, and with the pleasant contemplation of a cup of hot tea in my immediate future, I headed for the wing where George and I were staying, pausing to knock on his door but receiving no response. I entered my room, shed my jacket, and took off my shoes, which were cold from sitting on the stone floor of the mudroom. I put on a pair of slippers, added another sweater to the layers I was wearing, and waited for my tea to be delivered. I remembered that George had given me the coroner's report on Flavia Beckwith—his gift—and retrieved it from my purse. I sat at the desk, turned on the lamp, and spread the pages out in front of me. Someone had lit the coals in my fireplace, and the room felt cozy. Nigel arrived and placed the tea service and a small, doily-covered plate of cookies on a table. "Dinner will be served in an hour," he said.

"Thank you, Nigel. Have you seen Inspector Sutherland?"

"Not recently, madam. Anything else?"

"Thank you, no."

With him gone, I returned to the coroner's report and began to read.

Coroner's Report: Postmortem Examination, Flavia June Beckwith

The body was not examined in situ. The body was delivered to the coroner's office in a white signature-sealed body bag. The body is that of a Caucasian woman appearing the stated age.

Clothing:

The body was dressed in a purple wool shirt dress, nylon stockings, and brown leather shoes. The apparel and shoes showed signs of water staining.

No bloodstains on clothing. Evidence of water staining on the back and left side of the dress. Dirt contamination within the water-stained area, on the left shoulder and upper sleeve.

External Examination of the Body

Female. Thin build. Hair, blond of medium length; weight 55 kg; height 167.64 cm.

On the left parietal scalp, at a point 8 cm above the ear, superficial abrasion of 2.5 cm x 2.5 cm in, consistent with bruise sustained in fall.

An area of reddish discolouration on the left shoulder, upper arm, elbow, and hip, consistent with fall.

Red stains were observed on the right distal phalanx of the index, long, ring, and little fingers. Samples sent for microscopic and chemical analysis. Evidence of bruising on the distal and proximal interphalangeal joints of index, long, and ring fingers. Also, reddish discolouration on the palmer side of the hand at the thenar and hypothenar region.

Two vaccination scars over left upper arm

Vertical surgical scar on abdomen

No tattoos

Clothing as described

No signs of sharp force injury. No signs of blunt force injury.

At crease of the left wrist, old scar approx. 2.5 cm long with parallel multiple stitch marks extending from one end of the wound to the other.

No other contusions or injuries observed.

Internal Examination of the Body

No evidence of cranial injury or fracture of the skull

Heart:

There was no aneurysm. The major noncoronary branches were patent. The great veins were unremarkable. Congenital floppy mitral valve observed. Ventricular septal defect.

Tissue samples taken from the heart and other internal organs sent for toxicological analysis.

Exhibits List:

See page 2 for list of tissue samples sent for microscopy and toxicological analysis together with other exhibits (hair, saliva, blood, and other organ samples, stomach contents).

Conclusion:

Interim conclusion pending pathological and toxicological reports: myocardial infarction caused by falling left ventricular oxygen uptake due to negative inotropic effect of hypothermia.

Fifteen minutes later I finished reading the final page, laid the report on the table, and wished for the time to pass quickly until I saw George. Based upon what I'd read in the report, we needed to have a serious discussion—and soon.

Chapter Twenty-three

George and I had just finished dinner and were sipping our tea when Nigel announced that Detective Sergeant Dudley Mardling was asking to see us.

We had been the only two at the table. The family had dined privately, we were told. Nigel had escorted us to an area called the "morning room," in one of the towers. It was a square space with a large round table. The room, usually reserved for the family's breakfast, had an old-fashioned dumbwaiter with ropes and pulleys for food to be sent up from the kitchen below.

I was relieved that we were not sitting in the state dining room. Occupying two chairs at a table that accommodated thirty or more would have made for an awkward meal. The morning room was decorated in shades of yellow and green, and probably provided a cheerful atmosphere on even the dullest of days. On this night, with the yellow silk drapes drawn over the windows, thus blocking a view of the snowstorm outside, it was an especially welcome atmosphere in which to dine.

Clover had served us chestnut soup, followed by potted shrimp, and then a mixed grill with glazed carrots and roasted brussels sprouts. The dumbwaiter saved her from having to carry our food up on heavy trays. I wondered how she managed with food for the family, and if there was another dumbwaiter wherever they had taken their evening meal.

"Do you think they'll be letting my boy go any time soon?" she'd asked George.

"If it were up to me, Mrs. Estwich, Archer never would have been arrested in the first place. But I promise to raise the question with the superintendent tomorrow morning."

"Oh, thank you so much, sir. I'll get his room ready as soon as I get home. He'll likely be exhausted from the experience. He usually is. Of course, he's never been arrested for murder before."

"Now, I can't guarantee his release, you understand."

"I know, but your being Scotland Yard and all, I'm sure the local bobbies will be guided by your greater experience." She'd carried our dinner plates to the dumbwaiter, whistling, and soon placed in front of us two pieces of chocolate cake with spun sugar curlicues left over from Chef Bergère's New Year's Eve dessert table.

Nigel brought in Detective Sergeant Mardling, and George stood to greet him.

"Sorry to interrupt your dinner, Chief Inspector, but we've had a bit of news, and I thought you might not want to wait for tomorrow's meeting to hear it."

"There's no interruption at all," George said, settling in his chair again. "We've finished our meal. Would you like to join us? Have you eaten?"

"Kind of you, but I've had my supper."

"I'd be happy to ask the cook for another cup of tea for you," George said as Mardling pulled out a chair. "She may even have another piece of this lovely dessert."

"You're welcome to have mine," I said. "I'm sure it's delicious, but I'm quite content as I am."

Mardling's eyes widened as I pushed my untouched plate over to him.

"Is Constable Willoughby with you?" I asked. "Perhaps she'd like a slice of cake as well."

"Willoughby went to the kitchen to talk with Mrs. Estwich. We're releasing her son tonight."

"That's good to hear," George said. "Thank you for coming to let us know."

We heard a whoop echoing up the dumbwaiter.

I smiled. "I take it that Constable Willoughby has just delivered the news."

A beaming Clover entered the room shortly, followed by Willoughby who was holding a plate with a different one of Bergère's creations. Clover set a second portion in front of Mardling. "I apologize for all the things I said about you, Detective Sergeant."

Mardling looked surprised. "No negative comments have reached my ears, Mrs. Estwich."

"Nevertheless, I didn't speak kindly of you, and it would soothe my conscience if you would accept my apology."

"Apology noted and accepted," Mardling said, "but it would

go a lot better with a cuppa. Do you think you could accommodate us?"

"Right away, sir."

Over tea and dessert, Mardling explained that the ingredients listed on the package of rat poison found in Archer's room could not have caused the symptoms that preceded the earl's death. "We determined that lack of more authoritative evidence required that we release the prisoner."

"A sound decision," George said.

"We took under advisement that several of the lads on the force vouched for Estwich, even though they'd arrested him before, and the judge who knew him quite well questioned the need to detain him further. We are, nevertheless"—he looked around to be certain Clover wasn't listening in—"keeping a weather eye on the fellow. I told him, the next time he was brought up on charges, he'd find himself in less comfortable quarters. I painted rather a severe picture."

"Oh!" I said.

"He's been a pest, if a charming one. But he has assured me of his intent to adhere to the letter of the law." Mardling pushed his empty cake plate forward and drew his teacup in front of him. He sipped delicately at the brew and smiled in satisfaction.

Nigel came in to clear the table. "I've given Mrs. Estwich the rest of the evening off," he explained. "She was eager to go home and cook a celebratory dinner for her son."

"Wonderful baker," Willoughby said, indicating her empty plate. "She made those, right?"

"If I am not mistaken, the recipe came from the French chef who was in charge of last night's meal," Nigel said. "But I believe Mrs. Estwich had a hand in turning them out."

Mardling waited for Nigel to leave the room before stating, "There was one more thing I meant to mention." He reached into his breast pocket for an envelope. "We got back an analysis of what caused the discoloration on the fingers of the deceased—Flavia Beckwith that is—of the deceased's right hand, and it was . . ." He unfolded a piece of paper.

"Oil paint," I said.

Mardling's mouth dropped open, and he scanned the paper in his hand. "That's right. How did you know?"

"Yes, Jessica," George echoed. "How *did* you know?"

I looked around at the three surprised faces and shrugged. "Really, I just thought of it now." I addressed Mardling. "You just said you 'painted a rather severe picture' for Archer, and I remembered that Elmore Jackcliff is painting the countess's portrait in oils."

"But how did you make the connection?" George asked.

"I visited Jackcliff's studio the other day. It's just down the hall from our rooms. I saw four white stripes painted over a red area on the canvas. I figured he was correcting an error he'd made himself. But now that I think about it, four fingers could have made that mark. I can't say for certain, but I doubt if Mrs. Beckwith made the marks on purpose. Perhaps she was in the studio and tripped. If she put her hand out to regain her balance and it made contact with the painting, it would have left the marks we saw on her fingers. It would be interesting to know if any of her clothing has paint on it as well."

"I'd like to see this painting you're talking about," Mardling said. "Do you think that's possible?"

"If the room is unlocked, I assume we can go in," I said. "I know where it is."

"I'd like to see it, too," George said. "Why don't you lead us there?"

At the top of the grand staircase, we turned left instead of right, toward our rooms, and walked down the deserted corridor. Before the ball, there had been other guests staying on this floor. I'd greeted a few when I happened to pass them as I went back and forth to my room. But I could feel the emptiness of the building now that they'd departed. The hall sconces still provided illumination, but the lights over each of the paintings on the walls had been extinguished, presumably to save on the cost of electricity.

I had no difficulty locating Elmore Jackcliff's makeshift studio. It was right next door to an arresting painting, a still life of a hare and two pheasants draped on a wooden table and surrounded by platters of raw vegetables. I suppose it represented the ingredients of a meal some centuries back.

I tried the knob, and the door opened into the darkened room. George walked in and fumbled around the wall until he found the light switch. The room appeared to be exactly as I'd seen it last: the chair under the window, the chaise in the corner with its throw pillow left on the floor, the drop cloth under the easel, and the battered table holding the artist's materials. I led our small group around to the front of the canvas. It, too, had not been altered. I must have come upon Jackcliff when he'd stopped working for the day. Or perhaps he preferred to have his model in front of him before adding strokes to the portrait.

"Quite skilled, isn't he?" Mardling commented.

"She looks a bit younger in the picture, don't you think?" Willoughby said.

"All in the eye of the beholder," her supervisor replied. "What are these things?" he asked, waving at the photograph and sketches of the countess's shoes, necklace, and ring that were pinned to the side of the canvas.

"The photo shows the position of the countess in the portrait," I said. "I assume it helps him position her correctly when she poses for him live, and lets him work on the painting when she's not here. Artists often sketch details of a painting they are working on. In fact, many museums display the artist's preliminary drawings—if they have them—along with the final work of art."

"And where do you see the marks you were telling us about?" George asked.

"Right here," I said, pointing to four narrow bands of white paint. "It's easier to see in the daylight. But look how he's outlined her figure in red, and here is a break where it appears as if the paint were smeared and then covered up in white." I put my fingers over the white bands, and they lined up perfectly.

Willoughby reached out and lifted the top of Jackcliff's metal paint box. "What does he keep in here?"

"Paints and brushes, I believe," I said.

"May I ask to what occasion I owe the honor of this visit?" Elmore Jackcliff leaned on the door frame and eyed us lazily. "I wasn't aware that I was supposed to provide studio tours to visiting policemen."

"Our apologies for barging in unannounced, Jackcliff," George said.

"And uninvited, I might add," the artist replied. He pushed himself off the door frame and entered the room, walking around and looking left and right as if he expected something to be disturbed. He picked up the fallen pillow and threw it on the chaise. Then he came around to where we stood and slapped closed the cover of his paint box. "And how may I help you? Am I correct in assuming that you are not here to determine my qualifications to paint your portraits?"

"Quite correct," Mardling said. "Would you mind telling us how these particular marks were made on your painting?"

"What marks?" Jackcliff asked. "The entire painting is full of marks."

"These, here," I said, fitting my fingers over the white paint as I'd done earlier.

"The constabulary has determined that red staining found on the fingers of the late Flavia Beckwith was actually oil paint," George said.

"And you believe she got those stains here in my studio?"

"We do," I said. "Did you ever invite Flavia here to your studio?"

"No, I can't say that I ever did."

"Did she ever come up here uninvited?" George asked.

"Well, now, I cannot be responsible for knowing the whereabouts of all the people wandering about the castle, can I, Chief Inspector?"

"Quit playing games, Jackcliff," George said. "Had Mrs. Beckwith ever come to your studio?"

"Not to my knowledge. No," the artist replied.

"Not to your knowledge, but perhaps without your knowledge?" George said.

"I doubt it."

"Then you won't mind if we take a sample of the red paint on your canvas, will you?" Mardling said. He reached in his pants pocket, drew out a jackknife, and opened it. "Do you have any cellophane on you, Willoughby?"

"I think so," the constable said.

"You're not planning to take a knife to my painting, are you?"

"We only need to scrape off a little bit of the paint," Mardling said. "I hope my hand is steady enough not to cut into the canvas."

"Wait!" Jackcliff said, moving to block Mardling from approaching his artwork. "It is possible Flavia may have been up here. I do seem to remember a time she came to see Lady Norrance when Her Ladyship was sitting for me. Or standing, as it were."

"Ah, and do you remember what occurred on that occasion?" Mardling asked.

"The ladies were having a discussion—I cannot recall what the topic was—and Flavia turned to leave. She tripped on a drop cloth and fell against my painting. I was concerned for her person, of course, and wiped the paint from her fingers, but it tends to leave a stain."

No concern for your painting? I thought, but didn't say.

"And then?" Mardling prompted.

"And then she left. Afterward, I noticed that the outline of the figure had been smudged, and I covered up the mess with some white gesso. I was concerned that she might have ruined the painting, but, I'm relieved to say, her carelessness will not spoil the final work, thank goodness."

"Remarkable the detail you can recall when, only a moment ago, you didn't even remember if the lady in question had ever been up here," Mardling said.

"Yes. Well, you jogged my memory," Jackcliff said.

"He's good at that," Willoughby put in.

"I think we can take our leave, ladies and gentleman, don't you?" George said. "Thank you, Jackcliff. We appreciate your cooperation."

"Not at all. Always happy to assist the authorities in whatever way I can."

The four of us vacated the room, and Jackcliff closed the door behind us. I heard the sound of a lock being engaged.

"I don't know that this information sheds any light on the demise of Mrs. Beckwith," Mardling said as we walked down the hall, "particularly in view of the coroner's conclusions. But it's always good to add pieces to the puzzle."

"True," George said. "Was there any other matter you wanted to go over tonight?"

"No," Mardling replied. "I believe we've accomplished what we came for. Willoughby and I will see you at the case meeting tomorrow morning?"

"Of course," George said, shaking his hand. "Allow me to walk you out." He turned to me. "Jessica, up for a stroll?"

I stifled a yawn. "If it weren't so dark and cold outside, I'd opt for a brisk walk to wake me up, but I've already had my fill of the elements for today. If you don't mind, I think I'd like to go to my room, read a bit, and maybe doze off."

"Feeling all right?" he asked.

"Yes, I feel fine—just tired. It's been a long day." *A long day, indeed,* I thought, cataloguing the events of the past twenty-four hours: a late night on New Year's Eve, my morning conversation with Clover, Archer's arrest, my social call with Hazel and Emmie, lunch at the Muddy Badger, our meeting with Fitzwalter, the excitement over the birth of a new foal, and the confrontation at gunpoint in the orchard with Angus. And then there had been the arrival of the officers and the visit to Jackcliff's studio to cap it all off.

"Go put your feet up," George said. "I could use an early-to-bed myself. We'll start tomorrow fresh as daisies."

I bid them good night, and George accompanied Mardling and Willoughby down the center staircase. I heard George say, "Nice bit of business there, Mardling, threatening to take a knife to the painting."

The detective sergeant chuckled. "We have a few tricks up our sleeves."

Chapter Twenty-four

Back in my room, I put off changing into my nightclothes and instead sat at the desk, reviewing the pages of the coroner's report on Flavia Beckwith. I made a mental list of what I wanted to discuss with George the next day when we could go over it together. But in the meantime, my mind kept rerunning the scene that had just transpired.

Jackcliff had remained in his studio, and I considered going back to continue the conversation with the talented but pompous artist. However, he'd become so angered at what he considered the unwarranted intrusion by George and the others that I thought better of it. At least I knew the source of the red stains on Flavia Beckwith's fingers, although I certainly didn't buy his version of the events.

Just how exactly had she tripped? Was it possible that someone—either Jackcliff or the countess—had pushed her into the canvas, or at least gave her a shove so she couldn't stop herself from falling? I doubted that Jackcliff couldn't remember the content of a discussion between Mrs. Beckwith and the countess if it ended in what he considered, if not an emergency, at least a matter of concern as to whether the painting had been damaged. Why was he reluctant to talk about it? What secret was he keeping?

My speculation was that someone had pushed Mrs. Beckwith in a moment of pique. But if that were true, what had prompted such an action? Was the countess even in the studio at that time, as Jackcliff contended? If she wasn't—if he was alone with Flavia—had he made advances that she found offensive and said so, which then generated a physical response from him? I hadn't heard anything about Flavia Beckwith that would indicate that she was a flirtatious woman. Yet Jackcliff had given me the impression he was making a pass at me, and I certainly hadn't given him any sign that such behavior would be welcome. A piece was missing from the picture, and not knowing what it was frustrated me.

All this speculation chased away my fatigue. I decided to make a fast trip up to the fourth floor to look in Mrs. Beckwith's apartment again to see if I could find what she might have been wearing when she fell against the painting, and whether there were still any traces of the paint on the clothing she'd worn that day. *It's not really important,* I told myself as I walked down the hall to the enclosed stairwell. *You really don't have to examine her clothing to prove that she fell against the painting. The paint on her fingers is proof enough,* I thought as I climbed the steps. *Why are you going there? This is just to satisfy your perpetual curiosity. If Mrs. Powter finds you, there will be another confrontation. George will wonder where you've gone off to.*

Even as I tried to talk myself out of going to Flavia's residence, my feet kept moving of their own accord, or perhaps at the demand of my subconscious.

While chiding myself for being so inquisitive, I also had another question in mind. The notation on the coroner's report that Flavia had a scar on her left wrist had been nagging at me. Such a scar could, of course, have resulted from an accident—*or* it might be the permanent reminder of a suicide attempt. If the latter was true, why would she have taken such a drastic step? She'd been a member of the household staff at Castorbrook Castle for many years. In fact, according to Lionel Fitzwalter, she'd been paid considerably more than other staff members, and at times received what appeared to be healthy bonuses despite the earl's fragile financial situation. Did the earl know of a suicide attempt? Was he more sympathetic to her feelings than he allowed others to see? Did anyone else in the household have knowledge of an attempt Flavia had made to take her own life? I would have to bring it up with Flavia's sister, Emmie, so making sure we got together soon was high on my list of next steps. Emmie must know the answers. Would she be willing to talk about them, assuming I found a tactful way to raise such a delicate subject?

I approached Flavia's apartment with trepidation, mindful of how angry Mrs. Powter had been when George and I first visited the rooms. She had toned down her consternation and her criticism of us once she knew that George was a ranking inspector at Scotland Yard. I assumed that she'd learned by now that I'm a mystery author, not a second-story burglar as she had suggested to Mardling and Willoughby. If she tried to stop me, I would be ready. I rationalized that when two suspicious deaths occur within days of each other in the same place, the rules of the house could be bent, if not broken, in the interest of justice. I've always been good at coming up with rationalizations.

The door to the apartment was unlocked, but it was dark inside. I put on the light in the anteroom and looked around. Nothing had changed as far as I could see. There was no fire in the grate, and the room was cold and damp. *A fitting atmosphere for a dead woman,* I thought. I walked to the bedroom door. It occurred to me that Mrs. Beckwith's belongings might have been removed by now. But who would do that? As far as I knew, she was alone in the world except for her sister and her nephew, Colin. Emmie had been trying to rid herself of a few of Flavia's possessions when I'd last seen her, but I didn't think she was emotionally ready to tackle her sister's living quarters just yet.

The room was as I'd last seen it. I flicked on the lamp, opened the armoire, and scanned the clothing it contained. The garments were neatly aligned on the rod, and I was careful not to disturb the symmetry as I pulled out each hanger and examined what hung on it. It was the fourth dress that contained some flecks of the same red paint that had been on Flavia's fingers when I discovered her body in the walled garden. Not that knowing this accomplished anything. Mardling had also said it didn't shed any light on her death. Still, it did satisfy my natural curiosity. At least, it confirmed that more than just her hand had made contact with the partially finished portrait of the countess.

As I replaced the dress, I felt the hairs on the back of my neck tingle. Someone else was there, and I knew who it was. I turned to see Mrs. Powter, the staunch, redheaded housekeeper, standing in the doorway.

"Good evening," I said.

"Good evening, Mrs. Fletcher. Is there anything I can do for you?"

"No," I said. "I was interested to know whether any clothing belonging to Mrs. Beckwith contained red paint from the portrait of the countess that Mr. Jackcliff is working on."

"And? Did you find such a piece of clothing?"

"Yes. As a matter of fact I did."

"I trust now that the question has been answered, you will promise to leave these rooms and not return again."

"I can't promise you that," I said. "In fact, I may return again and again. The next time I come here, I may be accompanied by Emmie Stanhope. Mrs. Beckwith's sister will want to remove Flavia's possessions and take them home with her, don't you think? You'd have no objection, of course."

"So long as she has permission from Her Ladyship. We cannot have anyone walking through the door and removing items from the castle without her knowledge."

"Is that what you told the officers that George and I were doing?"

"I beg your pardon."

"I don't think I want to pardon you. When Chief Inspector Sutherland and I first visited up here," I said, "after I'd discovered Mrs. Beckwith's body, it was obvious that someone had been searching for something. This room was turned upside down, drawers emptied, linens scattered, nightstand toppled."

"Which shouldn't have been a concern of yours," she said. "The members of the household are entitled to their privacy."

"You might want to take a second to think about that, Mrs. Powter. The sudden, unexplained death of someone who'd been on the staff for so many years would pique anyone's interest. It certainly did for the police required to conduct an inquest under such circumstances. That can hardly be news to you. Yet, when we brought the officers up here, this room had been straightened to within an inch of its life. There wasn't a pillow out of place. Did you trash it and then clean up your own mess? Or did you clean up someone else's mess?"

"That's not your business," she said, but I sensed her bravado wavering.

"Either way, what you did was not only underhanded; it was illegal. That's tampering with evidence—a criminal act. You could be brought up on charges."

"It's not tampering with evidence when there's been no crime," she said, gritting her teeth. "Only a writer of sordid murder mysteries would come up with such a scenario."

"Have you appointed yourself constable and coroner?" I asked mildly. She was trying to insult me, to provoke me to respond with the same anger that she was barely concealing. But I'd always found that if I kept a cool demeanor, it was more likely to put my opponents off balance, and perhaps prompt them to reveal more than they intended. Mrs. Powter was a formidable adversary, but I was through with letting her push me around. "It sounds as if you've already decided the results of the inquest," I said. "You, Ginger Powter, have determined that no crime took place; therefore you can do as you please. I wonder if Detective Sergeant Mardling would agree."

"I've already been interviewed by Mardling and his assistant, and I told them to investigate you," she retorted.

"Which they did, and now they can turn their attention back to the housekeeper who lied to them. Expect another call, Mrs. Powter. You have a lot to account for."

"I have nothing to hide."

"Oh, yes? Then it wasn't you who ransacked this room? But who would you clean up after? Was it the earl? Somehow I can't envision him rummaging through the belongings of a staff member. The countess?"

"Sh—"

I cocked my head. "She? The countess?"

"What Her Ladyship does within her own home is her business and no one else's."

"So you say it was the countess who came to the room looking for something following Mrs. Beckwith's death?"

"I'm not saying anything to you. Are you quite finished here?" she asked.

"Did she?" I pressed. "Did the countess visit this room and rummage through it? Why would she do that? What was she looking for?"

"I think that there is nothing to be gained by further conversation. You'll find your way back to your own room, I trust."

"Of course, Mrs. Powter."

But as she turned to leave, I added, "I hope you understand that I'm well aware of how important you are to this household. Contrary to what you may think, I'm not your enemy. Two people who lived in Castorbrook Castle have died, and I'm sure that you don't want to see any more deaths in this house. I'm hopeful that you want to see justice prevail."

She'd stopped to hear my final comment. Then, without another word, and with her head held high, she left the room.

Chapter Twenty-five

The next morning, I found George browsing the floor-to-ceiling bookshelves in the castle's library.

"I listened at your door last night," he said, "but assumed you were catching some much-needed rest, so I didn't knock."

"I took a detour," I said, "and made another visit to Flavia Beckwith's room."

"Oh? Find anything of interest while you were there?"

"Only that the same red oil paint that stained her fingers was also on one of her dresses. Of course, my nighttime examination of Flavia's clothing was interrupted by the ever-vigilant Mrs. Powter. She must haunt that floor."

George laughed. "Still as abrasive as ever?"

"Yes. She lectured me again about not intruding on the Grant family's privacy. I'm afraid I pushed back a bit this time."

"Good for you, Jessica." George looked at his watch. "Let's go in for breakfast. I have the case meeting this morning at the superintendent's office. I've already told Ralph to pick me up here at the castle at nine. What are your plans for the day?"

"I was hoping that we could go over that gift you gave me yesterday." I patted my shoulder bag into which I'd tucked away the coroner's report.

"When I get back, perhaps?"

"All right. And if you don't mind, I'd like to catch a ride into town with you. I'm hoping to find time with Flavia Beckwith's sister, Emmie."

"The reason?"

"I haven't formulated one yet," I said. "I'll give it more thought on the way."

After a sizable English breakfast set out by Nigel, we climbed into the back of Ralph's London taxi and headed for town.

"Hope you don't mind a question," Ralph said.

"Fire away," said George.

"I was wondering how much longer you'll need me here. Not that I'm complaining. You've been more than generous, and I love staying in that Muddy Badger inn—made lots of friends there. But the little woman back in London is missing me and—"

"Hopefully, it won't be much longer," I said, looking to George for confirmation, who nodded. "With any luck the three of us will soon be heading back to London."

"You sound confident," George said to me.

"Better than lacking confidence," I said as we neared Chipping Minster.

"So, you're going to look up Mrs. Beckwith's sister. Emmie, is it?"

"Yes. There's something missing in what we know about Flavia Beckwith. Her sister might have the answers, provided she'll share them with me."

"Go to it, Jessica," he said, taking my hand and giving it a squeeze.

After dropping George off for his case meeting, Ralph drove me to Chipping Minster Antiques, where Hazel Fortunato was out front, sweeping her sidewalk. I asked Ralph to wait as I got out and approached her.

"Good morning, Hazel," I said.

"Jessica, what a surprise to see you so soon again. Are you here to pick out your souvenir?"

"Hope you don't mind if I come back another time. I just stopped by to ask you a question."

"Just as well. I'm getting in a shipment today. You might find something of interest in it once I've had a chance to put the items on display. Anything new about the murder up at the castle?"

The word "murder" had a jarring effect. "Unfortunately, no," I said.

"Then what was your question?"

"I was hoping to call on Emmie Stanhope today."

"Shouldn't be difficult," Hazel said while pushing a small mound of debris into her dustpan. "She's around." She leaned on her broom. "Colin stopped by to show me pictures he took on his mobile of the new foal up at the castle."

"I was there when he was born."

"So he said."

"What a wonderful event to witness." I sighed at the memory. "To see a beautiful new life brought into the world, so full of promise and possibilities. Well, it was just—"

Hazel's eyes glistened with tears.

"What's the matter, Hazel? What have I said to upset you?"

She waved a hand in front of her face. "Oh, I'm such a sentimental watering pot. They're naming the colt Good Fortune. Colin suggested it. Told me it was in honor of Mr. Fortunato, who gave them—him and Jemma—their first lessons about horses."

"That's so thoughtful."

"He's such a fine fellow, that Colin. Wish I had an eligible granddaughter for him. Would love to have him as a member of my family."

"Emmie must be proud of him, too."

"That she is."

"Where does Emmie live?" I asked.

Hazel pointed. "Take that second right and go up the hill a hundred yards or so. Can't miss it. She lives in a gray stone cottage with a green door. You can recognize it by the ivy vines growing up the chimney. A five-minute walk at worst."

"Do you think she's home?" I asked.

"I know she's home, Jessica. Colin was on his way to have breakfast with his mam."

I called back to Ralph, "I won't be needing you for a while. I'll call you on your cell."

He gave me a hearty wave. "I'll be at the inn."

"Hazel, before I talk to Emmie, do you mind if I ask you a question about Flavia?"

"I don't know if I'll have the answer," she said.

"Did Flavia ever have any children?"

Hazel's eyes widened. "Why would you ask that?" she said.

"I just wondered."

"Well, then, my answer is that if she did, she kept it a well-guarded secret from me."

"Thanks. I'm off, then. Second right, you said?"

"Yes, second right. And please say hello for me."

Hazel had been right. In five minutes I stood in front of a row of gray stone cottages, each with ivy vines covering the chimneys, and in some cases, the entire front of the house. Luckily, Emmie's home was the only one with a green door, plus a small sign outside that read STANHOPE. I knocked and she came to the door. She was dressed in a multicolored housecoat and slippers, the front of her hair up in old-fashioned curlers.

"Good morning, Jessica," she said. "What a nice surprise, but I'm afraid I'm not fit for visitors." She waved at her housecoat.

"I'm so sorry to barge in on you like this without having called first."

"That's all right. I guess." She pulled two rollers out of her hair, put them in a pocket, and ran her fingers through her bangs. "Hazel just rang me up to say that you were on your way. Come through to the kitchen." She led me into a sunny room with remnants of a morning meal still on the table. "I've just finished having breakfast with Colin. He's been up all night with the new foal. He said you were there to see it."

"It was a wonderful experience."

"He's gone straightaway to bed, poor thing. He could barely lift the fork to his mouth, he was so exhausted."

"A well-deserved sleep," I said.

She picked up two plates and carried them to the sink. "Would you like tea?" she asked. "I'm afraid I don't have any coffee."

"Tea would be lovely." I took the chair she indicated at the kitchen table.

She poured water from an electric teakettle into a mug, dropped in a tea bag, and sat in a seat opposite mine, pushing the mug in my direction. "So," she said, "what brings you here this morning?"

Although her tone and smile were warm and welcoming, I

sensed a certain defensiveness on her part. The smile remained, but she sat with her arms tightly crossed over her chest, a classic defensive pose in Body Language 101.

"I realize that I have no official standing to ask this question, Emmie, but my friend, Chief Inspector Sutherland, and I have found ourselves smack-dab in the middle of two cases of unexpected deaths—your sister's unfortunate demise, and what we believe may have been the poisoning of the earl."

She nodded. "Go on."

"I had occasion to read the coroner's report about your sister."

Emmie looked startled. "I wasn't aware that it was freely available information."

"It isn't exactly."

"Then how did you get it?"

I began to regret my visit. If Emmie complained about a breach of privacy on the part of the local police, it would put George in an awkward position with his colleagues, once again because of me. I didn't want a repeat of the embarrassment he had suffered when the Bermuda press put pictures of the two of us together on their front page.

"Please don't be upset, Emmie. I would never discuss this publicly. Chief Inspector Sutherland and I are, well, we are close friends, and just as I confide in him, he trusts me to keep confidences he shares with me. In this case, the coroner observed some items that captured my attention."

"Such as?" No smile now. Her eyes took on defiance to match her crossed arms.

"The report cites a scar on Flavia's wrist. While it could have been the result of an accident, it could also indicate a—well, a suicide attempt."

Emmie said nothing in response, but her expression told me that I had not plucked something out of thin air.

"Forgive me if I've touched a raw spot, but had Flavia ever attempted to take her life?"

Emmie stared down at the table. She unlocked her arms and gathered some crumbs with the side of her hand. She swept them into her palm and dusted them off into her empty teacup. "I must admit, Jessica, that your question has taken me by surprise. My sister never had a reason to entertain ending her life. She was quite content with her position at the castle and—"

"Is that really true, Emmie?" I asked.

"Why would you doubt it?" she asked, but her eyes stayed focused on the tabletop.

"Because of something else on the coroner's report."

"I'm listening."

"The coroner also reports that Flavia had a vertical abdominal scar. I wouldn't have thought anything about that, except there was a moment during the foal's birth when the possibility was discussed of the mare needing a cesarean section. In women, a vertical incision is rarely used now, but it used to be more common. Your sister's abdominal scar was the result of a cesarean birth—wasn't it?"

Now, Emmie's demeanor changed from defiance to discomfort. She glanced nervously in the direction of the hallway.

I leaned across the table and placed my hand on her arm. "Please don't misunderstand why I'm raising this," I said. "Under ordinary circumstances, whether your sister had a child or not should remain only the business of the woman involved, and her closest family. But we're dealing here with the murder of a lord, and the tragic death of a lovely woman under mysterious circumstances."

"That's just a coincidence."

"I wish I could be certain it was. These two deaths so close together change the rules, Emmie. I'm afraid the only excuse I can offer you for probing into your personal business is that speculation such as what I've raised could amount to crucial evidence."

I fully expected Emmie's warm welcome to change into a brusque request that I leave. I was wrong. Tears filled her large green eyes. She lowered her head and slowly shook it back and forth, as though denying what was occurring.

"Was Flavia employed at the castle when she became pregnant?" I asked.

Her nod was barely discernible.

"Did she have the child here in Chipping Minster?"

I saw an equally subtle back-and-forth head movement this time, an unspoken no.

"Who was the father of Flavia's child?" I asked in a low, sympathetic voice, my hand still on her arm.

She started to answer but held back. I understood her reticence. If I was right—that Flavia Beckwith had had a child—it had been kept a deep, dark secret for all these years, and my intrusion into what was a family matter was understandably wrenching for her. But as I'd said, we were also dealing with the murder of the Earl of Norrance. If Flavia's secret had played any role in that murder—and could possibly help bring the murderer to justice—it had to be revealed.

"You've opened a nightmare," Emmie said softly. "I wish you hadn't."

"Which certainly wasn't my intention, Emmie. I stress again that I'm not snooping into private family matters out of morbid curiosity. I would never do that. But as I said—"

"Yes, I know. There's been a murder, and my sister has met an untimely death. But surely you can understand how delicate this matter is for me—and for others involved."

I withheld further comment to allow her to regain her composure. When she seemed calmer, I said, "I've also learned that Flavia received considerably higher pay than any of the other staff at Castorbrook Castle, and that she received large sums of money from time to time from the earl, bonuses of one sort or another. Do you know why he paid her so much?"

She let out an exasperated stream of air before pressing her lips tightly together and closing her eyes. When she opened them, she said, "There's no way for this not to become known, is there?"

"Whatever the truth is, it will come out in one form or another. My motive isn't to cause you or anyone else grief, Emmie, but the local constable, as well as Chief Inspector Sutherland, have an obligation to bring the earl's killer to justice. The circumstances surrounding your sister's death might help them, and I have an obligation to tell them what I've come to know."

When she didn't respond, I asked, "Does anyone else know the truth about Flavia and her child?"

"Not that I know."

"Hazel, at the antiques store?" I asked.

"I doubt if Flavia ever confessed to her. She was usually good at keeping secrets." Emmie swallowed hard. "Mrs. Fletcher, Jessica, I know you mean well and are not out to hurt anyone, but I really would prefer that you leave."

"Don't make her go." It was Colin, who stood in the doorway.

"I thought you were sleeping," Emmie said.

"I tried but couldn't. Too wound up from last night at the stables. I heard your voices and came downstairs. I've been listening to the conversation."

"It doesn't concern you," Emmie said.

"Who else, if not me?" he said, coming to the table and wrapping his arms around her from behind. "I'm a big boy, Mam," he said. "No need to protect me from the truth. Aunt Flavia was really my mother, wasn't she?"

"Colin, please, there's no need for you to be upset by what you've heard," Emmie said.

"I'm not upset," he said. "I've suspected it for a long time."

Emmie jumped. "What do you mean?"

"Don't take it amiss. You've been the most wonderful mother a lad could ever ask for." He hugged her tighter. "You taught me to be thankful for what I receive, to appreciate the opportunities I'm given that others don't have. You taught me to be observant, and I am. There've been hints, nothing Aunt Flavia ever said, but I'd catch her over the years watching me with a wistful expression. And so often people would remark on how much I resemble my aunt."

"Lots of people look like other family members," Emmie said.

"There were other signs. She would always lecture me that I was as good as any of the Grant children, even though I could clearly see that they lived a more privileged life."

"Oh, Colin."

"I wasn't jealous. Don't think it for a moment. I was grateful to stay home when they got trundled off to boarding school. But

I heard Aunt Flavia arguing with the earl about me. And she told me that when the time came, to remember to demand my rights."

"She wanted the best for you, just as I do."

"Why do you think she told you to demand your rights?" I asked.

"No more questions," Emmie said.

"Oh, Mam, let's just get it all out in the fresh air. It's time, don't you think?" He looked at me. "You've put two and two together, Mrs. Fletcher, and that's okay."

"The earl is your father, isn't he?" I said.

"I always wondered why Lord Norrance treated me so *patiently*, when that was never a word you could apply to him as a rule." Colin chuckled. "But he tried to keep me away from Jemma, and now I know why."

"Colin, you don't have to say any more," Emmie said.

He disengaged from her and leaned against the kitchen counter. "The earl treated me *almost* like a son. Jemma and I used to laugh about it. She'd say I was more like him than Rupert and Kip. I wasn't sure I liked that, but I wanted us to be brother and sister, so I allowed myself the fantasy. It's true, isn't it, Mam?"

Emmie looked at her son sadly. "I didn't want this to come out. He never acknowledged you. I was so afraid you'd feel rejected, unwanted," she said.

"I knew it! I just knew it. But is there anything to prove he was my father, any official paper, or something?"

"There was your birth certificate. Flavia put his name on it, and the hospital officials insisted on getting a confirmation from the earl before they would send the form to the General Register Office."

"Where is the certificate?"

"I've no idea. Flavia kept it. I don't know where she put it."

Colin looked deflated, but then brightened. "But we could send away for it, couldn't we?"

"There's no need for that," Emmie snapped. She glowered at me. "You've opened some can of worms, Mrs. Fletcher. I hope you're satisfied."

"'Satisfied' is the wrong term," I said. "I never brought this up to seek satisfaction."

"For whatever reason you've elected to delve into our family secret, you've done a good job of it," Emmie said. "Next question?"

I was tempted to leave things as they were and depart, but I did have more questions and decided to take advantage of the openness that now filled the kitchen.

"Where did Flavia have Colin?" I asked.

"You don't need to know that."

"*I* need to know that, Mam." Colin took a seat at the table and pulled his mother's hand into his.

"In Birmingham," she replied stiffly. "That's where we were from. Flavia studied nursing at the university, where my husband taught. After the first countess died—she was a sickly thing—Flavia came back to live with us. When she found out she was pregnant, she called him. I'll never forget it." She looked at Colin with tears in her eyes. "He refused to marry her, said he'd never recognize the child, and advised her to get rid of the baby. She was so distraught. I thought she'd never recover."

"Is that when she tried to take her life?" I asked.

Emmie nodded, the tears coursing down her cheeks.

"Lucky for me she wasn't successful," Colin said with a wink, eliciting a watery chuckle from his mother. "Tell me more."

"Are you sure you want to talk about this in front of Mrs. Fletcher?"

"She seems to know more than both of us, so I'd say she's earned a place at the table."

Emmie sighed. "My husband and I couldn't have any children. We convinced Flavia that we'd raise the baby as our own and she'd need never tell a soul. It was a difficult birth that necessitated a cesarean section. I was with her. We took the baby home, and everything was perfect that first year. But then my husband passed away. Flavia wanted to bring Colin back to Chipping Minster. I resisted, but she won. She usually did. But I made her promise that we'd tell people that Colin was *my* child. And she agreed."

"What was the earl's reaction?" I asked.

"At first, he was furious, but he came 'round to it." She put her hand to Colin's cheek. "He saw what a lovely lad you were."

Colin covered her hand with his.

She withdrew her hand and stared down at the table, recreating what had happened.

"After the earl and his new wife had three children in quick succession, Flavia went up to the castle and suggested that she could be their governess. The earl was pleased with the idea. He took good care of Flavia financially, and she shared the funds with me and Colin. She resumed her place on the Castorbrook Castle staff as though nothing had happened."

"Did anyone else know about the relationship between Flavia and the earl," I asked, "or that he was Colin's father?"

"I can't speak for the staff. I think Hazel suspected the truth. She was a friend to us both. But I never told her, and I'm certain Flavia didn't either."

"Hazel said you and Flavia had a falling-out several weeks ago. What was that about?"

"Is there no part of my life that's my own?" she moaned.

"You don't have to answer if you don't want to," I said.

"We had an argument. She threatened that she was going to tell the countess everything. I told her I'd never speak to her again if she did. She was going to break her promise to me that Colin was to be my son forever. But she was sure if she revealed everything to the countess, the earl would be forced to acknowledge Colin." Emmie looked up, her eyes pleading for understanding. "She couldn't take him back now. I'm his mother."

"You are, Mam. And you've always been."

Emmie put her head down on her arms and sobbed, the tension of holding on to an important secret all these years finally released in a torrent of tears. Colin patted her back and kissed her hair. "There's nothing to be ashamed of," he told her in soothing tones. "You're my mam always, the best mother ever."

It was time for me to leave. I wanted to ask Emmie if Flavia ever carried out her threat to tell the countess that Colin was the earl's son. What would she have accomplished other than making Marielle feel like a fool for not knowing that the earl had fathered a child with the woman she'd thought was her friend, someone who'd been a governess to her children and who functioned as her lady's maid and was with her every day?

Emmie seemed to anticipate my question. She raised her head, wiped her eyes, and looked at me. "I know what you're thinking. You'll have to ask the countess yourself."

Which was what I intended to do at the first available moment.

Chapter Twenty-six

I called George's cell phone to see if he was ready to return to the castle.

"Afraid not, Jessica. This case meeting still has a way to go. But I'll ring up Ralph and have him pick you up wherever you are."

"No need," I said. "I'll walk down to the Muddy Badger. It's a lovely sunny day. Ralph said he'd be there."

"Sounds good. I'll join you later at the castle."

I put my cell phone in a side pocket of my blazer where I'd been keeping it since the day I was locked outside in the frigid garden. Although Flavia's heart condition had caused her death, if I had read the coroner's report correctly, the inclement weather had been a contributing factor. If she'd had a cell phone with her, she would have been able to call for help instead of futilely pounding on the door. It was a lesson I had learned the day we arrived, and one that remained with me.

Ralph was playing darts with a woman in the pub when I arrived. I encouraged him to finish his match and ordered lunch.

Doreen slid a bowl of cream of lemon soup in front of me. "This is a classic English soup," she said, "going back to the seventeenth century. It's one of the cook's specialties."

I picked up my spoon and tasted it. "It's wonderful."

Doreen grinned. "I knew you'd like it. Oh, I almost forgot." She disappeared into the kitchen and returned a few minutes later, holding a tiny tin. "Would you like some caviar as a garnish? We have a little left over from New Year's Eve." She opened the tin and placed it in front of me. It contained a small number of the precious black fish eggs. Before I could answer, she took a spoon and stirred what was left in the tin.

I laughed and said, "I learned from the chef at the castle never to stir caviar."

Doreen laughed, too. "I don't know why people raise such a fuss over this stuff."

Although I'd eaten only some of my soup, I dropped the spoon in the bowl, turned, and called out, "Ralph!"

"Is anything wrong?" Doreen asked.

"No, it's delicious, but we have to go. I just thought of something."

"Darts have never been my strong suit," Ralph said cheerily as we left the pub, got in his taxi, and drove back to Castorbrook.

I hadn't seen any members of Lady Norrance's family since the day before when they'd bid adieu to their remaining guests—all except George and me and Elmore Jackcliff—in the castle's entry hall. It wasn't surprising. People in mourning often isolate themselves; families may feel the need to cling together to share the grief they hesitate to display when visitors are present. Of course, George and I had been out of the house most of the time. It was possible the family had received condolence calls from neighbors and friends that we were not aware of. Still, I hoped to find time to have a private talk with the countess. How much or how little she knew of her husband's relationships before they married could be pertinent. And were any of her loyal staff members aware of the history between the earl and Flavia? If so, could that knowledge have spurred someone to take revenge on her behalf?

Ralph left me off in front of the castle. The media that had been camped outside the gates were not in evidence, perhaps scared off by Angus's shotgun. The officer in the one remaining police vehicle had waved us through.

I hadn't been back to the conservatory since I'd shown Detective Sergeant Mardling and Constable Willoughby where I'd found Flavia Beckwith's body. I remembered feeling that there was something I should notice, but I couldn't put my finger on what it was. I decided another visit to the scene of the first death might jog my memory.

By now, the layout of the castle had become familiar. I made my way to the stone-floored corridor that led past the auxiliary larder where Nigel and Angus had taken Flavia's body, and walked toward the end of the hall and the heavy drapes that sealed off the entrance to the greenhouse. I pulled aside the curtain and let myself into the glass-enclosed space. Sunlight flooded the room. It felt like stepping into a jungle. The air was warm and moist; the palm trees and other exotic plants gave off an earthy aroma that was at once appealing and slightly sour.

I looked to my right and studied the door to the enclosed garden. The heavy glass panes effectively sealed off the weather outside. I closed my eyes to bring back the first time I'd been there. I remembered that I'd moved the plant, which was on a wheeled stand, to use as a wedge to hold the door open before

I'd entered the garden, but had neglected to position the wheels to prevent it from rolling away.

That was it!

That was what I'd been struggling to remember when I showed the officers where I'd found Flavia. The wet tracks on the floor from the wheels of the rolling stand had given me the idea to use it as a wedge to hold open the door. Clearly, I was not the first person to use the plant for that purpose.

Flavia had lived in the castle a long time. She must have known that the door to the garden needed to be propped open. Yet when I first entered the greenhouse, the plant on the stand was at least twelve feet away from the door. It couldn't have rolled that far even if Flavia had neglected to position the wheels properly. It would have rolled only a short distance. Which meant someone had to have put the plant stand back in its usual place when Flavia was outside.

I wandered over to the grouping of metal furniture underneath the glass cupola that crowned the roof of the conservatory. I shrugged off my overcoat and sat on the garden bench, occupied by my thoughts.

"There you are," said a voice from the door. "I'm so glad it's you. I'm afraid I owe you an apology."

It was the countess. Nigel stood behind her, holding a large silver tray.

I stood. "I can't imagine what you'd need to apologize to me for."

"For having neglected you since your arrival."

"I'd say that you have had other things on your mind. I haven't felt neglected at all."

Lady Norrance settled herself on one of the metal chairs. "Please sit," she said, waving me back on the bench. "I must also apologize to your handsome companion, Inspector Sutherland. It's been extremely comforting having him here during such a frightful time. The children and I are most appreciative."

"How are your children doing?"

"Just as I am. We're muddling through."

Nigel set the tray on the table with the pineapple base. It held plates of scones, tea sandwiches with the crusts removed, and cookies, in addition to sugar and cream. "I'll be back shortly," he told her.

When he left the room, I said, "I've just come from visiting people in the village, people whom I've gotten to know since arriving in Chipping Minster."

"Aren't you the clever one to make friends so quickly."

"I came back this afternoon, hoping to find some time with you," I said.

She beamed. "Then we're thinking alike."

Nigel returned with a china pot of piping hot tea and cups. "Anything else, my lady?" he asked.

"Thank you, no. That will be all for now." She poured tea from the silver pot into a delicate china cup, handed it to me, poured herself a cup of tea, leaned back against the cushions of the chair, and took a deep breath. "I do love my conservatory. You Americans call it a greenhouse. It's so soothing to see all this greenery when it's cold and bare in the gardens, don't you think?"

"It's a lovely space," I said.

Lady Norrance picked up a plate of cookies and held it out. "Would you like one? These are Clover's newest experiment in biscuits. I'm delighted to say she has picked up quite a few pointers from working with Chef Bergère. I'm thinking seriously of allowing her to be the head cook again."

I took a cookie. Even though I had abandoned my lunch, I wasn't very hungry. There was too much on my mind.

"Help yourself to tea sandwiches and a scone. Afternoon tea is one of our nicest traditions. It always helps to put one's day in perspective. I feel terrible that you and the inspector had to experience these dreadful events on your first visit to Castorbrook. What was intended to be a festive celebration to usher in the New Year turned into a terrible tragedy."

"I'm afraid that we can't always control events," I said.

"Yes, you are absolutely right, Mrs. Fletcher."

"Please call me Jessica."

"Of course, Jessica, and I am Marielle. My position as Countess of Norrance calls for so much formality, I sometimes forget to tell people my name. With the staff, of course, it's 'my lady this,' 'my lady that.'" She laughed. "I am delighted to have this opportunity to chat with you, Jessica. I'm well aware of your fame as a writer of crime novels. Pity you had to encounter a real crime this time around."

"It's happened before, unfortunately," I said. "Lady Norrance—"

"Marielle."

"Marielle, I realize the strain that you've been under, losing your husband as well as your lady's maid of so many years, but there's something I feel I must raise with you."

She sipped her tea. "My goodness!" She lowered the cup and plucked a cucumber sandwich from the tray. "I hope it isn't something ghastly. We've already suffered enough bad news, and it's only the second day into the new year. I presume it's about James."

"Actually, it's about Flavia Beckwith."

"Flavia? What could you have discovered about Flavia? She was such a drab soul, a stereotypical childless old maid. I suppose she may have been attractive in her youth, but recently she had become so morose. I was seriously considering giving her her walking papers. One doesn't like to have negative people around all the time."

"I assume that you haven't been informed that the coroner's report on Mrs. Beckwith's death has been released."

"Has it? You're quite right. I have no knowledge of it. What did it say? Heart attack? Stroke?"

"Yes, she died of a heart attack, hastened by exposure to the elements."

"Foolish woman, allowing herself to get locked in the garden in the frightful weather we've been having." She looked up at the arched glass ceiling and the sun streaming through it. "Sunshine always makes things seem better, doesn't it?"

"Marielle," I said, "Mrs. Beckwith may have been unmarried, but she was not childless."

She'd raised her cup halfway to her lips, but my blunt comment stopped it in midflight. She looked at the half-eaten cucumber sandwich in her fingers, and dropped it on her plate.

"Wasn't she?" She took another sip of tea. "What a scandal. Had I known, I doubt I would have let her be a governess to my children. Whatever happened to the child?"

"Colin Stanhope is her son."

She stared at me over the rim of her teacup and said, "Colin? My, my, are you sure that you don't write lurid romance novels, Jessica, rather than crime books?"

"I'm quite sure," I said.

"Colin's last name, you know, is Stanhope, not Beckwith."

"He was raised by Flavia's sister, Emmie Stanhope, since the day he came into the world."

"You've been here—what?—three or four days? How did you come by this information so quickly?"

"I had access to the coroner's report on Mrs. Beckwith."

"How? Oh, of course. How indiscreet of Chief Inspector Sutherland."

I ignored her comment and continued. "The coroner referred to a scar that would have been acquired during a cesarean section. Unfortunately, that wasn't the only scar she bore. She'd tried to take her own life when she learned that she was pregnant and the father wouldn't marry her."

There was dead silence in the steamy conservatory. I slipped my hand into my jacket pocket, feeling around for the cell phone.

Marielle broke the awkward hush. "I knew there was something unbalanced about her. Go on. I'm eager to hear what else you've discovered in the short time you've been here as our guest. Remember that, Jessica. You came to Castorbrook as our guest, and guests have certain obligations to their hosts and hostesses."

"I'm mindful of that, Marielle, but when a murder—or possibly two—takes place, social niceties take a backseat to finding the truth." When she didn't respond, I said, "It was your husband, the Earl of Norrance, who fathered Flavia Beckwith's child. When did *you* learn of it?"

She tossed her teacup on the tray. It broke in half; the tea left in the cup dripped onto the sandwich platter. "Your inquisitiveness knows no bounds, does it, Mrs. Fletcher?" That she had reverted to my title and name wasn't lost on me. "Mrs. Powter has kept me informed about your need to snoop where you have no business being."

"Mrs. Powter is protective of you and your family. She interrupted my visit to Flavia's living quarters following her death."

"More than once."

"True. The first time was after *you* had gone there searching for something and left her room in a mess. What were you looking for?"

She didn't reply.

"You have no obligation to answer my questions, but I'll ask again anyway. When did you learn that your husband had fathered Flavia's child?"

During our confrontation, Marielle had been leaning toward me, a furious expression on her face. Now, she sat back, and what passed for a satisfied smile crossed her lips. "I'll consider this conversation my contribution to your literary efforts, Mrs. Fletcher, giving you an exclusive glimpse into the turmoil into which some families are thrown, even aristocratic ones like ours. Flavia revealed her tryst with James when I tried to dismiss her from the staff. She told me that I couldn't sack her because the earl, her former lover and father of her beloved son, would never allow it. She spilled everything, all the nasty secrets she'd been harboring for years. She seemed to delight in doing so, watching me vacillate between rage and misery, hatred for her and disgust with my darling husband."

"And she did so in front of Elmore Jackcliff, adding to your humiliation. Was that when you pushed her into the painting?"

"She was lucky I didn't have a gun in my hand; I would have shot her on the spot. Elmore hustled her out of the studio before she could do any more damage."

"You must have been very angry at Flavia after she told you about her affair with your husband."

"Wouldn't you be, Mrs. Fletcher?"

"Angry enough to lock her in the garden in freezing temperatures?"

A mocking laugh came from her. "I can account for every minute of my time that day. Did I send her to look for a sprig of holly for my hair? Guilty! I wanted to punish her for all the years she had deceived me, for all the years she'd pretended to be my friend. Some friend! She put a cuckoo's egg in my nest, bringing her *nephew* to play with my children. Getting my husband to give him a job, send him for special training. And then she said she'd convinced James to acknowledge him, that *her* son was entitled to a portion of the estate, a piece of Castorbrook. Castorbrook! My home. The one I gave up everything to secure. No interloper was going to stake a claim on my children's inheritance. No ambitious by-blow was going to challenge Kip's birthright. I'd never allow it. Never! So yes, I was angry with her. And yes, I had her locked in the garden."

"*Had* her locked in the garden?"

"You don't think I'd get my hands dirty moving plants around, do you?"

She'd become increasingly heated as she related the betrayals of those she thought she knew and loved. Then she stopped, her eyes focused on a picture I couldn't see. She sighed. "How were we to know that she had a weak heart?"

"*We*? You and Angus?"

She shrugged.

"You're saying Flavia's death was unplanned?"

"How fortuitous that Mother Nature stepped in and spared us the unpleasantness, although I would dearly have loved to kill her. It was an accident. That's what the inquest will say. We could have prevented it, of course, but that will remain our little secret, won't it?"

"Are you going to say your husband's death was an accident as well?"

"Ah, James. So many years. So many secrets. What a feckless fool he was, weak-kneed and without conviction, used by everyone, chasing his ridiculous dreams of breeding champion racehorses, gambling money we didn't have on races, and owing his soul to the bookies at the track. I don't know why I put up with it for as many years as I did. I certainly didn't need his money, if he had any after his foolish ventures. I wanted him to sell to the hotel people, and he was fighting me. I didn't think he had the capacity to surprise me anymore. But I was wrong." She waved her hand in a gesture to reinforce the disgust in her voice. "Good riddance to him!"

"I can understand why you were furious with him," I said. "Furious enough to kill him?"

"Are you accusing me of poisoning James? He was so apologetic, so bereft at having disappointed me, eager to make amends, to put this sordid episode behind us. He said he never loved her and that she'd been blackmailing him all these years. But she was gone now, and he was sending the fellow off to Wales. He wouldn't be here as a reminder of James's indiscretion. Wouldn't I please forgive him?"

"But you didn't. I saw you stirring the caviar. Caviar doesn't need to be mixed. In fact, your chef warned Clover to be especially careful not to break the eggs and spoil the taste and texture."

"Ah. You're such a knowledgeable woman. I would have enjoyed getting to know you better. But we'll never be friends now."

"So you did poison your husband."

"You were there. How could I possibly have done that? It was a New Year's Eve ball. I was in a formal gown, no pockets, no purse. Where on my person could I hide poison? In my shoes?

Down my décolletage?" She plucked the front of her dress away from her chest and looked down. "I don't see a place here."

"As it happens, I've recently been reading a book about the Renaissance when a great many poisonings of political figures took place."

"Is this relevant?"

"Sometimes the poison was concealed in a ring. You were wearing an interesting domed ring the night of the ball. I noticed that it was missing when you took off your gloves in the drawing room while waiting for the police to arrive. I wondered where you had put it since, as you say, you had no pockets and no purse."

"And what did you conclude?"

"I concluded that your friend and lover Elmore Jackcliff took it from your hand when he threw himself at your lap in a paroxysm of supposed grief."

"I have to say I am impressed. You are very observant, Mrs. Fletcher. Yes, I killed James. It's too bad that no one will believe you if you try to communicate all this fascinating information to the authorities. It's your word against mine. Flavia died of a heart attack? Oh, what a terrible thing, I'll say. Angus will have to replace that awful door next spring. What did Mrs. Fletcher say? Well, you know about those writers. They have such extravagant imaginations." She tilted her head and smiled at me. "You wouldn't like to take a little walk in the garden yourself, would you? Re-create the scene of the crime, as it were?"

I resisted the urge to pat the pocket where I'd put my cell phone. "How will you explain the poisoning of Lord Norrance?"

"I don't have to explain the poisoning. I'm the innocent widow. James had a lot of, well, I don't want to say enemies, but he owed money to quite a few men of questionable morals. I will point your friend Detective Sergeant Mardling in that direction, and see what the little man can come up with."

"And what do you plan to say when your ring is found to contain traces of cyanide?"

Marielle looked at me wide-eyed. "My ring? What are you talking about?"

"You may have gotten rid of the ring, but I'll tell the authorities that they can find the poison that killed the earl in the box of mole killer in your garden shed."

"Is it there? Really? Angus usually takes care of those sorts of things." She waved her hand.

The gardener pushed opened the heavy glass door and stepped into the greenhouse. I'd been facing away from the enclosed garden and hadn't known he was outside. He was carrying a large plastic bag.

"Angus was just cleaning out the potting shed in the garden, getting rid of all those nasty insecticides and other poisonous chemicals," Marielle said, smiling at the man she'd brought with her from her father's house when she'd married the earl.

Angus shuffled closer to where we sat and glared at me. "Everything all right, my lady?"

Marielle nodded. "Yes, Angus. I am most appreciative of your tidying the garden cupboard. It will be nice to have it in good nick when the police take a look inside."

Angus lifted the bag. "Anything for you, my lady. There's nothing dangerous left behind."

I watched the exchange between mistress and servant. "It's really remarkable, Marielle. Mrs. Powter, Nigel, Angus. They're all devoted to you. You inspire such great loyalty on the part of your staff, even to the point of allowing someone to die because you desire it."

"How nice of you to notice."

"Even so, it's the rare criminal who can completely cover up the crime. There are always loose ends, little details that you've neglected. You've concocted a nice alibi, but the police are very thorough. You'll never get away with this," I said, hoping that I was right.

"I don't know any such thing," Marielle said, getting to her feet. "I've been getting away with things for a long time. This little discussion was just your sharing the plot for your next mystery. I am most amused that you are using our historic home as a setting, and flattered that I have inspired your fictional visions, but I really believe you have carried your imaginings too far. Using the Norrance title to bolster your sales. Well, it's just reprehensible, that's all. I'll have to consult my solicitor. We can always use the few dollars you may have put by to salve our ire and repair our reputation."

"That's a fine fairy tale you've written for yourself," I said. "Murderers often deny any culpability. They construct elaborate excuses for why their actions were justified, and they dream up revenge scenarios. The psychopathic personality tends to create its own version of the truth regardless of the facts."

"Are you calling me names now?"

"You're an intelligent woman, Marielle. I think you realize that there is just too much evidence piling up against you."

"I've had enough of your fanciful accusations. Angus! Mrs. Fletcher is just leaving. Would you kindly escort her to her room and ensure that she is out of this house within the next ten minutes." She glared at me and lowered her voice. "You're nothing but a hack, a writer of cheap crime novels, and I won't have you spreading your malicious rumors about my family. It's disgraceful. I told James not to invite you. Rupert doesn't need advice from base, self-centered Hollywood types."

Angus waved at me. "Go along, Mrs. Fletcher. It's time for you to leave."

I turned toward the door and was grateful to see a figure standing there.

George had swept aside the drape covering the entrance from the hall. "Mrs. Fletcher isn't going anywhere just yet. We have a few questions for you, Lady Norrance."

"Lucky you," Marielle said, a smile breaking out on her lovely face. "The cavalry has arrived."

Angus hoisted his plastic bag and started for the door.

"I think the authorities may want to ask you about Flavia Beckwith's death, Angus. And I'm certain they'd like to see what's in your sack." I looked at George. "One of the garden chemicals is likely to contain cyanide."

Mardling came through the curtain with Willoughby and another constable, who took Angus's bag and escorted him from the room.

"Lady Norrance, will you please come with us," Mardling said.

"And why should I do that? You have no cause to arrest me," Marielle said as Willoughby took her arm. "Just what are the charges? You have no proof of anything." She smiled in satisfaction.

"Did you hear it all?" I asked George.

"We heard enough."

Marielle laughed. "What you heard were my suggestions for Jessica's next book. Isn't that right, Jessica? It was just a made-up story. An amusing exercise."

"I'm afraid it was more than that, Marielle. I have recorded your whole confession." I pulled my cell phone from my pocket and looked at the screen. "Chief Inspector Sutherland was my last call. I pressed one button to redial him. I knew he wouldn't answer if his meeting was still taking place. Everything we talked about will be on his voice mail."

The countess straightened her shoulders. "James always hated those mobiles. I rather think he was right."

Mardling extended his hand to her.

"I'll have nothing to say until my legal representation arrives," she said, ignoring Mardling's hand and sailing out of the room in front of him.

Despite her crimes, I couldn't help feeling sympathy for the countess. She had been hit with two terrible blows one after the other—betrayal by a woman she'd thought was her friend, compounded by the betrayal by her husband. Even though Lord Norrance was no longer involved with Flavia and hadn't been for years, he'd been disloyal to Marielle by keeping his former lover in his employment, by allowing her to befriend his wife, by supporting his illegitimate son's mother financially without telling Marielle, and by giving Flavia the terrible power to tear down his wife's trust and love.

The situation reminded me of the badgers that Farmer Melton was intent on wiping out. Flavia had tried to destroy Marielle, and the countess had responded like a mother badger defending her nest. She had gone on the attack, killing those who threatened her home and her children. It was not defensible, but I understood what drove her.

Chapter Twenty-seven

The arrest of the countess and her gardener naturally became big news, and the media descended on Castorbrook Castle once again. Detective Sergeant Mardling and his trusty aide, Constable Willoughby, took charge and arranged for a contingent of uniformed officers to provide security and keep the idly curious away.

George was busy with Mardling and Willoughby when I received a phone call from Colin. He and his mother, Emmie Stanhope, had heard the news of the arrests on the radio.

"Did she admit it?" he asked. "Did she admit that the earl was my father?"

"Yes, Colin. The countess admitted to that, as well as to having poisoned him."

"Did she also murder my aunt—I mean my real mother—I mean Flavia?"

"She's responsible for her death, yes. She had Flavia placed in a dangerous situation that was too much for her heart to handle," I said. "The countess contends it was an accident, but it's likely that she—and Angus—will be charged with manslaughter."

"That doesn't really make it any better, especially for me mam."

"No. I don't imagine it does. I was wondering if you and your mother—I mean Emmie—can find time to meet me here at the castle today."

He laughed. "We don't have to juggle the words around. Emmie is me mam, now and forever. But I'm a lucky chap to have had two mothers claim me."

"Yes, I'd say that you are."

"Coming to the castle won't be a problem, unless Rupert and Kip object," he said. "Why do you want us there?"

"As Flavia's only relatives, you inherit her possessions. I'd like to be with both of you when you go to her living quarters to collect her belongings."

"I'm sure I can talk Mam into it. An hour from now all right?"

"Yes," I said. "I'll alert the police that you're coming."

"You don't have to do that, Mrs. Fletcher. The officers know I work at the stables. Mam and me, we'll walk up to the castle from there. She wants to see our new colt anyway."

I told Nigel that Emmie and Colin would be arriving and that I would be in Mrs. Beckwith's quarters. I would have also alerted Mrs. Powter but didn't know where to find her. If another visit to Flavia's rooms upset her, so be it.

I stood in what had once been the fourth-floor nursery that Flavia Beckwith had turned into her apartment, and I tried to put everything that had happened into perspective. I didn't know what I was looking for, but there had to be *something* of importance to have motivated the countess to turn the bedroom upside down immediately following Flavia's death. If she'd found what she was looking for, it would be gone, and going through Flavia's things with Emmie and Colin could be a wasted exercise. But maybe Lady Norrance hadn't found what she was seeking. If so, could we figure out what it was, and could it be found in Flavia's rooms?

I started looking at the volumes on her bookshelf, well aware as I did that I wasn't family and had no legitimate reason for doing so. But I rationalized—once again—that there was still a loose end to the events that had transpired, and I've never been one to be comfortable with unresolved issues.

"Can't keep your nose out of her things, can you?" Mrs. Powter stood in the doorway, her hands fisted on her hips.

"Whom are you protecting, now?" I asked. "Mrs. Beckwith's relatives are coming to gather her things. The countess isn't here to give or withhold her permission."

"The new Lady Norrance may not like it any better than I do."

"By all means, please inform Poppy and ask if she'd like me to explain why I'm looking through Flavia Beckwith's belongings. Do you think my presence in Flavia's rooms would be topmost on her agenda today? Her father-in-law has been murdered. Her mother-in-law has been arrested. Her husband, the new earl, must be overwhelmed by grief. She is now in charge of a household in turmoil. Yet you would add to her troubles by complaining that a nosy guest is looking at Mrs. Beckwith's books."

The housekeeper's shoulders slumped, and she seemed on the verge of tears.

I chided myself for speaking so harshly when she was clearly grieving herself.

"Look, Mrs. Powter, you and I may never see eye to eye on whether I should be permitted to search Flavia Beckwith's apartment. However, I'm sure you understand that criminal acts have taken place in Castorbrook Castle."

"She would never do what you have accused her of doing."

"I'm not accusing her. The police are. And they have her confession recorded. But didn't you find it strange that she came up here and tore Flavia's room apart? Did you ask her what she was looking for?"

"It was none of my business."

"Didn't you even wonder why she did it?"

"I thought Mrs. Beckwith might have stolen something from her. It wouldn't have surprised me. She was such a cold, calculating woman. You could see she was jealous of Lady Norrance, although that never registered with Her Ladyship. She always thought well of everyone."

"Never registered? Of course. That's it." I smiled at the housekeeper. "Thank you, Mrs. Powter. I was trying to picture what Mrs. Beckwith may have been hiding. She didn't steal anything from the countess; I promise you. The countess wanted something that was Flavia's, and now I think I know what that was."

"Then I'll leave you to it. The rest of the family needs me right now. They are all in a state of shock, as is the staff."

"I don't doubt it," I said. "I know you won't believe me, but I'm very sorry for your loss. You were and are an important member of Lord and Lady Norrance's staff, and I know they appreciated your loyalty."

She sniffled, but no tears fell. Instead, with an erect back, she turned and walked away. I felt very sorry for her. I was at least partly responsible for the tumultuous situation the household found itself in.

I'd turned back to the bookshelf when Nigel delivered Emmie and Colin to the room.

"Thank you, Nigel," I said.

"My pleasure, ma'am. If there is anything I can do for you, you need only to ask. The new Lady Norrance has instructed the staff to cooperate with the constabulary in any way we can. I am at your disposal night and day."

What a lovely gentleman, I thought as he departed and Emmie and Colin entered.

"I hope you don't mind my going through Flavia's things here," I said. "I have no legal authority to do it but—"

"Not another word," Emmie said. "Colin and I have discussed this. Even though I resisted it, you've done us a great service. It was time that Colin's true heritage be established. Was there something of Flavia's you wanted in particular?"

"No. I don't want anything." I explained how after the countess had Angus lock Flavia outside, she searched the apartment. "Lady Norrance was desperate to find something."

"Do you know what it was?"

"I think I do."

"Look at this, Mam," Colin said as he picked up the framed photograph that George and I had looked at during our first visit. "That's Aunt Flavia with the four of us. It must have been taken before the earl sent them off to boarding school. Look how young we were."

"How much you look like Kip," Emmie said, although her smile was wistful. "And how beautiful Flavia was. This must have been taken twenty years ago, Colin. What a handsome lad you were."

I joined them.

"That's me, Kip, Rupert, and Jemma," he said to me. "I remember when it was taken. I didn't know that Aunt Flavia still had this picture."

Emmie idly pulled on the tape that held the damaged frame together.

"Careful," Colin said. "It'll fall apart."

Emmie handed the photograph to me. "I suppose you want me to take stock of what Flavia has left behind," she said, heading for the bedroom. "I hated having all her things in the house. Now, I'll have even more."

I reached to replace the photograph on the bookshelf, when I wondered why Flavia had kept it in a broken frame. I pulled on the tape, and the backing came off completely. *What's this?* I thought as a piece of paper wedged between the photo and the backing slid free. The paper that had been hidden had an official seal on it, and a florid signature at the bottom.

"I think I've found what Lady Norrance was looking for. Come see," I called. I couldn't keep the excitement out of my voice.

"What is it?" Colin asked.

I handed it to him and his mother, and I read it over his shoulders. We were looking at Colin's birth certificate from the General Register Office. Flavia Beckwith was listed as the mother; the space for the father's name read "James William Edward Grant, seventh Earl of Norrance."

"You wanted proof that you're the earl's son, Colin," Emmie said, holding back tears. "Well, here it is."

Chapter Twenty-eight

George and I made plans to depart Castorbrook Castle that evening. I didn't relish still being a guest in the castle should Lady Norrance somehow be released.

The police had searched the countess's rooms but hadn't been able to locate her domed ring. At my suggestion, they also searched Elmore Jackcliff's studio and found the piece of jewelry at the bottom of his paint box. They had taken both the ring and the artist's box to a laboratory for testing.

Jackcliff swore he hadn't put the ring in his paint box, but the police charged him as an accessory to murder anyway. The artist was expected to make bail and would be allowed to return to his gallery in London until his court date drew him back to Chipping Minster.

I was fairly certain that Jackcliff must have wiped clean any fingerprints that could have been left on the ring. But even if he had taken the time to wash out the ring's secret compartment, it was unlikely he'd have been successful in ridding the ring of all traces of the poison that the countess had poured into it. How much the artist had known in advance of Lady Norrance's murderous plans we might never discover.

There was no doubt that the ring was a crucial piece of evidence, although between Marielle's taped confession and the plastic bag of chemicals Angus had taken from the garden shed, the officials had enough to hold both of them.

George and I declined to dine with what was left of the Grant family that evening. Kip and Poppy as the new earl and countess apparently felt it was incumbent upon them as our hosts to extend the invitation, but we knew that the duties of their new titles notwithstanding, they wouldn't really want to have those responsible for the arrest of the countess sitting at the table with her children.

George had secured two rooms at the Muddy Badger. "I told the young earl that we'd been imposing far too long on their hospitality but would swing by in the morning to say our final good-byes."

"I like the way you think, Chief Inspector," I said lightly.

"Pleased that you agree. Let's get packed and call for Ralph to deliver us to our new lodgings."

As it turned out, Emmie Stanhope and Colin Stanhope Grant, as he planned to call himself, joined us at the pub for dinner, as did Ralph, our perpetually upbeat driver. It was a lively, almost festive dinner. At one point, Ralph, slightly in his cups, stood and delivered the classic ode to the London taxi, written by Ogden Nash.

When he was finished, I joined the others in their applause.

"I have something to say," Colin said, getting up, coming around behind Emmie, and placing his hands on her shoulders. "I had an opportunity this afternoon to speak with my half brothers and half sister, Kip, Rupert, and Jemma. Jemma is happy to discover I'm her brother, Rupert less so, but I'm hoping he'll come around. Kip, of course, is the new Earl of Norrance, as it should be." Colin smiled wryly. "He actually said he's sorry I'm not eligible to inherit the title. I thought his wife, Poppy, would strangle him right then and there."

George and I looked at each other, and I imagined that we were both thinking that Kip had better get his drinking under control if he was to be an effective heir to the title of Earl of Norrance.

"You wouldn't want to be earl anyway," Emmie said to Colin. "It's too heavy a burden to bear."

"You're probably right, Mam. We were a pretty sober group, everyone missing the earl and upset about the countess. But Poppy said we'd better plan for the future if we had any chance of saving Castorbrook. Kip asked Jemma and me to continue running the stables. He said he had confidence we could take a direct role in bringing Castorbrook Castle back into financial stability. Jemma and I had discussed turning the castle's stables into a top-flight breeding stable and training grounds. Those were, um, *our* father's plans," he said, stumbling a bit at the unfamiliar relationship. "Anyway, we had already started working toward that goal. Our new colt, Good Fortune, is going to be the first of many winners for us."

"Does Kip have any other tangible plans for helping bring financial stability to Castorbrook?" George asked.

"Not Kip exactly," Colin replied. "But Poppy, Kip's wife, has some splendid ideas."

"I think that's exactly what Castorbrook Castle needs," I said, "fresh young blood bursting with ideas."

"Glad you agree," Colin said, retaking his seat at the table. "And I assure you that you and Chief Inspector Sutherland will always have the best of rooms whenever you decide to visit again."

I wasn't as convinced that we'd be so welcomed in the future, but I didn't want to contradict Colin so early in his days as an official member of the Grant family. Instead, I asked him, "Has any decision been made about selling the castle and grounds to a hotel chain?"

"I believe that's been put off for the time being," Colin said. "Kip and Poppy are determined to keep Castorbrook in the family, and I'll do anything I can to help bring that about. After all, I now have an official stake in the future of Castorbrook Castle."

Emmie, beaming, gave him a hug.

"I imagine that will be a mixed blessing for the Dowager Countess of Norrance," George whispered to me.

Colin overheard him. "The eldest Lady Norrance is not ready for me to call her 'Grandmother' yet, but she came in while we were meeting and lectured Kip on how he'd better live up to his father's reputation. I'm not sure that's the wisest of advice, but it's nice that she remembers her son that way," he said.

"What will Rupert and his wife, Adela, contribute?" I asked.

"Kip said that Rupert has dreams of turning Castorbrook into a world-class film studio, and he will be moving to London to seek financing," Colin said as dessert, orange trifle, was served. "Adela wants to stay at the castle and open a spa. They're both great ideas, don't you think?"

George and I lingered in front of the fireplace after the others had left.

"Turned out to be quite a New Year's celebration, didn't it, lass?"

"It's one that I'll certainly never forget," I said.

"It seems we've spent what was to be a joyous holiday together tracking down a murderer, much the way it was when we first met during the Ainsworth investigation."

"And here we are together in this charming inn after all those years."

"That says something about how we get along, doesn't it, Jessica? We should spend more time together, a *lot* more time."

"Maybe one day," I said, aware of where the conversation was leading.

"Yes, maybe one day," he said.

As promised, George and I stopped at the castle on our way to London where I would catch a plane back to the States. There was a meld of mourning and optimism in the air as the earl's children, including Colin, bade us farewell.

I sympathized with them, but they appeared to have discovered inner resources for handling the death of their father, and the incarceration of their mother. Was it the British stiff upper lip at play, or was it that they had been roughly forced into adulthood and realized that more was expected of them?

"Quite a melodramatic situation," Rupert said to me. "Adela said I should write about it—that it would help me cope with all the emotions. I'm thinking she may be right. It would make quite a thrilling screenplay—don't you agree?"

As Ralph slowly pulled away from the castle, I glanced back and saw Honora standing in an upstairs window, looking as formidable as ever. I hoped that she would live many more years; the children of Lord and Lady Norrance would benefit from learning her no-nonsense approach to life.

We stopped by Chipping Minster Antiques so I could say good-bye to Hazel.

"I have the perfect souvenir for you," she said. "It just came in. I put it aside so no one else would get it first." She set a box in front of me.

What was inside the box was swathed in tissue paper. I unwrapped it carefully and pulled out a porcelain figure of a foal and mare.

"Aren't they lovely?" Hazel said.

"Just beautiful," I said, and gave her a quick hug. "Look, George. It's Lamia and her colt, Good Fortune."

I tried to pay Hazel, but she insisted that the horses were a gift. "I'll never forget what you did for Emmie and Colin," she said. "And I'm sure Flavia, wherever she is, is grateful, too."

A few days later Ralph drove us to Heathrow Airport, getting me there in plenty of time for my flight to Boston, where Jed Richardson, who runs a charter air service in Cabot Cove, would meet me and fly me home.

"Is there anyplace we can rendezvous in the future where a murder isn't likely to take place?" George asked as we prepared to say good-bye once again.

I had to laugh. I was wondering the same thing. "I'm sure that we can come up with a place," I said.

"Promise you'll work on it, lass?"

"Yes, I promise, if only to hear you call me 'lass' again."

"I'd be happy to do that for the rest of my life," he said.

I let that final comment of his linger as I kissed him goodbye and disappeared into the security line. I was tempted to look back and wave, but knew that if I did, the tears would flow. If there ever was a man I could love as much as my late husband, Frank, it was George Sutherland.

"Please empty your carry-on bag," a British security guard ordered.

And thus, I was transported back to the real world.